TURN TO STONE

Jonah heard something behind him in the darkness of the cave and stole a look back. There was a sharp point of white light that grew so quickly Jonah felt like he was falling into a dream. The whiteness did not hurt, it was not blinding. There was simply nothing left wherever the whiteness touched.

The temperature of the cave fell and the iciness covered him as the walls and floor emptied of stone and color and shadow. In a moment the whiteness had swallowed the barrel of his gun and raced toward him. When he tried to move the gun, he found he could not. When he tried to get out of the way he was unable to bend. When he attempted to scream he could not open his mouth. Soon there was only the white and then, moments later, with a cry locked in his throat, there was not even that . . .

OPERATION MEDUSA

A UNIT OMEGA NOVEL

JIM GRAND

JOVE BOOKS, NEW YORK

This is a work of fiction. Names, characters, places, and incidents either are the product of the author's imagination or are used fictitiously, and any resemblance to actual persons, living or dead, business etablishments, events, or locales is entirely coincidental.

OPERATION MEDUSA: A UNIT OMEGA NOVEL

A Jove Book / published by arrangement with the author

PRINTING HISTORY
Jove edition / June 2004

Copyright © 2004 by Jeff Rovin.
Cover art by Tony Randazzo.
Cover design by Erica Tricarico.
Book design by Julie Rogers.

ISBN: 0-515-13749-9

A JOVE BOOK®
Jove Books are published by The Berkley Publishing Group, a division of Penguin Group (USA) Inc., 375 Hudson Street, New York, New York 10014.
JOVE and the "J" design are trademarks belonging to Penguin Group (USA) Inc.

PRINTED IN THE UNITED STATES OF AMERICA

10 9 8 7 6 5 4 3 2 1

PROLOGUE

YOUNG JONAH MONDAY crouched in the dark bowels of the cave, one knee on the hard stone floor, his carbine across the other knee. It was miserably hot, which is why he never entered the cave during the day. But while sweat ran from him like water from the weeping rocks, the Apache youth stayed still and attentive, as he faced the distant mouth of the cave.

Monday had been washing in the cove of trickling water when he saw the horses in the valley below. He had gone through brush, hunting a wild hare for lunch, and needed to clean the burrs from his hair. Naked, he grabbed his rifle and came to his cave. It would protect him on all but one side. He had been here long enough to see the black-amber shadows lengthen in the mouth of the cave. Yet he did not mind the wait or the discomfort.

How could he? He was home. Except for the belligerent men, this was a place where his spirit and flesh and the land were in absolute harmony. Even their own holy man had said so. Father Gonzalez had given Monday his white name in the hope that his own white god might look favorably on their prayers. So far, this god did not help. But the padre agreed that this land was Apache, that it was "traditionallyso." Monday even memorized the word. He did not understand a great deal of the language of English. He only knew enough to tell men who came by the mountain ridge with increasing regularity that it was his "traditionallyso."

Perhaps they did not think he would fight to protect it. Unlike his warrior father, Monday possessed a tranquil nature. He cut silver from the rocks, formed it into healing and protective ornaments in his dwelling, and sold them to those who came through the area by pony-coach. He had recently discovered a fat new vein of the metal and was able to make even more charms. He liked sharing his culture and artistry with the whiteskins. He hoped they would learn to appreciate it, and let him and other Apaches live in their homes as "traditionallyso."

That did not happen. So he also formed the silver into bullets for the Colt 44-40. It was the only material readily available to him. It bothered Monday to turn a substance of good fortune into a tool for killing. The spirit fathers had not put it here to destroy. But he would not leave his home as the others had done. They had been moved to a "reservation" not long after his Nantan had disappeared. Nantan was Monday's father, the strong root that had kept the tribe anchored to the valley. Nantan used to tell of a time before there was English and the soft men and women who spoke it. When the land was without boundary, without the smell of wood-dust and metal, and the restrictive clothes that the soft men milled. These people tried to overcome nature rather than join with it. Nantan did not want that to happen to them.

Not long after the outsiders came, Nantan was approached by men who were different than the soft ones. They wore gray clothes and had gray hair—"rebil vetruns," they called themselves. They happened into the valley and asked if someone could show them the way to Mexico. These men were old, but strong and determined. They said they still "hadfight" and wanted to join the war against Spain. Nantan did not know of this war but he liked them. He agreed to lead them because the Mexicans would let white settlers go where the Apache could not. Nantan hoped to find former tribe members who had left when the outsiders first came. He thought he might get them to come back and help resist the intruders. Nantan went but he never returned. Monday suspected that the men had found their war and his father had been caught in it. If so, then at least he had died a warrior. Eventually, the others lost the will to fight. They moved to the place far nearer the smell of the sea. To the "reservation."

Monday did not intend to leave. Two days before, several men had ridden out from a ranch to tell him that they had bought the cave. They said he no longer "leagly" owned what was his. They said he had a new home, with his people, and that they would come to take him there.

Monday did not agree to go. He did not care what the sheriff said. He did not care what the maps from "Washingtown" said. This was not "ranchland" or "Sedona." It was "the land of gleaming hills." It was Apache land. And this was his precious corner of that, from the stream above that fed the weeping rocks to the cave and the dwelling beside it. So it was and so it should always be. He would not surrender what he had built here. His was a life in harmony with his surroundings, with the invigorating power of the baking sun when he slept and the peacefulness of the cooler night when, by torchlight, he made his way ever-deeper into this cave. A cave to which he had been drawn at first when he was a small boy and in which he always felt happy. He had even accepted being alone, since none of the tribal women shared his passion for the work and some seemed afraid of this place. Not he. There was energy here, not just in the flaming sun and wandering stars but in the walls of the cave, in the red rock beneath him, in the silver itself. To give this up would be the same as giving up sustenance; Monday would die. The young Apache shot small game to survive. He could, and would, shoot these men if he had to.

Perspiration dripped into his ear, clogging it. He cocked his head hard to the right to snap it out. That was something he did on warmer nights when he didn't want to stop chipping with his stone axe and handmade hammer. He listened. He heard the men ride up the narrow trail from the valley. There were four of them. He knew they wouldn't use their thunder to close the cave, since the cave was what they wanted. He thought they might light a fire to choke him out, but he was prepared for that as well. He had used some of their iron to hack a hole in the soft stone of the side wall, then inserted a reed so he could breathe. He would close his eyes to keep them from burning. The men would never think to look for a breathing hole. And if they came in with weapons he was ready for that too. He had tucked himself into a very narrow section of the cave. They would have to enter single file. Doing that, they would be easy targets and at very close range. He would warn them first, of course. And when they did not retreat—

He heard the clack of the hooves and the fearful complaints of the horses as they scaled the last, steep section of the passage. The men did not dismount because of the rattlesnakes that dwelt here. Their ignorance made them afraid. Monday knew where to step so he did not bother the animals. He did not hurt them and they did not hurt him. It was a rule the white men did not understand.

The horses stopped and he heard the men dismount. They spoke to each other, though Monday could not understand much of what they were saying. Like its speakers, the English tongue was rough, fast, and strident. Monday heard someone enter his home. It was made of deerskin and bark, huddled against the side of the cliff. There were trinkets hanging just inside the flap. When the flap was raised the wind caused the trinkets to stir. Monday was angry at the men's boldness. They had no right to enter there. But he stayed where he was. His father had taught him that if you are patient an enemy will always come to you.

Monday's naked flesh tickled with the constant flow of sweat. The trickles were like harmless little snakes. Though they were bothersome, they were not annoying. Ignoring them took concentration and, concentrating, he was better able to focus on what the men were doing.

"Jonah Monday, this is Sheriff Bradley," someone said slowly from the opening. "I'm here with Frank Hartford and Father Gonzalez. We need to talk to you. You are trespassing."

The sheriff's deep voice was further deepened by the cave. That did not make Monday any more inclined to listen. Besides, they had called him two names. He did not recognize "trespassing."

"Father Gonzalez is putting together some of your belongings now. Mr. Hartford has title to the cave," the sheriff went on. "That means he owns it. He would like for you to leave." He was silent for a moment. "It would be easier, son, if you cooperated. Like the rest of your people did."

"Father is Nantan!" Monday shouted. He knew what son meant and he did not like this viper calling him "son."

"I don't know what that means, Mr. Monday. I can tell you that Father Gonzalez is not this "Nantan," whatever the hell that is. He's a good man, a man of god, and a friend. He wants to help you."

"Go!" Monday shouted.

"We won't do that, Apache!" another man yelled. That must be the man from the wooden office, the strange one with inside windows that had bars where they kept their "money."

"I am Apache!" Monday yelled proudly. "This Apache home."

"Not anymore, Mr. Monday!" the sheriff yelled back. "Don't make this ugly, boy. I've got a paper that says what I just said and I'd like to show it to you. It has a stamp and signatures and it's all done according to the law. Maybe you'll understand when you see it."

The man's words were annoying. "Go!" Monday cried again. He sensed that if he knew what they meant they would be even more annoying.

"Mr. Monday, I'm coming down to see you," the sheriff said.

Monday saw a shadow appear in the part of the cave mouth that was visible to him. There was a round in the chamber of the 1866 Lightning. Monday raised it from his knee and cocked the hammer.

The shadow stopped.

"I heard that," the sheriff said into the cave.

"Ears work. Good."

"Son, I don't want this to get nasty but I am obligated to remove you from Mr. Hartford's property."

"Wait!" Father Gonzalez said. "Let me go in and speak with him." The priest's voice was urgent, then compassionate. "Jonah? May I come to see you?"

"Come," Monday replied. "Alone."

Monday watched as one shadow receded and another entered. He kept the carbine raised in case one of the other men decided to run in. He was not giving up his home. Monday hoped he could convince the padre of that.

The Apache youth heard the distinctive scrape of the holy man's sandals on the dusty floor of the cave. With a friend between himself and the enemy Monday relaxed slightly. He acknowledged the cramping in his legs and rose. The cave was very low here and though he was not a tall man he had to bend his neck forward to stand. He kept the carbine pointed ahead, waist high.

As he watched for the padre himself to appear behind his shadow, Monday felt his perspiration grow icy—the way he felt when he was higher in the mountains and the rain fell as pellets, stinging him. There was a strange sound from ahead, from where Father Gonzalez was. It sounded like a captured bird sizzling on an open fire. The ringing, hissing noise grew louder and Monday raised the carbine to his shoulder. He watched through the site, unafraid and serene in his conviction that what he was doing was right and honorable.

And then, in a moment, everything changed. The cave began to tremble, as though it were afraid.

"Father Gonzalez?" he said.

There was no answer. Monday's eyes could not focus on the rocks near the light, they were moving so quickly. Yet his hands and his rifle were steady. His bare feet felt solid on the gritty cave floor.

"Father, are you there?"

Suddenly, the young man heard something behind him. He stole a look back. There was a sharp, sharp point of white light. It grew so quickly that Jonah Monday felt as if he were falling in a dream. The whiteness did not hurt, it was not blinding. There was simply nothing left wherever the whiteness touched. The temperature in the cave fell and the iciness covered him as the walls and floor emptied of stone and color and shadow. In a moment the whiteness had swallowed the barrel of his gun and raced toward him. When Monday tried to move the gun he found that he could not. When he tried to get out of the way he was unable to bend. When he attempted to scream he could not open his mouth. Soon there was only the white and then, moments later, with a cry locked in his throat, there was not even that.

CHAPTER 1

"DR. JACKSON SAYS he is on the way," Tally said as she flipped the cell phone shut.

"That's great," Collins croaked.

And it *was* a croak, dripping with insincerity. Tally saw his throat move over his necktie, but not his lips. *Well, let him croak,* Tally thought. She was doing the best she could.

Blonde, twenty-six year-old Tally Randall tucked her cell phone back into her handbag. She hung "big floppy" over the back of her seat—it held everything from her palm pilot to printouts of the manuscripts she was editing for *Natural History* magazine. Then she took a sip of coffee. She looked at her sullen breakfast companion. Harold Collins was like a car with three gears: unhappy, which was reverse; preoccupied, which kept things in neutral; and obsessive, which was breakneck-forward. None of them matched her own gears of upbeat or busy.

"You could be a little appreciative," she added. Her amber sunglasses turned Collins into a human pumpkin, like something from a Tim Burton movie.

"You mean I should be glad that he's seeing us at all?"

"No, that I'm trying to help," she said.

"I am," he grumped.

"And you can give *him* some elbow room too," she went on. "Dr. Jackson was on a conference call with European scientists. It's tough to organize those things with different time zones and schedules and all that."

"Tally, I know a little something about different time zones," Collins reminded her.

It took her a second to get what Harold meant. That was why they were here—because there was compelling if not persuasive evidence that while they were in Scotland, exploring Loch Ness, Harold had traveled back in time. Way back. To a period when dinosaurs lived. That's why they wanted to talk to Dr. Jackson, to see whether any of their thinking made sense.

Collins sat across from her at one of the three outdoor tables. He was slowly rubbing the edge of the funky lavender tablecloth and breathing hard through his nose, which tended to flare his nostrils and create the jack-o'-lantern effect. That plus the fact that he was grimacing and his dark eyes, which were staring at the steam from his coffee cup, seemed even darker with the morning sun behind his head. At least there were no other diners around to wonder if anything was wrong with him. It was nine-thirty and most of the Parkhut's business during the week was takeout. Upper Westsiders came for the fat egg-bagels, which were the best in New York. Coffee was free, making the wise little hole-in-the-wall on Seventy-seventh Street the first eatery in the city to have put a Starbucks out of business.

"I have to tell you, Tally, I'm still not convinced this is the way to go," Collins said.

"Getting an expert to corroborate our rather bizarre initial conclusions before we publish anything about what we think happened, or look for funding to explore them further? What a brilliantly stupid idea, Harold."

"Hey, I'm an expert too," he said. "I've considered the quantum physics of what happened."

"And you know everything there is to know about the subject."

"I didn't say that—"

"Dr. Jackson knows a little something about white dwarfs," Tally went on.

"I know. But getting him up to speed—"

"What you're saying is you don't think he'll believe you," Tally said. "Well, guess what? I've still got one eye on that exit too."

"Tally, I got sucked backward through a hole in time. While I was there I got chased by an aquatic dinosaur. That is a fact."

"No, it's a leading explanation."

"It happened," Collins insisted. "The only things we're fuzzy about are what caused the temporal rift and whether this creature was the origin of stories about the Loch Ness monster. And the latter isn't even a question, as far as I'm concerned, since it happened *in* Loch Ness and since the animal looked a whole lot like reliable eye-witness accounts of the monster. Which means we're wasting time that we should be spending looking for other anomalies like the one we found there. In fact, we may be doing worse than that."

"What do you mean?"

"One scientist is an explorer. Two or more are an argument. If we bring other scientists into this, we'll only muck things up."

"Harold—that is the lamest defense of territorialism I've ever heard."

"It's true. What I said, not what you said."

"I've known lots of scientists who agree on things," Tally insisted.

"Yeah, after they're proven."

"No. Scientists are very methodical and goal-oriented. Cure a disease, split the atom, go to the moon. The only time they fight is when someone jumps to a conclusion before doing the groundwork, like 'It was an asteroid hitting the earth that caused the extinction of the dinosaurs,' or 'Every human on earth comes from this one Homo sapien mother in Africa,' or 'The Neanderthals didn't become extinct, they went into the Himalayas and became Abominable Snowmen.' "

"Or 'The earth isn't the center of the universe,' " Collins said.

"I'm not saying radical ideas are necessarily wrong," Tally said. "You just need to present them a certain way or you end up on the defense instead of the offense. You were the only one to witness whatever happened to you. None of the other people who were out on the loch can verify our story."

"They're not scientists," Collins said through his teeth.

Tally motioned to the waiter to refill her coffee. "You know, I shouldn't even be dealing with this."

"What do you mean? You want to know what happened."

"Yes, but I don't need to do the legwork," Tally said.

"Your boss is the one who couldn't be convinced that what we said happened actually happened. Remember?"

"I remember."

"You should be sitting there all smiling and pleasant and glad that I'm working on this with you."

For the first time Harold Collins looked up from his steamless coffee cup. "Okay. *Now* I'm pissed off."

"Why?"

"Because when we eventually take the cork out of this bottle, Tally Randall gets to tell the greatest story in human history. So where do you come up with you're doing *me* a favor?"

"That wasn't what I was saying at all!" she protested.

"Yes. It was."

"No."

Or was it? Tally wondered. Collins was doing the rational scientist thing of working backward from a goal. She was taking a reporter's step-by-step approach from the other end. Still, Harold was right. When they got to the same place, this story *would* make her career.

"Look," she went on, "let's take a step back from the edge. We both want the same thing: to get the ammunition to give to Sam Bordereau so he can go to his bosses at the United Nations and get you the resources—"

"Us."

"Okay, get *us* the resources *we* need to investigate the phenomenon properly. Better?"

"Yes."

"Good. Dr. Jackson is one of the world's foremost astronomers. You saw the show he wrote for the planetarium. *Star Trek*-y and wormhole-y and far out. If Dr. Jackson thinks there's any possibility that there's a particle of white dwarf matter tucked inside the earth somewhere, and that it's bending time and space out of shape, he'll be in our corner one hundred percent. I guarantee."

"And did he give you any indication that he thought it was feasible when you told him?"

Tally waited as her cup was refilled and took a sip. Then she took another. She started to say something, then stopped.

"I have to assume he did if he's coming to meet with us," Collins pushed.

"Not actually."

"What?"

"I didn't tell him what the meeting was about," Tally blurted.

Collins was looking at Tally. His eyes and mouth were open and frozen. "No. No, don't say that."

"There was a reason I did it this way—"

"Yeah, what?" Collins asked. "Because he would have laughed until his lungs collapsed?"

"No," Tally said firmly.

"What, then?" Collins demanded. He was practically shouting.

"I wanted to see his face when you told him."

"His face? This isn't *The New Candid Camera*. He's gonna look at me like I'm a talking dog when I tell him I just *traveled through time!*"

"He won't do that," Tally assured him.

"Sure, Right."

"I'm good at people-reading. I'll know right away whether we have an ally or whether we need to continue shopping."

Collins looked up, looked down, shook his head, then looked back at his coffee cup. The cup was apparently his personal white dwarf, taking him from this terrible situation to a safe place somewhere in his head.

"It's going to be okay," she assured him.

"It's going to be a disaster," he said.

"It won't be. I promise. If nothing else, we'll learn something."

"What?"

"How to present this story," Tally said. "Until we can offer commuter tickets to one million B.C., this is *not* going to be an easy sell."

Collins sighed once again. The grimace returned with what appeared to be more pain than before. "I'm going to learn something else, I bet."

"Really?"

"Yeah," he said. "Not to tell the story to someone who's drinking their morning O.J."

"I don't follow."

"You'll see, watcher of body language."

"See what?"

"A spray of Minute Maid across the table," Collins said.

Tally shook her head, and drank more coffee, and looked at her watch, and waited for Dr. Jackson. She didn't confess her own feelings to Harold Collins: that though she had been there on Loch Ness, even *she* wasn't convinced that Harold hadn't bumped his head and dreamed some, if not all, of what happened, and that the videos they took and the sea creature they thought they saw were something else entirely. . . .

CHAPTER 2

BLOSSOM "RUSTY" WANG was the great-great-granddaughter of a Chinese railroad worker and a barmaid from Ohio, a first generation transplant from Norway. Growing up in Arizona in the late 1940s, Blossom used to get put into classes with the Chiricahua and Apache kids because no one knew what to make of her blue, blue eyes set in Asiatic features and golden skin. That was okay, though. Her Native American friends liked to talk about the past and that interested her. She used to go out looking for arrowheads and lead-ball bullets with them. That was how she got her nickname. People used to say she wasn't interested in anything that wasn't rusty.

Family lore had it that her great-great-grandmother had been taken against her wishes by a refugee from indentures, caught as she left the privy one night on her way to her apartment above the saloon. How else to explain what would otherwise have been an improbable union between a hardworking young woman from the Midwest and a laborer who, according to another part of the story, was wanted by the law.

But five years ago, Rusty had found out that wasn't quite the case. There was a gambler who had moved through the American Southwest during the latter 1800s, a dandy by the name of Boston Tremont. He'd kept a diary of his winnings in different towns in which he also noted anything else of interest that grabbed his eye. That journal was kept by his family. By happy chance the family, and the trunk with the diary, ended up in Sedona. The family brought the chest to Rusty, who owned an antiques store, and who bought both the trunk and its contents. Rusty read the diary first, just in case there were artifacts or letters tucked inside, ribbons or clipped tresses or currency that told a separate story. Entries for 1875 referred to a barmaid named Augusta—not a common name, and the name of her great-great-grandmother—who was "with yield," as Tremont had put it. According to the gambler, the young lady had been visiting her well-to-do "mister" at the railroad he was building. That was when said "mister" had become violent about her desire to terminate their relationship—which he suspected was more business than romantic. A young worker named Wang, hearing the altercation, had come to Augusta's aid and seen her safely back to town. Because he had saved her by beating the boss with an iron spike, Wang could not return to the train. He stayed with Augusta. When he moved on two weeks later—to the Barbary Coast, it was rumored—Augusta was not quite alone. She became less alone as the months passed.

The names were right, the areas were right, and the
time was right. After reading the diary, Rusty proudly
and legally changed her surname from Shubert to Wang.
She was even able to find out what had happened to her
great-great-grandfather, thanks to a friend who wrote
about antiques for the *San Francisco Chronicle*. According to a report in the *San Francisco Call* from October
14, 1875, a former railroad worker named Wang was
killed in a fight with a fellow washerman at Wah Lee's
Wash'ng and Iron'ng Establishment. The dispute was reportedly about a lady who had dropped off shirts one
morning. The other guy wanted to go home with her. After closing, when it was dark, Wang made sure he didn't
get there.

What Rusty took from all this was one rule above all:
never believe any story until you investigate it. She tried
to do her homework on every piece that came into her
store, and then she wrote up what she discovered on index cards. She kept those with the items, so people could
get a sense of just how special each chair or knife set or
water pouch or desk was.

That care and devotion to detail was what gave her
shop its international reputation. Orders and artifacts
came from around the world. But what she liked best
was when something reached her from Arizona. This
was her home, and she loved learning about it on a very
personal person-by-person level.

That was how she happened to be at Snake Mountain
outside of Sedona on a dry, hot morning just after sunrise. A deputy sheriff, investigating a rockslide in the region, saw that the point of origin appeared to be a cave
about a hundred feet up the slope. Since there was no
cave noted on the map, and his global positioning system
had no idea what it was, he took his jeep up an old dirt

road to investigate. It appeared to him that the rocks had been piled in front, since a few still remained in the mouth of the cave. They had become dislodged for reasons that were not clear: there was minimal dampness, so erosion was probably not a factor. There were no nearby trees whose roots might have nudged them over, negligible seismic activity, and no bike or SUV tracks that might have rumbled them loose. The only thing he could think of was that they had been knocked around by sonic booms from the Flying Angels Squadron making their runs to or from Luke Air Force Range. His report, which Rusty had read, said they seemed to have been knocked over from the inside—which was unlikely, since the only opening he found in there was a small, ancient hole that had been hacked through the side for reasons he couldn't quite figure out. Perhaps as an air hole in the event of a cave-in. Marks on the cave walls suggested that this was, at one point, a working cave. Silver, he had guessed, from the thin lines that remained embedded in the rock.

But that was not all the deputy had discovered. He'd also found a statue. Life-sized and very strange. When the deputy returned to the station he called Rusty. Whenever they found cave paintings or potential grave sites, or former settlements, Rusty usually got the call to come and give them a first-look evaluation. Micah Michaels from Northern Arizona University charged a couple hundred bucks an hour for his time. Rusty did it for free, for the love of it.

The white-haired woman went up to the cave with her two Jack Russell terriers and her hiking stick. The animals had been trained to respect the sites. They also had been trained to bite hard behind the heads of rattlesnakes.

Rusty went in with her dogs and her industrial-size, high-intensity, shock-proof LED flashlight. She made her way to the back, poking cautiously with her stick at the walls and the six-foot-high roof to make sure they were secure. They were. This was a natural cave, not a man-made one.

The cave whistled quietly as wind came in through the hole the deputy had told her about. It was an eerie sound and it obviously unnerved the dogs. They walked close beside her ankles, their tails low, their respect having cycled through reverence to awe to being just a little afraid.

"It's okay," Rusty told them.

They were unconvinced. So was she. There was something "off" about this place, though she couldn't figure out what it was. It was almost as if there were a slight pull on her from the rear of the cave, like the attracting end of a magnet.

After a very slow walk that took less than a minute but seemed like five, Rusty spotted the statue. It was around a bend, about five feet from her, standing in a corner. It was holding a carbine and looked remarkably alive. Part of that illusion was due to its flesh-like color—which, she saw as she neared, was due to sand that had blown in through the open hole. The sand also coated the back wall of the cave, which is where that "pull" seemed to originate.

The dogs slowed, stopped, sank, then began to creep away.

Rusty turned the light on them. "What are you doing?"

They stopped, bellied down on the cave, and waited. When she turned the light back on the statue, they resumed their slow retreat.

Rusty ignored them now. The statue was too damn fascinating.

"What the hell are you doing here is only one question I have," she muttered to herself. Her voice carried through the shallow cave. She blew the dirt from a shoulder of the statue and examined the material. She wet an index finger and touched it. She looked at her fingertip in the light. "It looks like chalk but it feels like marble and it isn't particulate." She put three fingers on the bare shoulder and held them there for a moment. "And it's warm, not cold. Very odd."

She took a step back and looked over the entire statue. It was naked and holding a cocked carbine.

"What was the sculptor thinking? And who the hell *was* the sculptor?"

She shined the light on the ground. There were no shavings, which meant it was hewn elsewhere and brought here. Which raised the question of *why* and also *when.* She knew this area. In sixty years she had not known there was a cave here. She examined the features of the statue more closely. They were Native American. They were also extremely lifelike, and not very happy.

"Okay, now I'm really confused," she muttered. "Who would sculpt a life-size, naked, Native American with a cocked hammer, looking like he just saw a grizzly eat his sister?"

Behind her, the dogs began to whine.

"Quiet!" she yelled. "You're supposed to be watching for snakes."

The statue was too tight against the wall for Rusty to get around it herself, so she angled the flashlight around it and lightly brushed dirt from the sides and arms. The mystery became more puzzling when she noticed scars. These were not imperfections in the material but scabbed

scratches—the kind you'd get from falling against rocks—
as well as what looked like healed knife-wounds.

"Demented self-portrait or Native American pornog-
raphy—you decide," Rusty said.

That last thought made her wonder. The weapon gave
it a Freudian edge, but this might have been some kind
of fertility site. Maybe there was a lodestone in here exerting that pull she was feeling, something that made
it stimulating to some group. Maybe even a renengade
group that broke from a tribe for religious reasons. Perhaps the naked statue was a virility totem of some kind.
Native Americans typically used animals to represent
emotions of human conditions, but maybe this was an
exception.

"Assuming it *is* Native American," she said. Rusty
had never seen a photo-realistic sculpture like this anywhere in the Americas. This looked almost Greek in its
detail and craftsmanship.

She loved enigmas like this. She went in for another
close look at the carbine. It was a 44-40 Lightning, from
the look of it. That would make the date of the statue no
earlier than the late nineteenth century.

As she contemplated the weapon, and admired the detail work on the lifelike hands, Rusty became aware of
the pull becoming stronger. She swung her light in a
one-eighty-degree arc along the back of the cave. She
didn't see anything.

The dogs were whimpering now.

"Guys, be *quiet!*" she snapped.

They were. Instantly. For the first time ever.

Rusty turned and shined the light on the terriers. They
were at the point where the cave turned. They were not
only silent, they were also very still. And white. She
moved toward them.

"Cracker?" she said. "Flap?"

The Jack Russells didn't react. As she neared, she saw something that caused her to stop. Motion, in a nook off to the east. An instant later something flashed in front of her, bright and white and piercing. At first she thought it was a glint from a strand of silver in the cave wall. But as she watched it, the glow grew brighter and larger. The pull she had felt was all around her now and growing more powerful by the instant. It was drawing her back, toward the statue, almost like someone had turned on a way-oversized vacuum cleaner.

"What the hell—?"

A moment later she felt like she did the one time she had eaten Chinese food as a tribute to Wang. Her head got tight, from her jaw to her temples, as though someone had filled it with cement. It was the MSG, her doctor told her. At this moment her entire body felt as if it were being pumped with the stuff. She tried to break away, to get out of the cave, but then something equally strange happened. It suddenly felt as if her arms and legs were going to sleep, but in reverse. They tingled painfully for a few seconds, then less so, then seemed to be full of sand, then went numb. She tried to move them but couldn't. Hell, she couldn't even feel them. All the while the glow continued to expand, filling the cave ahead, then her peripheral vision, and finally—

The thin cave hole was to the right of Blossom Rusty Wang. The wind blew through the flute of an opening, carrying fine bits of sand into the cave. Some of them landed on the ground and some of them landed on Rusty, Flap, and Cracker.

They didn't feel them. Or the wind.

Or anything else.

CHAPTER 3

DR. FRANK JACKSON did not arrive like Mr. I. M. Late. He approached reading a carefully folded *New York Times*—Science of the Times, of course—walked past the table, and had to be called back by Tally. He did not seem surprised to have gone too far. He simply doubled back, stepped through the low gate that surrounded the outdoor tables, and took a seat.

"Good morning," he said—formally, as though he had just put on his robe and were greeting his butler.

Tally replied cheerfully, Collins less so. He studied the scientist as if he were looking at a menu, superficially from top to bottom. Okay, so maybe Tally was right. Scientists didn't get along, as a rule. Jackson had a long, pale face made longer by upswept gray-going-on-white hair and a downswept gray-with-some-black-left goatee—and full, mad eyebrows that were gray with improbable splashes of reddish-brown in the center. He was thin and dressed in black and, to Harold Collins, he looked like he belonged behind the conductor's podium ten blocks south at Lincoln Center instead of publishing highly regarded papers on quantum theory.

Jackson ordered a fruit plate and milk and then asked why he was here. To Collins's surprise, the scientist listened very carefully as he described what had happened in Loch Ness and finally why he thought it had happened:

"I was thinking there could be a speck of white dwarf behind all of this," Collins told him.

"Which is why we wanted to talk to you," Tally added.

"A hypergravitational piece of a collapsed star inside the earth," Jackson said. There was nothing in his expression or tone to suggest belief or disbelief. It was simply a statement, like *"Oh, they have sourdough French toast on the menu."*

"That's right," Collins said.

Jackson forked a section of honeydew into his mouth. He didn't chew it but sucked it, crushing it to pulp within his cheeks.

Tally watched him eagerly. "Well?" she said. "What do you think?"

"What do I think," he repeated. He speared a second piece of honeydew into his mouth. "I think that Mr. Collins hit his head on a rock, passed out, and drifted in and out of wakefulness for a couple of hours."

"Not what happened," Collins snapped and sat back. He wanted to throw the bread basket at Jackson—or maybe at Tally, he couldn't decide. Which was probably what stopped him.

"Dr. Jackson, with respect, there are several reasons why that isn't likely," Tally said.

"Oh?"

"Tell him, Harold," she said.

Collins was impatience personified. The words popped out like bubbles in a pot of boiling water. "For one thing, I would have run out of air. For another, I sent the video camera back through the opening with pictures of the dinosaur that was trying to make me a coprolite."

"There have been seventy-odd years of pictures of the Loch Ness Monster," Jackson noted.

"Not from reputable sources," Tally said.

"That may be true, but even credible individuals can misinterpret evidence."

Collins moved the chair back. "Sir, I'm sorry to have wasted—"

"As for the air issue," Jackson went on, "perhaps Mr. Collins ended up in an underground cave. Methane gas could have caused the delusions."

"They. Weren't. Delusions," Collins said. "They were Big pops. Big hot bubbles."

"Dr. Jackson," Tally added quickly, "what about Harold's theory that earth accreted around a particle of white dwarf, or that a piece of one collided with earth and buried itself in the crust or mantle somewhere."

"A white dwarf has a mass equivalent to that of the sun, a radius equal to that of the earth, and a density one million times greater than water," Jackson said. "If a grain-sized piece of one came near an object—say, a human being—it would tear him to pieces. Very tiny pieces, subatomic size. He would look like a cartoon character being sucked into a vacuum cleaner."

"But what if—" Tally said.

"Not finished," Jackson said, holding up his fork to silence her. There was a piece of cantaloupe on it and the juice ran down the side.

"Sorry."

"Theoretical scientists don't work by instinct or first reactions," Jackson went on. "We 'what if' ourselves from place to place, make the big leaps by imagination and then use science to fill in the road. 'What if there were a three-dimensional shadow of a four-dimensional object. What would it look like? We have to suppress what is animal and reach for what is divine. Multidimensional thought, thought of the places where angels and gods dwell. That is where we start our quest."

"We're coming into the light," Collins said. He pushed his french toast aside and leaned forward. "You're not saying you believe me. But if I'm hearing you correctly, you're not saying you don't."

"I'm saying I can't not believe you," Jackson replied. "It is plausible, therefore it cannot be discounted. By definition, intense gravity fields such as black holes or even white dwarf stars suck in everything around them, matter and energy alike. It's like pulling a rug toward you. Whatever is on it comes with it. In theory, everything in the universe should be drawn to their event horizons. Yet they aren't. And one reason, we think, is that there may be internal *counter*forces at work. Not from the objects themselves, which are one-way streets, but by hidden energy, black energy, perhaps from the parallel dimensions that they may open into. Sort of wormhole riptides, if you will."

"Wormholes being—?" Tally asked.

"Theoretical shortcuts in space caused by black holes pulling the area between them together," Jackson said. "It's like touching the ends of a string together instead of traveling along its entire length."

"I see."

Collins's appetite was definitely returning. He cut

a hunk of side-dish apple sausage and tapped it in the syrup server.

"The interesting thing here is that Dr. Collins's theoretical wormhole is not just between places but between times," Jackson said.

"Hold on," Tally said. "Why wouldn't it just be between times? Harold was in the same place, only a few hundred million years earlier."

"But he wasn't. That's what's so remarkable."

"I'm lost," Tally said.

"A few hundred million years ago—or five minutes ago, for that matter—earth was in an entirely different spot in the universe. It revolves around the sun, the sun moves through the Milky Way, the Milky Way moves through the universe—our planet is nowhere near wherever it was in the Devonian era, if that's where Dr. Collins went. Let us imagine that, for some reason, his theoretical particle made an impression at that point, there and then. In effect, then, the earth has dragged that spot along as it moves through the void."

"It's like a bookmark," Tally said.

"Exactly."

"So then we should be able to go back to Loch Ness, find it, and go back through it," Tally said.

"Maybe," Jackson replied.

"Why maybe?" Collins asked.

"And before you answer that," Tally said, "I have to ask you this. I've seen time-travel movies. What about the whole traveling-to-the-past-and-changing-it thing? By stepping on Dinosaur Beach, Harold may have done something that affected the course of evolution—"

"I believe the past is irrevocable," Jackson replied confidently. "If it's 'then,' you already did it. It was written, published, codified."

"That *really* seems hypothetical," Tally said. "If Harold changed things, we may not know it because we've changed as a result. I could have been a guy before Harold left, and he screwed that all up. In fact, each time he goes back, things could change again."

"Not possible," Collins said. "I would have noticed. I'm the one constant."

"Exactly," Jackson said. "Harold would have noticed if the North had won the Civil War or Italy had lost World War Two."

Collins froze. "Wait. What did you say?"

"Just kidding," Jackson said.

Collins tasted syrup. From his stomach.

Jackson ate a trapezoid of pineapple and talked around it. "Philosophically speaking, that very idea can work for or against your claim of time travel."

"How so?" Collins asked. "I've considered these time-dispacement effects on a quantum physics level, but not the ontology of it."

"If you did indeed go into the past, you disturbed sand on the beach, stepped on foliage, distracted a dinosaur, breathed modern bacteria into prehistoric air, or let it wash into prehistoric seas. Any one of those would have caused domino-like changes, perhaps even given rise to the modern world. Skin cells you left in the water or on the beach may have given rise to mammals."

"That would make Harold the most important man in history," Tally said.

"It would indeed. Which is what I meant about philosophy. Those are the works of God and nature, not men."

That was very unsettling. Being the father of all things warm-blooded was not something Collins could get his mental muscles around.

"But getting back to the *why* one may or may not be

able to go back through the wormhole," Jackson said, "the thing we have to ascertain—apart from whether or not it exists—is whether or not it's a stable wormhole."

"Why wouldn't it be?" Tally asked.

"The power source, your theoretical white dwarf particle, isn't just radiating in one direction. It's like the sun, reaching in all directions. Now, let's assume the particle preexisted the formation of the earth. Maybe its gravitational pull drew together the rocks that made us, attracted the comets that may have brought us water, maybe even the building blocks of life."

"Assuming they weren't me," Collins said.

"Which we cannot assume," Jackson said.

"What do you mean? Life was already here when I got there."

"Yes, but we don't know what you may do—or more accurately, may have done—on a future trip."

That was true. That was *really* scary.

"If an already-formed earth had suffered a collision with a white dwarf particle, said particle would have sucked up our planet like that cartoon character I described," Jackson said.

"I know," Collins said. "That's been bothering me. It would have torn us up, atom by atom, in seconds."

"Correct," Jackson said. "If this anomaly exists it was probably here from the get-go."

"So why didn't this powerful anomaly pull earth apart?" Tally asked.

"Because if this phenomenon exists here—and that is still, for me, a very considerable 'if'—there is obviously some kind of buffer," Jackson said. "And that buffer could be our bookmarks, the rips in time-space. They got locked in place by the pull of the particle and stuck to it."

"Like a rubber-band ball," Collins offered helpfully.

"Exactly."

" 'Rips,' " Tally said. "Plural."

Jackson and Collins both nodded.

The waiter ambled over. "More coffee?"

Tally nodded. "The check, too, when you have a sec."

"You bet," he said, smiling, and walked away.

"Just like that," Jackson said.

"Sorry?" Tally said.

"The time-space tears," Jackson said. "You have been connected to that waiter since you got here. Wherever he went, you had access to him. And he to other diners, for that matter."

"Are you suggesting that there are multiple pathways to the past?" Tally asked.

"Not just necessarily the past," Jackson said. "To the future, to other dimensions, to deep space. One of these links might intercept another, preempt another, bounce another one to yet another location."

"Needing *wormholequest.com,*" Tally said.

"You would need something very much like that if this phenomenon proves to be real and, if real, not an isolated link," Jackson said, as he ate a grape. "What I'm suggesting is a complexity of the patterns, the mathematics of which is mindnumbing. But the most remarkable, and terrifying, fact is that were it not for this big bundle of yarn around your particle—"

"We'd be sucked into the vacuum cleaner," Collins said.

Jackson nodded as he cheek-drained another piece of melon.

"Is there any danger of us doing damage to these wormholes?" Tally asked.

"No," Jackson replied. "We're like dust hitting Everest."

"So then what I went through was not the particle itself but one of the threads around it," Collins said.

"If there is such a structure as I've described, then that's how you moved through it, without question," Jackson said. "Either that, or—"

"Or what?" Collins asked.

"You passed out underwater and imagined all of what happened."

"I didn't," he insisted. "Look at the videotape. See if you don't think that's a dinosaur."

"It may well be," Jackson said. "That still wouldn't prove anything. It is not unknown for people to 'think' images onto film and tape."

"Say again?" Tally asked.

"I read a thesis paper not long ago, from Duke University, about fiercely emotional individuals, especially *terrified* individuals, who are able to project their fear as radiant energy. What they see as ghosts are actually electrical manifestations generated by their agitated brains. What the cameras of ghost hunters record as spirits of the dead are actually energy imprints from said brains."

"Do you believe that?" Tally asked.

"It's either that or believe in ghosts," Jackson replied.

"Do you?" Tally pressed.

"No," he said as he finished his milk. "Primitive people believed in ghosts and demons. That's usually my barometer to go in the other direction."

"I guess the idea of disembodied beings is a pretty big leap," Collins said. "Unless."

"Unless what?" Tally asked.

Collins said, "Unless they were coming through wormholes."

CHAPTER 4

AS SHE WALKED the four blocks to her office at the Museum, Tally was not sure what to think.

Dr. Jackson at first firmly trashed, then cautiously encouraged—or if not encouraged at least validated—Harold Collins's belief that he had traveled into the past. The physicist hadn't actually said, "You *did* it!" but he did say, "You could have done it." She wasn't sure what the psychology was behind the trash-and-sift approach, or even if there was psychology behind it. Maybe that was just how he was: look at one side (bah!) and then at the other (hmmm . . .).

Regardless, Dr. Jackson's low-heat endorsement meant that they could actually take this exploration to the next level: Collins could seek additional funding from his boss at the United Nations and, if that were approved, she could then try to get the Museum magazine to shovel in additional monies in exchange for exclusive reporting rights, perhaps in partnership with a newspaper like the *New York Times* or the *Washington Post*. That would be a helluva coup for her, a byline in one of the Big Ones. It was an incredible opportunity, but it was also a huge responsibility.

What if we're wrong?

She expected that. It was still too incredible to believe. What troubled her more was, what if they were right? How do you report time travel? How do you *control* time travel? How do you stop people from streaming to Loch Ness to vacation in the past? No one could stop *Titanic* opportunists from grave-robbing. What would wealthy collectors pay for a hatchable dinosaur egg? And despite what Dr. Jackson said, he didn't know for absolutely sure that those trips into the past wouldn't screw up the present. Maybe Harold was lucky. Or maybe he just screwed things up in ways that weren't apparent. Perhaps he had caused the extinction of an offshoot of the creature, one that no one had missed yet. Or he could have brought *back* some prehistoric virus that had not yet begun turning people into scaly, tongue-flicking hybrids. Or maybe the transformation *had* occurred. Maybe there were now millions of merpeople living in the North Sea who hadn't been there before.

It was all too much to contemplate. Yet it *had* to be contemplated before any of the findings were widely discussed, let alone reported. And those were just the things she came up with walking four blocks to Eighty-first Street.

Tally listened to voice-mail messages while she

started checking E-mail. Her mother had called, remind-
ing her—"as a courtesy, not that I expect you to actually
show"—that her cousin Blaine's engagement party was
that weekend on Uncle Moore Randall's side of the family's estate in Westport, Connecticut. Mrs. Thompson
Canyon Randall IV was right. Her daughter would rather
have her gums tattooed than go to a family gathering. She
had no intention of explaining, again, to Aunt Dona-with-
one-"n" or cousin Lance why she was happy to be associate editor of *Natural History* magazine instead of a
country-club wife married to a Yale grad who had bought
his grades with endowments anyway, and probably spent
his few sober morning-minutes a day downloading fetish
porn in his wood-paneled home office when he was supposed to be on-line checking his portfolio.

Or something along those Randallesque lines.

There was a voice-mail message from her editor asking for the article on the Chumash Painted Caves of
Santa Barbara; from the writer of the Chumash Painted
Caves of Santa Barbara article asking for another day to
fact check; and from Harold, in his cab, thanking her for
a great breakfast and for being a stalwart friend.

Very few people could use the word "stalwart" and
make it sound natural, but Harold Collins was one of
them, the strange-duck Ph.D. physicist with a Hawaiian
mother and a retired-navy father, and working now for a
one-time foreign-exchange-student friend from France
who had become a big shot at the United Nations. Sam
Bordereau was the one who had set up UNIT Omega for
Harold to run. Though UNIT was an acronym for United
Nations Institute of Technology, the one-person division
was really a weird-fact-gathering bureau. Bordereau
felt that the United Nations should have a firsthand

repository of data about international phenomena such as UFOs and Yeti sightings, and that the analyses conducted by said repository should be the last word on these wonders—hence the epithet "Omega," for the Greek letter "Z." Bordereau also felt that his longtime friend was the man to run it. Based on the fact that recent MIT graduate Collins had been considering a career as a short-order cook while he wrote hard science fiction—"science fiction with rivets," as Harold described it, stuff that was believable—Tally wondered if UNIT Omega had been a mercy job created to keep "Harold Collins" and "Burger King" from appearing on the same paycheck stub. The fact that Harold's office was several stories below the East River, next to but smaller than the Domesticated Animal Rescue Office, provided telling clues.

Not that it matters now, Tally told herself. Maybe after all this became public being underground, closer to the white dwarf particle would become a prestigious place to be. Maybe Scotland would become the next economic superpower. It was more than she could contemplate. It was more than she wanted to contemplate. In his first turn at bat, his first field trip, Harold Collins had not only found the road map to the Outer Limits, he'd made a round-trip. After listening to Dr. Jackson, Tally realized that however large it seemed, this could be just a very small beginning.

Or a knock on the head.

She was annoyed at herself because, despite the evidence, she still doubted Collins. Partly because she was hard-core "show me" and partly because she was afraid. Though she had lent her presence and the reputation of *Natural History* to the initial trip, that had been more to get out of town for a weekend than because she believed they'd find the Loch Ness Monster, let alone the Time Tunnel. She had always imagined herself a big-time rebel, turning her back on the family name and fortune to be a Working Jane and live in a tiny subsidized apartment in Manhattan's trendy but still not upper-class West Village. Compared to Harold, Tally was a freshman at the University of Sticking Your Neck Out.

The nearly fifty E-mails were the usual notifications of papers about to be published, papers newly published, writers with article ideas, scientists with article ideas, publishers wondering if the magazine would be interested in excerpting this or that book, and press releases from universities, foundations, institutions, and laboratories. She pretty much read the subject headings and then deleted them. Then she checked the on-line news headlines, since she rarely had time to read the *New York Times* except on weekends. It all seemed strangely mundane. And chillingly irrelevant. If they had actually found a way to travel through time, maybe soon—and what did "soon" mean when time wasn't really a factor?—maybe they'd be able to go back and manipulate events to turn them from bad to good.

Or maybe someone found a white-dwarf wormhole and was already using it to turn good events to bad, she thought.

Tally's head hurt and it wasn't even 10 A.M. A very small, unambitious, frightened part of her hoped that this whole thing about time travel turned out to be just a load of bushwah.

In the meantime, there was an item that caught her attention in the on-line travel log, under "This Just In!" It seemed like something that would give Harold a moment's distraction, which he could probably use before he went upstairs to meet with Samuel Bordereau.

It was an item about a woman in Sedona, Arizona—
where else, except perhaps Roswell?—who went to examine a statue in a cave and disappeared, though she left
another statue behind.

Of herself.

CHAPTER 5

HAROLD COLLINS SAT in the sun-splashed office of
Sam Bordereau. The big, square, windowy room was
ten times as high over First Avenue as Collins's office
was below. Collins sat with his legs crossed, his foot
jumping impatiently as he looked across the room. He
had just told Samuel about the breakfast meeting and
summarized what had been discussed. Now Samuel was
thinking. His slender fingers were steepled in front of his
lips, a practiced gesture that said, in any language, "I've
listened and am seriously considering what you just
said," even if he wasn't. Collins had always been patiently impatient with his friend. Whether it was pursu-
ing a woman, getting a grade changed in high school, or
even ordering food at a restaurant, Bordereau used a
kind of circuitous charm rather than hard reason to get

what he wanted. That was not Collins's way. He didn't need to know a waitress's life story. He just needed lunch.

Bordereau lowered his hands to the desk. That meant he was going to be defensive. If he had put them on his lap or on the arms of the chair, it meant he was going to be more receptive. Collins wanted to yell at him before he even spoke.

"It's a good start. A very good start," the United Nations assistant-deputy secretary-general told his friend and colleague. He told him in the same silky, seductive French accent that had convinced Collins to take this post in the first place—told him in a way that pat him on the head but made absolutely no promises.

"But?"

"But it's only a start," Bordereau said.

The young physicist uncrossed his legs, set them firmly on the plush white carpet, and leaned forward. "Sam, you came to Scotland. You talked to Dr. Castle. She told you what happened in Loch Ness. Now we've got another scientist, Dr. Jackson, saying, 'Yeah, this is possible.' "

" 'Possible' is not 'likely.' "

"Not if we can't do the research," Collins said. "Please. We've got to go back to Loch Ness with some artillery. Not just me and a reporter whose testimony is also being ignored—"

"It is not being ignored, not by me."

"—but with a team. A *bunch* of scientists. People with knowledge and equipment I don't have."

"Harold, I hear you very clearly and you have my support. But UNIT Omega has only been in operation for four months. We're lucky we have the money to pay your salary, let alone your plane ticket—"

"Okay, screw this," Collins said. He put his hands on

his knees and pushed up. "Save my salary. I can't work like this."

"Like what? As part of a team?"

"As low man on a bureaucratic totem pole. I'm going to get a real job."

"Where?" Bordereau asked. "At Wendy's?"

"Why not? Better to get burned with grease than by a supposed friend and supporter, the guy who wanted this stupid division in the first place."

"Harold, sit down," Bordereau said. "No one is burning you. You're screaming because you're impatient, not hurt."

"Are you kidding? We're sitting on the greatest scientific discovery *ever,* and you're having trouble getting bus fare for a few experts. That hurts!"

"Tell me, Harold. What great discovery has ever been thoroughly researched *right away* and then announced *in a hurry?*"

"I'm not asking for the Manhattan Project, Sam, though that would be the smart thing to do," Collins said. "I'm being practical. I'm asking for the resources to go back to Loch Ness and do research. Not even killer stuff, just more preliminary work. Measurements of electromagnetism, currents—"

"And I will get it for you, the same way any scientific grant is obtained," Bordereau promised. "*After* you've written a convincing report that I can present to the Financial Oversight Committee for Emergency Funding, and after they tell me what else they need—data, budget, letters of support—to approve your research."

"Bullshit, you mean."

"No. *Process.* Harold, ask your friend Tally, or Dr. Jackson. Is there a scientific or government institution on Earth that funds projects any differently?"

"If they knew what we were sitting on—"

"Harold, you are not sure what we're sitting on."

"I am."

"Like God."

That was the second time he had been described in those terms today. The karma was weird and made him uncomfortable.

"Be just a little reasonable," Bordereau said. "The United Nations is not going to change nearly sixty years of chartered activity because you say they must."

"No," Collins agreed, quietly. "That's *your* job, to convince them."

"Then let me do it," Bordereau implored. "On a timetable that will bear long-term results, not temporary solutions."

Collins was still standing. He put his hands on his hips. "What kind of time frame are we talking about?"

"Harold, I really don't know."

"Guess."

Bordereau scrunched his mouth and shrugged. "Three months."

"Realistically?"

"Optimistically," Bordereau admitted.

Collins scowled. "That's not acceptable."

"Then I recommend that you go back to Scotland, back in time, and start this process three months ago," Bordereau suggested. "Then you and Dr. Jackson could leave today."

"*That's* not funny."

"What do you want me to say?" Bordereau asked. "You're asking for something that isn't possible."

"Okay, let me ask *you* a question. Give me a reason why I shouldn't go to private investors and promise them the secret of time travel in exchange for five million dollars in research money?"

"Because first of all, you couldn't make that promise. You don't know how this time gateway works, or even— and you'll forgive me—*if* it works. Or will work again. Secondly, it would take you months to find the right financiers, months more to convince them to put up the money, and then years of therapy when they push you out and take over the project because they want their own people investigating and running it. And Tally won't be too happy when they insist on controlling all of the ancillary rights, including book publication and motion-picture rights."

Collins looked down. He had done the quantum physics thing: come to a conclusion then found that the step-by-step didn't work.

Bordereau walked from behind his desk. He lay a hand on his friend's shoulder. "I'm not your adversary, Harold."

"What are you?"

"Your ally."

"Allies help you," Collins said, with a tinge of disgust.

"That is true. I want to help. But you don't want to help me."

"Balls. I did. Just a week ago we stood in this office and you said to me that if I found the Loch Ness Monster you would have 'no trouble' boosting my budget. So where is the boost?"

"Where is the monster?" Bordereau asked.

"What?"

"Show it to me."

"That's not fair," Collins said.

"Why?"

"What was I supposed to do, bring a dinosaur home with a leash, have it clap its flippers for fish?"

"That would have gotten you your money," Bordereau said.

"It's vulgar and disgusting," Collins said.

"Welcome to the world of finance and politics. Welcome to reality—which is something I tried to shield you from for years," Bordereau said.

"Thank you, My Bodyguard."

"You *should* thank me. Do you think I like this way of operating?"

"Frankly, yes."

"Alors, I enjoy the fencing but not the reasons for it," Bordereau said. "I dislike all the patronage and territorialism, the pettiness and revenge. The reason I'm successful is because I look at it as a challenge, not a moral issue. I don't take things personally the way you do."

Collins did not reply. Bordereau had a point.

"Harold, I repeat. I want to help you. Look at me. Do you believe that?"

"I want to," Collins admitted.

"Then do. But getting the kind of money you require is something I have to finesse. You must give me a bit of breathing room. Just a little, all right?"

"Sure, Sam," Collins said.

The Frenchman was *so* damn sincere. Collins felt like a bad friend, though that surely hadn't been Bordereau's intention. And if it were, at least it wasn't malicious. Just manipulative. In a good way. Collins believed that Bordereau wanted to make UNIT Omega an important part of the United Nations, a part that was not tangled in the present but was proactive about the future.

"I'll give you time," Collins went on. "What's a few weeks when we're talking about eons?"

"That's a good attitude," Bordereau said.

Collins thanked his friend for punching a hole in his

busy morning to see him. Who else but Samuel Bordereau could deny Collins what he wanted then get him to thank him for it? The guy was good.

Bordereau's secretary Galit Lopatin was an exotic young beauty who was one of the few U.N. employees who happened to be from the U.S. of A. She gave Collins a wicked look as he left. Not exotic-sexy wicked, and not just nasty. It was nas*tay*—inconvenience plus disgust. She was in charge of the assistant-deputy secretary-general's schedule and Collins had a way of showing up and screwing it up. That was one area, at least, in which his friend never told him "no."

Collins passed several people who were waiting to see Bordereau, waiting with the kind of patience that ambassadorial types needed. Expressionless and unhurried, like poker players. Instead of cards and cash they played with words and favors. Collins took the executive elevator—the elevator reserved for diplomats and officials—to the main floor, then walked past the guard, through the always crowded public area, to the stairs that led to the gift shop. Off in a corner on the east side of this floor was another guard and an elevator that led to Collins's floor, sub-level three. It was beside the elevator the custodial staff used. Going to his office was like taking a subway from the Upper West Side to the Lower East Side: you had to transfer at Times Square. There was no direct way to get from one to the other.

Exhausted and dejected when he should have been uplifted and excited, Collins went to his office to brood. He had heard the words, he had understood the argument, and he had grasped the reality. But Collins still couldn't believe that he had discovered a means of going back to prehistory and studying dinosaurs, and he couldn't get someone to say, *"That's incredible! We'll*

*invest in that instead of new wallpaper for the security
council or new helmets for peacekeepers who don't do
anything or go anywhere."* What Collins really should
do was present his case to the Pentagon. Tell them he
could bring back dinosaurs to turn loose on enemies of
freedom. That would get him a billion dollars before the
week was out. He could see it now. Triceratops-tanks,
dive-bomber pterodactyls, G.I. allosauruses. . . .

Collins sat down in his windowless office and decided
to check his E-mail. It was necessary, diverting, and
even the spam was more satisfying than ruminating on
the antivisionary nature of bureaucracies. His parents
usually sent him digital photos from the banana planta-
tion that doubled as a bed-and-breakfast that they owned
in Maui. Just photos of them and the sunsets and the
dogs and the guests and whatever else grabbed his
mother's eye. The twenty-seven-year-old loved seeing
them. The photographs made him feel like he belonged
somewhere. Knowing how proud his parents were also
gave him strength. To his mother especially, working for
the United Nations was something transcendent. It rep-
resented both rarefied air and higher purpose. If he told
her the truth, she'd never believe it. These were the people who invented UNICEF. In her mind, they all had
pure souls and big hearts.

There were a total of forty-three E-mails. Four were
from his parents, and he saved them for last. He deleted
the spam first then went through the rest. All three of
them. One was an MIT alumni request for donations.
Collins was about to delete it but felt like a hypocrite: after all, wasn't he asking for financial help, too? He wrote
his alma mater a fifty-dollar check and slipped it into an
envelope. There was another confirming dinner tonight
with an old college flame. He replied that he'd be there.

Might as well take a personal beating to match the professional one. The last E-mail was from Tally Randall. He was not looking forward to opening it. She probably wanted to know how things had gone with Bordereau. She probably already knew.

He didn't have the heart to read it. Instead, he opened the E-mail from his parents and looked at the pictures from home. They didn't make him feel good, but they made him feel better. And right now, that was a lot.

CHAPTER 6

ASSISTANT CHIEF OF Police Grant Rhodes was not happy as he drove home along U.S. Highway 89A. It had nothing to do with the fact that his wife's ever-yammering aunt Claire was staying with them. He would say he had paperwork and vanish into the bedroom to watch TV with the headset on.

No. He was unhappy because he hadn't been able to get out here sooner. He could not go while he was still on duty because this was not, strictly speaking, a Sedona Police Department matter.

Rhodes was pushing eighty in the vintage Corvette. There was a stop he wanted to make in Red Rock Country—in Oak Creek Canyon in particular—which was six miles north of Sedona. He wanted to get there before it got dark. He wanted to see the thing for himself and not only find his friend but find something the Coconino County Sheriff's Department had missed.

There had always been, was, and probably always would be a territorial rivalry between the Sedona Police Department and the Coconino County Sheriff's Department. It was clear who investigated what outside the boundaries of the incorporated town of Sedona. That was CCSD business. But it got a little fuzzy when citizens of Sedona were involved.

Blossom Wang was a citizen of Sedona. She was also a longtime friend of the forty-four-year-old officer. Firearms were Rhodes's passion. For a long time he couldn't afford to buy the weapons she was selling so she let him borrow them. It was just "Go on, take it till you're done with it." The rookie liked to—and still did, in fact—put the guns under a magnifying glass and study the workmanship, determine how much use they may have gotten, get the feel of what it must have been like to be a rancher or a sheriff or a gunslinger back in the 1800s. Rusty knew he would bring the guns back—it was a small town and he *was* an officer of the law. But he could have dropped one and busted it, or Rusty might have lost a sale while he had it out from the shop. Not only didn't she care, it made her happy to make him happy.

Now she was gone. Not just missing, according to Sheriff's Deputy Abe Tlaquepo, but gone, without taking her vehicle and having left behind a very strange memento: a life-size statue of herself and her dogs, in chalky marble. Rhodes didn't know how she would have gotten a statue of herself up the dirt road, or unloaded it by herself, or even when or why she could have had it made. Rhodes stopped by the shop at least once a week. He and Rusty talked about things. A self-portrait was a commission she would probably have mentioned, especially if it included her Jack Russells. They were her little loves, her heralds and her guardians.

And, really, it just wasn't *like* her. A statue? Rusty hated having her photo taken. She had issues with her appearance. The few antique mirrors she sold were behind the counter, so she wouldn't have to look at herself.

Rhodes reached the turnoff, headed to the site where Tlaquepo had found the statue that had brought Rusty out here, then used his cell phone to call Sgt. Donna Pratt, head of dispatch.

"Any news from county?" he asked, as he stopped at the foot of the road.

"Not a poop," she said. "Missing persons E-mail went out, photo attached, no response as yet."

"What about the interviews?"

Detective John Givens was handling the talks with Rusty's neighbors and family. He hadn't begun them until early afternoon, however, when the deputy went back to see how Rusty was doing and found the statues. The police hoped to find out whether she was supposed to meet someone somewhere after going to the cave, or if maybe she had ticked someone off—Rusty could do that, being as direct as she was—or if there might have been a family emergency.

That she went to without her damn van? What happened, the friggin' family whirlybird came and got her? Rhodes didn't think she even had any family. Except in Shanghai somewhere, which she was checking on. And he thought she would have mentioned if she were going there. From the side of Snake Mountain.

Rhodes parked behind the slope, where no one was likely to see his 'vette. It was a tempting target for car thieves and he'd be too far to stop them. Coming around to the eastern side he made his way up. That was one of the problems with having an SUV by day and a sports-car by night. You got spoiled. He eased his five-foot-ten-inch self from the vehicle and, flashlight in hand, made his way to the cave. He wasn't as familiar with this area as the deputy was, though Snake Mountain itself had been easy enough to find. There were yellow signs posted starting a half-mile away, with black silhouettes warn-ing hikers of rattlers.

Rhodes was wearing his twenty-year-old, oft-resoled Fryes. There wasn't a snake on earth that was going to get his ankles.

The sheriff's department had put yellow "crime scene" tape across the mouth of the cave. The forensics unit hadn't come up here yet. They were working on the van, which had been secured and flat-bedded to Flagstaff for review by the evidence technicians. They didn't want to come out to the mountain because the winds would have made it difficult to search for fingerprints, hair strands, and fibers. They were working under the assumption that this had been an abduction, since an aerial search had not turned up any trace of Rusty or her remains.

Rhodes ducked under the yellow tape and entered the cave. He got a strange feeling as he did that. There was something safe and familiar but also unsettling. There was fading daylight behind him, with changing colors, wind, and the occasional hawk crying out, and dark, ominous stillness ahead. It was almost as though he were entering a haunted attraction at a theme park.

He switched on the flashlight and held it shoulder high. He shifted it slowly from side to side. He was star-tled by a faint, low whistling sound coming from within. But then he remembered something from the deputy's second report, about his return to the site. Tlaquepo said he noticed a hole in a rear wall of the cave. That was probably what was whistling.

"Either that, or it's mutant snakes," Rhodes said. Aloud. To himself. Just to hear something other than that eerie recorder-like sound.

The burly officer rounded a corner in the cave. He half expected to see Rusty there with some strange, Rustyesque explanation: "Oh, I fell into this limestone pit and it got in my eyes and I couldn't see and I ended up in the river and as I walked back here to look at the statue the powder hardened and I couldn't move—"

Rhodes stubbed his foot on something hard. He turned the light on it. He looked down. He had toed one of the dog statues. They were facing backward. He went around and crouched in front of them. He shifted the beam from one dog figure to the other and back.

"Damn if you don't look just like Cracker and Flap," he said.

They did. A lot. The detail was amazing. He leaned closer. He touched what looked like a curled, stray hair sticking from one of the eyebrows. It shattered with a delicate *snick*.

"I don't get it," he said.

Rhodes rose, turned, and walked deeper into the cave. He walked slowly. The whistling was louder and the dogs freaked him more than a little. He was thinking—hoping, really—that this was a joke. Rusty wasn't like that on her own. But maybe she had worked up some kind of nutty happy-twenty-first-year-with-the-department thing with the chief, just to pinch Rhodes's ass. Not that the chief had a sense of humor either. But it was the only thing he could think of. Or hope for.

In just a few steps the light found Rusty's statue. It, too, was a perfect likeness. He moved closer and turned the light toward her left ear, right below the lobe. The real Rusty had a mole there.

So did the statue Rusty.

He moved around the statue, scanning it top to bottom with the light. The artist had carved all the hairs in her head. The wrinkles in the fabric were right, even the texture of the fabric. Rhodes touched the back of Rusty's vest. It felt like damp clay. It was uncanny.

Rhodes moved back the statue and shined the light around the back of the cave. He saw the other statue, which was just like the sculpture of Rusty. It was a Native American with a carbine. He touched the barrel. It felt almost as though there was carved rust. Which was insane and impossible.

He ducked and edged around the figure to the wall behind. Rhodes touched the rock. The stone was cool and clammy.

Like damp clay.

Except that there didn't appear to be a water source that might bring minerals down here. He ran his fingertips along the cave ceiling and the ridges along the top of the wall. They felt exactly like the face-stone. He wondered if the rock might be porous and leaking water from behind. He took out his Swiss Army knife and ran a blade across the stone. It came away in large dollops, like putty.

"Hard flesh, soft rock," he said. "This is not making sense."

Rhodes removed a handkerchief from his jeans pocket and wrapped a piece of stone inside. He was annoyed that the sheriff's deputy hadn't written anything about the malleable rock in either of his reports. Or maybe he hadn't bothered to check the wall. Abe Tlaquepo was probably in here just long enough to see the Rusty statue and leave. In fairness to the deputy, he was trained for first contact. The deputies made discoveries, secured a site, then left it to the CCDS detectives or the Sedona PD to figure out what had happened.

Rhodes felt air from the bore-hole on the side of his neck. The sun was setting and the temperature was dropping. He backed away from the nook-like area and turned toward the mouth of the cave. His light struck the statue of Rusty again; the thing was just plain weird. Though it wasn't as strange as what was in front of it. Rhodes saw what appeared to be a beam of light.

"Deputy Tlaquepo?" he said.

There was no answer. He squinted. The beam was much brighter than his and coming closer.

"Who's out there?"

Rhodes shined his own light ahead. He saw nothing but an enlarging cone of light. He thought he heard a faint hissing, like air escaping a tire.

"Okay, funny people. You got me. Who the hell's behind this? Rusty? Donna? Givens?" He waited. "*Talk* to me, dammit! I give!"

Rhodes shielded his eyes and tried to peer ahead.

He was still in the cave, still shielding his eyes three hours later when, answering a concerned call from Barb Rhodes, Grant's wife, the chief of police called the CCSD and asked them to have a man go up to Snake Mountain to see if Rhodes was still there.

CHAPTER 7

TALLY WALKED HOME from work. It was a straight
shot—three and a half miles south from West
Eighty-first Street to West Tenth Street. But it was a
beautiful early evening and she had barely left her seat
all day. Executive editors got to go to meetings every
day, during every part of the day. Assistant and associate
editors went to one meeting a week. The rest of the time
they got to edit.

Tally got to edit. She got to edit the work of scientists
who, as a rule, were not writers. Years of thesis-writing
enabled them to put thoughts together, though not often
using words or phrases non-Ph.D.s could follow. Since
Natural History was not *Scientific American* or *Paleobiol-
ogist Quarterly,* that was important. For one of her journalism classes at Vassar, Tally had to edit an article called

"Ion Propulsion Drives" so that it could be publishable in *Highlights for Children*. She got a B, not because it wasn't successful reduced and redacted, but because she had used Goofus and Gallant as narrators. That had changed the third-person narrative to first person.

Walking down Ninth Avenue, it seemed both reassuring and trivial to see people having dinner, talking on cell phones, selling things from vending carts or storefronts or blankets that got scooped up when a police officer turned the corner. Her own world had been changed by the knowledge that there might be—*all right, probably was*—a hole into one or more times and places. Both immediate and long-term goals suddenly seemed unambitious.

And yet, if there is such a thing as time travel, wouldn't every moment be exactly the opposite of meaningless? she asked herself. *If there's a record, so to speak, of everything that is done, was done, or will ever be done, then everything we do is immortal.* The good stuff, bad stuff, personal stuff, public stuff—all of it was available for viewing, as if the universe were a temporal Blockbuster. That was unnerving. To think that her first-grade play, *Our Body,* in which she played Wendy Wisdom Tooth, was locked in time somewhere was chilling. But it made sense. Even the grandest staircase was useless without each step. All of time wasn't "all" if it was missing even a nano-second. If there was a brief gap in time, nothing could get past it. Or move forward through it. Even words were screwing with her now.

Spicy Chinese food was always good for a reality check, so she stopped for Szechuan take-out at Eleventh and Hudson before going to her brownstone. She rented a room from Winston Kolb, a former publisher, now a philanthropist, who leased apartments to bright students or up-and-coming youths who needed a break. Or whom he liked having around because they were charming and smart. Or maybe, as Collins had suggested, he felt guilty.

"I've heard of a lot of starving writers but never a starving publisher," Collins had said at some point.

Well, maybe that was the case with Kolb. Tally didn't care. The courtly old gentleman was good to his tenants. Though she wasn't exactly needy, Kolb seemed impressed by the fact that she had given the back of her hand to the family fortune. Kolb himself had his own son tossed out the door to get him to do that, and also to make room for Tally. He also had the locks changed as well as the telephone numbers. Even so, the twenty-four-year-old still came back, pleading poverty, and occasionally bellowing "Stella!" when his dad wouldn't open the door. Tally admired the elder Kolb's resolve to make a man of his man-let.

Tally did not have voice mail at home so there were never any messages to return to. This was her haven. Anyone she wanted to hear from knew to ring once, hang up, then call again. She flipped through her mail, compulsively paid the bills right away, then planted herself and her container of sesame chicken behind a copy of *Gourmet*. She tried not to think that every bite was being burned into the annals of history. Therein lay the road to indigestion. Fortunately, she couldn't imagine that anyone would want to come back in time and see her chew.

Gourmet was followed by *Vogue,* then the comic-book magazine *Wizard,* and then *Cigar Afficionado.* Magazine reading wasn't like magazine editing. It was like rehearsing a play all day and then going to the theater. She wanted to be entertained and informed. Tally had subscriptions to over two dozen titles. It didn't matter what the subject was, Tally loved slick, handsome magazines. Slick paper was important: she didn't like pulp or newsprint. It seemed impermanent, like newspapers.

Wormholes make all the moments of the universe like slick paper, she thought happily.

The idea that a magazine could be beautiful and have substance excited her. And a good editor could make any subject interesting. She liked to see how they did it, even subjects in which she had no interest, such as cars or videogames. *Natural History* would never let her mess with the style of the magazine, which she described as "mint tea": Pleasant and wholesome, produced by the earth. Never anything disturbing, like the fighting animals and body-modified natives in *National Geographic*. But one day she would make changes, get it out of the museum-member-subscriber ghetto and into the mainstream. Maybe sooner than she had planned, if Dr. Jackson was right that Harold Collins wasn't crazy and they had a comet by the tail.

She was interrupted by a one-ring, then silence, then ring-ring call. It was from a guy she had met at a party at the South Street Seaport. A fund-raiser for a local aquarium. Tally was not a drinker but she must have had one too many chocolate daiquiris because she had given a yachtsman her number. He was young and tall with blue eyes and moussed hair carefully askew in front and a capped-teeth smile that he used as bait. At the time, she thought it would be fun to have dinner and a sail on his boat, on which the party was being held. But then she realized that all they had talked about was the places he'd been and though that had been fun when she was a little buzzy, it seemed lame now. Besides, he was the kind of guy her mother would have totally approved of. Wealthy and sharp and full of himself.

She let him invite her on a trip out to the family compound in Newport, Rhode Island the following weekend. She declined.

"Was it something I said?" he asked, with tongue in cheek.

"Actually, it was what you didn't say."

"I'm sorry?"

"Never mind," Tally said. She wasn't even sure what she had meant by that. It had sounded right in her head and just came out. "Listen, I'm really kinda busy right now." A beat. He didn't ask with what. *Now* she knew what she meant. What he didn't say. He didn't ask a damn thing about her.

" 'Kind of busy right now' as in 'this moment' or 'this week'?" he asked in a wounded tone.

"As in 'I may have found a way to travel through time, and I really have to check that out,' " she said. "Also, I'd probably make a mess of your stateroom."

"Why?" he asked with a lascivious little laugh. "Do you eat pretzel rods and mustard in bed?"

Jesus, Mary, and jumping Jehosophat. He was even worse than she remembered. "No, Dirk Pitt," Tally replied. "The mess would come from me putting a bullet in my brain."

There was a confused pause. "Excuse me?"

"Look, that doesn't matter either."

"Tally, are you 'on' something?"

"I wish—"

"This is Farley Rapp, not 'Dirk Pitt.' "

Fahley Rawpp, the guy said it. *Uggh.* "I know who it is. What matters is that I'm busy."

"What about the following week?" he asked. "We'll be off to my aunt's in Nantucket."

Tally resisted improvising a limerick. She had already

been crueler than she should have been. She told him she was busy too then hung up. She went back to the latest issue of *Rolling Stone.*

Almost immediately, guilt tried to get a beachhead on Tally's conscience. *Farley Rapp didn't deserve that treatment from her,* it informed her. She answered back that he probably deserved it from someone.

"And, lord God, he's *so stupid!*" she said aloud. He was one of those guys who had probably paid for his prep-school term papers and Yale theses and didn't care because he was inheriting dad's business anyway.

Still, she fought the urge to call him and apologize. She put the magazine aside and turned on the tube. She wasn't a big TV watcher, since most of it was dumber than Farley. But it was nearly eleven o'clock—time for the news. She watched one story, then another. The "another" got her attention. And as suddenly as he'd intruded on her evening, Farley Rapp disappeared. She reached for the phone and speed-dialed Collins's cell phone. He didn't answer so she called his home phone. He didn't answer there, either, so she left a message.

As Tally hung up, she half-wondered if he had booked a flight back to Scotland. That would be like him. She envied him that impulsiveness.

One day she would do something impulsive.

That was something she wanted to have recorded for eternity. . . .

CHAPTER 8

COLLINS HAD NOT spent the afternoon writing a Loch Ness report. Before he did that he wanted to read up on wormholes. He had a feeling his argument would be more persuasive garbed in techno-babble. He also wanted to be able to talk intelligently with Dr. Jackson on the subject. Or without him, if the scientist bailed.

The Internet had a lot of sites, even after you eliminated the *Star Trek*-related references. They all seemed to agree on one thing. A wormhole would by definition be an extremely unstable corridor.

" 'A wormhole cannot be a static, unchanging structure,' " he read on a site affiliated with the Mt. Palomar Observatory. " 'It's a construct that expands from a singularity, a point in space-time at which gravity—a black hole or white dwarf—creates a core of matter with infinite density but infinitesimal volume, causing time and space around it to become distorted.' "

So far, so good, he thought. Unfortunately—

" 'This construct would have a virtually nonexistent throat radius due to the intense gravity of the causal object. In theory, any matter which attempted to pass through would close the wormhole by the pull of its own gravity.' "

Yet Collins had traveled through one. Not only that, but he had traveled back through the same one. Something had held the door open. The more he read, the more it occurred to him what it might be.

Physicists theorized that black holes created wormholes that terminated in white holes—that is, collapsed stars that caused space-time to move in reverse. Sort of like matter and antimatter. A wormhole couldn't just open to "nothing." That made sense. Even in basic geometry, it took two points to determine a line. Thus, it would take two terminals to define and create a wormhole.

"What if we're only dealing with one particle of white-dwarf matter here, and countless others in different places?" he thought aloud. Jackson had alluded to one or more interlacing wormholes. Perhaps they were exerting sufficient gravity to keep each other open. A network of singularities.

The mental image it created was like the inside of an atom, with electrons whizzing around a nucleus. They were independent, yet interrelated. Nature liked symmetry, and it was conceivable that a design writ small could also be replicated on a larger scale. He wondered, though, if the theoretical interweaving of these wormholes would be sufficient to support the structure or if they needed a nucleus of their own somewhere. Scientists had recently proven that there was a black hole in the center of the Milky Way. Could the white dwarf have been ripped apart by that black hole? Could these particles be orbiting that phenomenon—not now, but in some future time when the Earth reached that point in space? Perhaps they had fallen through and gotten shot through time-space like marbles. One of them ended up here, one of them in the Devonian, others in who-knew-what time or space?

It was certainly possible.

Collins finished his preliminary research, checked a few paranormal websites to see if there were any interesting ghost sightings—he wanted to check out rattling flatware instead of time-and-space-warping, fluctuating wormholes—and came away with nothing worth filing. He went out for a long contemplative sit by the East River, then met a college friend for drinks. He and Rose Coronado had had a short-lived romance in their first year at MIT, one that ended with a debate—over drinks, as it happened—about whether anything in the universe could be proven. Collins had said no. Everything was subjective, even science. He had used, as his example— ironically, given his earlier thoughts about atoms, or perhaps not ironically, since subconsciously he knew he was going to be meeting Rose—he had used as his example electrons. If you stopped them to look at them, to prove they were there, they were no longer in motion. And an electron in motion was no longer an electron. If you didn't stop them, you could see the results of their motion and *infer* they were there from that, but not prove it. To Rose, who was a chemist, that was philosophical horseshit. She said you couldn't selectively isolate data. You had to take the electron in both states.

Collins argued that that was still an inference. Early paleontologists had found the tusks of prehistoric mammoths near the bones of primitive horses. They had assembled them as unicorns. That didn't make unicorns real.

From that conversation Rose had determined that Collins didn't trust women. He wasn't sure just how she had arrived at that, but she was wrong. Which, when he thought about it later, actually proved her point.

He and Rose didn't talk to each other for a semester-and-a-half after that debate. When they finally did get back together—they were both dining alone at McDonald's— they decided to be friends, not lovers. Rose said she couldn't be with a man who did not believe that anything was provable—especially love.

Collins had felt blindsided by that observation, but decided not to fight it. *He* couldn't be with someone who would not accept love as an idea but, apparently, would need overpriced flowers, overpriced dinners, and grievously overpriced jewelry to prove its existence. He wanted someone like his mom, who was happy with her man, her sarong, and her garden. Or whatever the New York City equivalent of that was, since he really didn't want to move to Maui.

The drinks were pleasant enough. They met at a Japanese restaurant on Forty-fifth and Third, and ended up having sushi with their brews. Rose was working for a pharmaceutical firm in the Midwest and was in town for a convention. She looked a little frumpier than when he had last seen her, though that could be due to a lack of sleep and white-collar clothing. He was used to seeing her in sweats.

When she asked him how he liked his new job, he

told her it was great. When she asked if he got to travel a lot, he said yes. He did not elaborate.

It was well after midnight when Collins reached his apartment on Twenty-third and Third. He had a "Did you catch the news tonight?" phone message from Tally Randall, who did not tell him what it was he should have seen. He called her back. Only after he had rung once, hung up, then started ringing again did he notice the time. He considered hanging up but realized the damage was probably done and, anyway, he wanted to know what she had been calling about.

"How'd you know I'd still be up?" she asked.

"I didn't. Were you?"

"Yes. I assume you were working late?"

"Actually, no," Collins told her. "I met an old friend for a drink that turned into sushi."

"An old friend as in 'female'?"

"Yeah. Look, I don't want to keep you up," Collins said. "What did I miss?"

"Something that sounded like it might belong in the UNIT Omega in-box for tomorrow," Tally told him. "Put on CNN. They usually repeat slow-news features every hour."

" 'Slow news'?" he asked.

"Same thing I E-mailed you about earlier, when there was just one."

"The statue?"

"Yes. There are more now."

"Really?"

Collins thanked her, wished her pleasant dreams, then turned on the tube. He dropped onto his tiny sofa, pulled off his shoes, and threw his feet up on his Workbench coffee table.

The story cycled around after just a few minutes. The news report treated the thing as if it were a joke, something to give the Arizona tourist trade a lift. Antiques dealer goes to check an antique statue, leaves a statue of herself behind. Police officer goes to check the statue of the antique dealer, leaves a statue of *him*self behind. The newscaster speculated that it was probably a promotion for an arts-and-crafts festival where the statues would be sold. Collins wondered what had happened to the days when anchors didn't offer opinions unless their signatures were being flashed across the bottom of the screen. Gone with the sugar barrel, pickle barrel, and milk pan.

It was an interesting story, and indisputably offbeat, but Collins just didn't know if it qualified as "the unexplained." Rose Coronado in business attire was also pretty strange. Still, Sedona had a reputation for being a place of spiritual relevance. He had never been there nor read much about it. This was as good a time as any. He would not be going to bed too soon. A lot of wasabi and a lot of soy sauce—not the sodium-free kind—had resulted in a lot of water being consumed. He booted his laptop, muted the TV, and went on-line to read about Sedona. He thanked the Lord for the Internet. He used to do this kind of stuff with the *World Book,* and hated those slick pages. They were a pain in the butt to turn without wetting your fingers. And then you stained them.

"Located high southwestern desert . . . mild weather and sunshine . . . blah, blah," he read on the official town website. He skipped to the history. "October, 1901, Theodore Schnebly and wife arrived with their kids. Very few settlers there, eager to get more, Ted writes to Post Office Department and gets p.o. approved, though he's informed that Schnebly Station is too long for the cancellation stamp." He snickered. "Thank God. So he suggests his wife's name, Sedona. Mostly ranchers living there, Native Americans, not incorporated until 1988."

He clicked on a link to tours, figuring that was what the New Agers would be interested in. There he read, " 'Sedona is the primary positive energy center of the world. When you stand among the vivid red rocks you can feel the spiritual auras, the vibration, of what the natives consider to be sacred ground. This vortex expands and magnifies your own energy, allowing you to meditate and absorb the power of the universe. Visit the cliff dwellings and also Jerome, which was once a thriving mining town and is now a virtual ghost town.' " He bookmarked the site. "Does that mean they only have virtual ghosts in Sedona?"

Collins frowned then slapped himself. He had absolutely no right to make light of Sedona. None. He went to the kitchen—which was two steps away; most things in his tiny one-bedroom apartment were within stretching-from-the-chair length—to get himself a bottle of water, which he shouldn't be having but needed. Actually, Collins told himself, he wasn't really making fun of Sedona or its energy. It was the *gravitas* of the presentation. New Agers tended to be overly sincere. Cracking the plastic cap of his bottle, he took a slug and went to another site, one that explained vortices.

Suddenly, the gravitas of the other website did not seem so inappropriate. He swallowed the mouthful then read aloud.

" 'A vortex is a funnel caused by surging, turning fluids or energy,' " he read. "It can be made of anything that flows, including water, electricity, or wind. In Sedona, these funnels are comprised of pure energy emanating from the Earth itself. Though the energy you will feel is not electric or magnetic per se, it registers on oscilloscopes and magneto-meters in areas where it is the most powerful. It is not known what causes the four specific locations of phenomena in Sedona. And while it is thought to be of terrestrial origin, a celestial agency cannot be dismissed.'"

"You mean, NASA?"

Collins, too, had experienced a strong, magnetic tug of some kind when he was deep in Loch Ness, right before he'd had his close encounter with a possible singularity. He wondered if the Loch Ness anomaly could be a vortex similar to the one described on the website.

Collins watched the CNN report when it came on again. The statues per se were not what interested him right now. They seemed almost to be a tacky, insincere sideshow, like the UFO cults that had grown up around the 1947 "flying saucer" crash in Roswell, New Mexico. It was Sedona that mattered. Sedona could be an outlet for a wormhole in the cluster posited by Dr. Jackson.

Collins couldn't tell that to Samuel Bordereau, of course. If he added too many supernatural "brand names" to the mix, the credibility of the Loch Ness report—such as it was—would be undermined.

Then again, what if all those places are considered strange and mysterious because *they've always been wormhole terminals,* Collins wondered. Loch Ness, Sedona, the Bermuda Triangle, Stonehenge, even Roswell. They might be anchored to vortices in time and space, thus causing objects or energy to shift from point to point. The young physicist couldn't quite get his mind around that—not the concept itself but the postmodern expression of it. He couldn't decide whether those so-called mystical places gave him a Unified Field Theory of the Weird or simply trivialized the one bonafide experience he did have.

There might be a way to find out, he decided.

He would go to one of them in the morning. And Sedona seemed as good a place as any.

CHAPTER 9

TALLY WAS LYING on her back in a small but fluffy bed, trying to think only good thoughts about Harold Collins. The momentum of that battle changed from second to second.

It was not quite six-thirty—the sun hadn't even reached the west side of Tenth Street—and she would have had another half hour of deeply cherished rest if he hadn't called. But then, she was the one who had given him the heads up. She had no one to blame except . . .

"That's a real nice theory, Harold," Tally said over the phone. "A *very* nice theory."

"But you don't want to check it out."

"I would love to but I have a job," she reminded him. "My employer likes it when I'm in the office."

What made the call worse was that she didn't know

whether Harold had really phoned to ask her to go or whether he was looking for some kind of blessing or permission or entente.

"But isn't this part of your work?" Harold pressed.

"White-dwarf-particle-number-two-hunting was not in the job description, no," Tally said.

"You're being glib," he said.

"I was being glib before, too."

"I don't get it," he complained.

"Look, Harold. I don't disagree with what you're doing. I was the one who turned you on to that news story, remember?"

"Yeah—"

"I think you should go to Sedona. It's a good idea and it is part of *your* job description."

"You may be missing out on an important part of the story you will one day be writing."

"I'll take that risk," Tally said. "Harold, I wish I could be that impulsive."

"You don't want to."

"I can't. But at least Arizona is closer than Scotland. I can get there quickly if I have to."

"Flying to the rescue to pull my head out of a honey pot."

"I think it was Pooh's hand that got stuck," Tally said.

"Whatever," Collins said. "Fine. I'll do all the legwork. Will you do me a favor, then?"

"If I can."

"Try and get to Dr. Jackson this morning, ask what he thinks of the idea that places like Sedona and Roswell may be loci in this theoretical wormhole rubberband-ball of ours."

"That's reasonable," she said.

"Thanks. I'll let you know what I find there," Collins

said. "And I still think you'll be sorry you didn't go."

"You know what? I hope you're right."

Collins *hmmmm*ed.

"I mean that," Tally insisted.

She did, too. It wasn't that she was disinterested in the mystery they had uncovered. Quite the opposite. But apart from finding herself jobless, she didn't want to go because she didn't want to became drawn into this quest the way Harold had. Someone needed to keep a hand-hold in reality. That was the problem with so many of the UFO looney-toons and conspiracy advocates. They had let hope rob them of checks-and-balances.

Tally wished Collins a safe trip and hung up before he shifted into a badgering or pleading mode. One thing she had learned about Harold was that "part B" of any conversation could segue into anger or appeasement but never got off-topic. He was Mr. Focus. A change in tactics didn't advance his cause, it just let him purge whatever he was feeling. And it left her feeling worked-over, as though she'd had a deep-brain massage in her pain center.

Tally looked at the clock again. Six-thirty-two. It was too late to go back to sleep, so Tally reached beside the bed and dragged out a manuscript she was going to start reading on the subway, about the early history of weapons in America, going back to prehistoric spears and Native American arrows. It was pretty fascinating how people who did not have sophisticated tools or knowledge of science were able to make such aerodynamic projectiles. She wondered how she would have done back then, what her specialty would have been. She wondered if she would have resented a society, however crude, in which men were so dominant. Or if that came from upbringing rather than some kind of genetic predisposition to indignation.

She wondered what career a man like Harold would have pursued in a prehistoric tribe. He probably would have been a shaman. He could have used science to scam the tribe into thinking it was magic. Or he could have sought real magic and convinced himself and the tribe that he had found it. Offbeat versatility. That was the odd marvel known as Harold Collins.

About whom you are thinking way too much, Tally reflected when she realized that ten minutes had passed and she was staring at the same second page of the manuscript. *Thinking about him with both frustration and inexplicable charity.*

Tally didn't stand by Harold solely for the chance to write about these wormholes, if that's what they turned out to be. There was something about Harold himself that commanded—it wasn't affection exactly, nor a desire to mother. She didn't know what it was. Perhaps it was exemplified in his devotion to Sam Bordereau, and Bordereau's to him. There was something sweet about that. Harold gave you the feeling that while he might not be the easiest friend to be with, he was a steadfast one. And that was pretty significant. Maybe that's what drew her to him. Harold put people and ideals above profit and acclaim. That was something new in her life. *And there you go thinking about him again . . .*

Tally pushed the manuscript back into her shoulder bag. She took a shower and swallowed her vitamins and got herself conservatively jacket-and-slacks-ed for another challenging but predictable day in the wood-paneled halls of the fifth floor of the Museum.

Maybe that was part of it, too, she reflected as she had a final half-cup of coffee and checked CNN before leaving for work. Unlike her, Harold was neither predictable or conservative. Dashing off to Sedona because of some unripe idea he had gotten while watching a curious news report at an hour when most people were asleep—you didn't just shut the door on a Cuckoo Salesman like that.

She finished her coffee and reached for the remote and was about to turn the TV off when an update from Sedona came on, one that made the salesman's pitch seem a little less "out there. . . ."

CHAPTER 10

THE UNITED NATIONS issued its employees cell phones that were made in Maun, Botswana. The UN Purchasing Committee believed in supporting up-and-coming economies instead of well-established ones, assuming that the quality of the products was somewhat similar, the operative word being "somewhat." The reception was pretty terrific for the most part, though it was much better outside than it was inside. Maybe that was because so much of Botswana was "outside," Collins suspected.

Regardless, he didn't get the 8:07 A.M. message from Tally until he was inside the terminal, where reception was not so good.

"Say again?" Collins said, huddled low in a seat at the

gate, facing a wall, a finger in his ear. "What did they find in the cave?"

"A *vet-er-in-a-ri-an*," Tally said.

"An animal doctor, not a soldier—"

"Correct," Tally said. "Apparently he's the one who looked after Ms. Wang's dogs. He must have seen the report on the news and went up to check out the statues of the animals."

"Gotta love those small-town doctors."

"Yeah, they still make cave calls. But that's not the strange part," Tally went on. "They found the doctor bent over one of the dogs. The other one is now in the vet's hand."

"Someone could have picked the dog up and put it there as a joke," Collins suggested.

"No. It is *part* of his hand and was obviously carved there."

"Oh." That was surprising. And inexplicable.

"The only words anyone is using to describe this are still 'elaborate joke,' " Tally said, "but no one is suggesting by whom or why."

"I'll find out," Collins assured her.

"Just watch out for the vortexes," she cautioned. "They may not go anywhere, but they apparently do strange things to people's heads and bodies."

"Are you saying I can't afford that?" Collins asked.

"I'm saying that scientists have to stay objective," she replied.

"Not a problem," Collins said. "I stayed objective in Devonian Park. I can handle some weird vibes."

"I guess. Hey, sorry if I was a little smart before," Tally said. "I tend to be that way so close to sun-up."

"Also not a problem," he said. "Tal, we're all just people trying to figure things out. It's like learning to dance.

Sometimes you get it and sometimes you step on peoples' toes."

They said good-bye. As Collins slipped the cell phone back on his belt he was amused at how uncharacteristically contrite she was. A lot of people were like that: attack, retreat, attack, retreat. Or in her case, sarcasm, sincerity, sarcasm, sincerity. He tried to be more consistent, staying committed to what had prompted the conversation in the first place, whatever it was. It was a philosophy that went back to his earliest major confrontation. It happened during high school, when Harold went round and round with a math teacher, claiming that he deserved a score of one hundred instead of a ninety-eight. To prevent cheating, Mr. Shawnee kept the tests in his head and wrote them on the blackboard. Collins insisted that what looked to Mr. Shawnee like a 7X in a chalk-written equation looked to Collins like a 74, and that he had computed accordingly. Mr. Shawnee argued that no one else in the class had made that mistake. Collins argued that the point was irrelevant: the test was about math skills, not reading, and whatever the element was Collins had performed the correct functions. And gotten the wrong answer, Shawnee shot back. Collins argued that if Mr. Shawnee wanted to make this issue about reading, not math, then Collins would also make it about penmanship—the teacher's, which was faulty. Both the principal and the superintendent of schools refused to hear his case, nor did the mayor, and Harold Collins did not get the two-point bump.

But Collins did get a mission in life. He dedicated himself, at that moment in the eleventh grade, to becoming a world famous mathematician/scientist so that he could continue this battle and one day humiliate his teacher in an international arena, such as accepting a Nobel Prize or giving a commencement speech at MIT. That—revenge, not the prize—was still a ripe, ever-present goal of his. And to achieve it, to achieve anything, required total commitment. But something Collins's father had said during that awful and dreary week stayed with him as well: "Unshakeable commitment is idealism and idealism is like pipe smoke," the elder Collins had told him. "It smells nice but you can't touch it. It's much better to be a realist and chew gum."

Collins did not agree, but he couldn't dispute the truth of his father's observation. Which was a paradox in itself, to concur with something and not embrace it. He wondered if anyone else in the crowded terminal was pondering their life's values or whether they were already checked in at whatever hotel they were visiting, planning their meeting or vacation or visit with the grandfolks. Not that there was anything wrong with that. Gum was a whole lot healthier than tobacco.

Collins went to a coffee stand, ordered black coffee and a thickly buttered bagel, sat down, and read the *New York Times*. There was nothing about the Sedona statues in the August paper, but that didn't surprise him. However, Collins made a promise to himself. He vowed that by the time he was finished in Arizona there would be. He had a feeling something was out there. Not because of the cave but because of the larger mystery that was Sedona.

Sedona, Sedona, it's my kinda town, he started singing to himself.

The tune got stuck in Collins's head as he made car and hotel reservations on-line. It was there as he boarded the plane and it stayed there through the four-hour flight and the landing in Phoenix. It moved silently on his lips as he picked up his rental car and found voice again as he drove out to Sedona. Just the one chorus, over and over. Wormholes he could understand. It was amazing to him that those things actually worked, that someone was out there receiving and processing the information.

Collins booted his laptop and glanced at the computer map as he rolled along 17N toward Sedona, a trip which the Internet—bless it again—had also told him would take about two hours and a quarter. Collins decided to go to the site before checking in at the Boots and Spurs bed-and-breakfast, since he didn't know what restrictions might have been placed on the cave site and he didn't want to go to town, go out to the mountain, then have to go back to town to get a hall pass or whatever the locals might require. He wondered if his United Nations ID would generate a lot of suction out here, whether the locals would think it was the Big Time or whether they'd think he was just an outsider clomping around in their private affairs. He bet on the former. Sedona was about places that generated a lot of strange and apparently pointless energy. The United Nations certainly fit that profile.

The trip to Snake Mountain was not quite as *How the West Was Won,* as Collins had expected. There were acres of blue sky and mountains in the distance, but the close-up roadside attractions were like in-your-face-tacky roadside attractions along any interstate he had ever traveled—except in Maui, where you could always see the ocean to overcome the kitsch that was humanity.

Collins turned on the radio to try and find the news. He couldn't find any and switched to FM. He picked up a station out of Flagstaff that had a talk show hosted by the mellow Percy Canali. Collins did not for a moment believe that was the host's real name. Flagstaff grew up around the observatory built in 1894 by Percival Lowell,

on what was now called Mars Hill. Lowell was a wealthy
Boston mathematician who read about sightings of
Martian *canali* by astronomer Giovanni Schiaparelli.
Whereas the Italian scientist was describing what he believed were "channels," his findings were misinterpreted
as "canals." From this, followed by research conducted
at the then-state-of-the-art observatory he built, Mr.
Lowell conceived of a scenario in which a heroic race of
intelligent Martians was undertaking to irrigate their dying world by constructing canals. These, of course, were
used to funnel water from the ice caps. In fairness to
Lowell, the undulating atmosphere of Earth did not per-
mit sharp visibility of the Red Planet. What he saw—or
wanted to see—as canals were apparently a smearing-
together of what later turned out to be craters on Mars.
Incredibly, the idea of Martians and canals persisted until *Mariner 4* flew past the planet in 1965 and sent back
the first close-up pictures ever taken of the world.

*At least, the first photographs ever taken by terrestri-
als,* Collins thought. He had to remember not to be so
provincial.

So Percy Canali was clearly not a name the host was
born with. And it made anything he said difficult to take
seriously. When it came to the subject of the Snake
Mountain statues—which was going full ahead when
Collins found the station—the ideas being discussed
ranged from angry and hostile subterranean rock leeches
that sucked the water from people leaving only "bodily
salts" to God doing "whatever He did that afflicted Lot's
wife." No one suggested that it might be a publicity ploy.
Percy Canali and his listeners did not appear to have a
sense of humor.

Collins wondered if he himself sounded like that to
other people. It was a disturbing thought.

The physicist followed his map to Snake Mountain, only to find that the road to the cave was blocked by a car from the county sheriff's department. There were no TV cameras around, no reporters, no hikers. Just the car. And a deputy inside. Collins got out of his Kia something-or-other and walked over. He stood by the driver's side door and the deputy opened the window. Air-conditioning whooshed out. The young man looked up through dark sunglasses.

"Good morning, Deputy—Woodward," Collins said, reading the name from his tag.

"Morning, sir."

"May I ask why the road is closed?"

"Someone keeps dropping statues off in the cave," the deputy said. A thick, dark eyebrow dipped sternly behind his sunglasses. "That someone wouldn't be you, would it?"

"No, sir."

"Yeah. I guess it would be tough to pull it off in that," the deputy drawled, nodding toward the Kia.

"Yes. But my other car's the Batmobile."

Deputy Woodward didn't get it. Or he didn't think it was funny. Collins could swear he heard tumbleweeds rolling behind the guy.

"This seems like a pretty strange place to put statues." Collins forged ahead, squinting up at the cave. "Does Snake Mountain have any kind of history involving things like this?"

"You mean artists going up there and sculpting?"

"That, or other strange occurrences."

"Not to my knowledge. But then, I wouldn't know about that sort of stuff," the deputy added. "I'm county. We have a pretty large patrol area and too few people to do the job."

"Why is the county involved and not the Sedona police?"

"Snake Mountain is located outside the city limits."

"I see. Then if I may ask, deputy—why aren't you investigating?"

"I'd like to be. This is boring."

"But?"

"I'm waiting."

"For?"

"A forensics person is coming from our Flagstaff HQ to have a look around," the deputy replied. "They want to look real close for fingerprints, try to find out who's doing this."

"Ah."

"Now it's my turn," the deputy said, looking over his sunglasses. "Why are you so interested in the cave, Mr.—?"

"Collins."

"You a reporter?"

"Good God, no. I work for the United Nations—"

"Really? In Geneva?"

"New York." Collins was surprised, first, to get an enthusiastic response, and second, that this sluggish deputy had heard of Geneva, let alone knew the United Nations had a presence there.

"My twin sister works for them in Switzerland," Woodward said. "She went over there to do her doctoral thesis on the League of Nations and they hired her when she graduated."

"Impressive," Collins said. He was being sincere.

"Yep. Works in their Office of the High Commissioner for Human Rights. Phoenix Woodward. Ever hear of her?"

"I have not," Collins admitted. "The U.N. employs a lot of people."

Woodward shrugged. "Well, it was worth a shot."

"Always."

"So why do you want to go up to the cave, Mr. Collins?"

"I head a U.N. division that investigates unusual occurrences around the world. This seemed to qualify."

The deputy regarded him suspiciously. "You flew out here for that?"

"I was coming anyway to have a little vacation," Collins lied.

"Good, because whatever you saw on the news this morning, that's pretty much all there is."

"I heard there is another statue."

"That'd be Dr. Fox."

"The veterinarian."

"Yeah. Pretty easy to remember that one."

"I'm sorry?"

"Fox . . . animal doctor."

"Right." Collins felt stupid for not having picked up on that. Especially after ranking on the deputy.

"His statue's here, but he's missing, just like Ms. Wang and her dogs," the deputy went on. "Or hiding, more likely. So, you have some kind of ID Mr . . . ?"

"Collins," he said. "Yes, deputy. I do."

Collins reached into his pants pocket, pulled out his wallet, and held his United Nations identification card to the open window. If he got past Deputy Woodward it would be the first time the laminated card would have done more than gotten him 15 percent off at the U.N. cafeteria and the book-heavy gift shop.

"That's you, all right," Woodward said, looking at the

tiny color photo. "Well, if you want to go up to the cave, pull off the road over there." The deputy pointed to a narrow section of rain-rutted, dusty dirt beside the road. "Then you can walk on up. Only don't touch anything inside."

"I won't," Collins assured him.

"You being U.N., that could make this an international incident. Then Interpol might have to get involved and everything."

"I'll be careful," Collins promised, and went back to his car. Maybe Deputy Woodward wasn't as humorless as he thought. Either that, or else he was really, really dumb.

The young physicist parked where he'd been told, then dug into his carry-on bag to get his employee-discounted United Nations powder-blue baseball cap. Fitting it on his head, he took out a flashlight—he'd brought a penlight so he wouldn't have any trouble getting it through airport security—then waved to the deputy as he walked past the police car and hiked up the dry dirt road that led to the cave.

CHAPTER 11

TALLY'S EDITOR, SEVENTY-two-year-old zoologist Dr. Kerwin Armstrong, was a gentle man with Ronald Reagan–black hair who collected mongoose memorabilia. He playfully referred to them as his "mongeese," even though the term was incorrect and chafed Tally's editorial skin. But then, the kindly scientist was not exactly an editor. He was a figurehead who lent prestige to the magazine at Museum dinners and conferences while Tally did all the work. Not that she minded. He was a good soul and he had given her this job.

That didn't make her like "mongeese" any better, though Dr. Armstrong avoided using it in an editorial he wrote for the magazine shortly after her arrival, telling the world about how he fell in love with them when his grandmother read him Rudyard Kipling's *Riki Tiki Tavi*.

"It's the tale of a mongoose who befriends a young man and protects him and his family from some very nasty cobras," Dr. Armstrong wrote, shortly before Tally arrived at the magazine. "I always thought of it as a response of sorts to the biblical story of Adam, Eve, and the Serpent. I felt that there is hope, that there is always a friend anxious to help redeem us. . . ."

Tally wasn't in a position to know whether that had been Mr. Kipling's intent. But she couldn't disprove it, and Dr. Armstrong believed it. He spent the rest of his life collecting mongoose books, taxidermied remains, key chains, paperweights, artwork, toys, vases, garments—anything with a mongoose image on it. He had lobbied Congress to lift the ban on mongooses; because of their ferocity, bringing them into the country from their natural habitats of Asia, Africa, and southern Spain was illegal. Even zoos were not permitted to import them.

Tally did not know whether it was just like dogs owners and their pooches, but the six-foot four-inch Dr. Armstrong also happened to look like a mongoose, with a long, slender frame and a prominently cheeked face. He was not deadly, however. At least, not as far as she knew.

"I was wondering if you've heard from your young friend lately," he said, after popping into her office to collect a short article on the origin of tacos. He insisted on hard copy, not diskettes or E-mails.

"My young friend?" Tally said, puzzled.

"The one you jetted over to Europe with, the one you took an extra day off for," he said.

"Oh, my young 'friend,'" Tally replied. Dr. Armstrong was so sweetly paternal. If only her father were like that. Tally hadn't told her editor anything about the nature of their trip to Loch Ness, only that she was going over with a "great guy." "As a matter of fact I have heard from him, Dr. Armstrong. We had breakfast today, and have been talking quite a lot."

"So glad to hear that," he said. "You need a life outside this office."

Yes, one that doesn't offer dinner and a show in the Twilight Zone, she thought. "I am learning to have one," she said.

"If you need another day or two, don't hesitate to ask."

"I won't, thank you."

"What's this lucky fellow's name?"

"Harold," she replied. "I wouldn't exactly say that he's a lucky fellow—"

"Like Mr. Macmillan, the British PM," Armstrong went on. "Good name. He joined Winston Churchill in condemning the apeasement of Hitler back in the thirties, you know."

"I did not know," Tally replied. She felt ashamed. The only other Harold she could think of on the spot was Harold Hill, the con artist from *The Music Man.*

"Is your Harold a writer?"

"No," she said. "He runs a technology division of the United Nations."

"The United Nations? Impressive."

"He's quite a guy."

"Well, he must be, to impress you. I'll leave you to your work," Dr. Armstrong said. "You'll have that piece on the Ringling Brothers next?"

Tally said she would.

"Tacos and circuses," Armstrong smiled. "We should translate that into Latin and use that as our motto. *Taconum et circi,* it would probably be—or maybe not. The 'um' doesn't seem right."

"It *sounds* right. I can look it up on-line, if you'd like," Tally said helpfully.

"Thanks, but not necessary. It was just a whim. Lord, it's been a half century since I've used Latin, except to refer to my good friend *Herpestes,* of course," he said, patting his mongoose tie.

Dr. Armstrong left, leaving Tally slightly exhausted. Not in the same way that Harold did. The older man had much more charm. But he took her brain places it was not accustomed to visiting, and along roads that were desperately unfamiliar. Which was not a bad thing, just tiring.

As Tally made calls to writers and went back to editing manuscripts, it bothered her that she didn't know a single British prime minister, other than Winston Churchill, who predated Margaret Thatcher. Who was queen before Elizabeth? Or was it a king? Then again, she didn't know which American president came before Franklin Roosevelt. Hoover? And before him? She had no idea. Wilson was somewhere in there. Speaking of Latin, how many Roman emperors did she know? Julius Caesar. Augustus Caesar. Caligula—but only because of the movie. Tiberius and Claudius, but only because of the British TV series. She only knew Harold Hill because of the movie, not even the Broadway show. Tally had a bunch of degrees, but she didn't know simple facts like that. It was disturbing.

Or maybe not, she thought defensively. It could also be that there was just way too much to know. Or maybe too much of the wrong thing, like sports scores, which she did not know, and how many threads were in her bedsheets, which she did know. Was this wormhole quest one of those misguided things? Sitting here in her office, reading about events and cycles that could be proven, her work with Harold suddenly seemed mad and frivolous.

Tally looked at the telephone. She had an overwhelming urge to call Harold and tell him to count her out of his ongoing search. And then the young woman had a curious thought. What if the phone beeped right now and it was Harold, telling her that he didn't want her to be involved in his research, that he found her a drag, not a devil's advocate but a sarcastic butt-pain, no help at all. How would she feel?

Peeved at being dumped. That was her first reaction. But feeling cheated was a close second. This was *her* story. She was a *writer*-editor. Maybe the search was nuts, but if Dr. Armstrong could find God in Kipling maybe there *were* giant monsters in white dwarfs. There was only one way to find out. You had to keep feeding the kitty to stay in the game.

While all of this muddle was going through her head, Tally latched onto something that Dr. Armstrong had jarred loose. It was a phrase she had heard in college. Not in a science class but in English, which was probably why it stuck with her. It was something the English poet William Cowper had written in the 1700s—a fact that Tally did remember. He wrote that knowledge was a rude, unprofitable mass, the mere materials with which wisdom builds.

The facts were the means, not the goal. The trick was to get enough of them to acquire wisdom.

Wacky or not, there was nothing dishonorable about this search.

She went back to work, confused but energized.

CHAPTER 12

SNAKE MOUNTAIN, SEDONA, was very different from First Avenue, New York.

New York was a city of sights and noises but also of smells. There were gas fumes from buses, urine from dogs, the whiff of foodstuffs in big, black garbage bags piled on the streets, the perfume or cologne of passing pedestrians, and most of all—best of all—odors of cooking food from restaurants. Like all its different people from different places, the city was a stew of this and that on every block.

Snake Mountain was not like that. Collins could taste the dry dirt each step puffed up, and it stayed in his nose so he could smell it and only it. The road was also toasty-hot by the time Collins was halfway to the cave. No bursts of air-conditioning from open office or theater or restaurant doors as in the city: just heat. Maybe it was dry heat, but his sweat was wet and it was leaking freely. That made it feel humid. He wished he had brought more than a carry-on change of clothes. Now he'd probably have to buy one of those "I Love A Sedona Vortex" T-shirts he was sure he'd find somewhere. Maybe he'd get an Arizona Diamondbacks tee for Tally. That would stymie her, to get something that wasn't weird-related.

With all of that thinking Collins felt as though more time should have passed, more progress made toward the cave. But it still felt as though he were only halfway up the damn mountain. He started walking faster, panting openly as the slope increased. He figured that though he would perspire more he would get into the cave faster, where it was probably cooler.

Unless I get sucked into a wormhole that drops me in the sun, Collins thought. That would be warmer.

As he walked on solid if dusty ground, Collins tried to imagine what that deputy would have said if he had been honest: "Deputy, there may be a door to another dimension up there. Mind if I have a look?"

What were the odds that the detective would say, "Hell, that's a possible explanation for the vortexes here, isn't it?"

Not good. Collins couldn't understand why people embraced religion, yet found it so difficult to accept the notion of secular phenomena they couldn't touch and see. Why did it make them anxious, the way people talking about sex did? Why was ridicule the near-inevitable result? Tally, for example. He was willing to bet she hadn't told anyone at the magazine why she went to Loch Ness. If she told them she went to Loch Ness at all. Because then the inevitable next question is, "Did you see the monster?" And then you have to answer. If you respond with anything but a rolling-eyed "Yeah, right!" you get a look that says, *Are you nuts?*

What was it? Fear? If so, of what? Death? It shouldn't be, not if they believed in a hereafter. Change? Discovering that they themselves had an imagination, one which would suddenly unhinge them? Did they hold reality so tightly, like a drink at a bar, because otherwise they would have to crawl from their cave and interact with the Unknown. Not simply what-lies-around-the-corner stuff, but creation in all its grandeur, without a guidebook, without a Bible to tell them what was up and where they belonged and what was expected of them? The ability to imagine was one of the things that separated humans from other animals.

Yet we run from it, he thought.

Now that he thought about it, maybe animals were more advanced. They didn't run from any kind of sex. They were certainly more forthright and adventurous. And they sensed things "out there" to which humans were totally oblivious. Maybe lobsters and honeybees and crocodiles and ostriches were the cream in Creation's coffee, not human beings. Maybe the Bible should have ended on page one.

There was yellow police tape strung from a pair of wooden posts. It was like a members-only club in hillbilly country. Collins stepped over the barricade and entered the mine.

It was not cooler in here. It was clammy. Collins touched the wall nearest him, to the right. He dragged his fingertips across the lumpy surface. There was a warm, oily dampness. It wasn't everywhere; he shined the light across the wall and it glistened in only a few of the deeper areas. He brought his fingers to his nose and sniffed. The odor was not unpleasant. It reminded him of the soft pretzels the vendors sold in New York. There was something chestnutty and salty about it.

Collins turned the flashlight light here and there as he walked further into the cave. He saw deep, long hash-marks on the walls where miners had once hacked out whatever ores they were after—silver, he imagined. The cave probably looked just the way they had left it when they mined their last, maybe eighty or ninety years ago. That was a lifetime ago, yet it felt so—so recent, given everything else that had happened or been thought about lately.

There was a bend ahead and he kept the light on it. Going around corners in dark places, especially when you were moving away from the way out, was something his instincts said was not good. Collins reminded his brain that it was probably more dangerous on dark New York streets than it was here, if for no other reason than that the uneven pavement could trip you up and taxis sometimes rode on the sidewalks. Still, his senses went on heightened alert, his body tense.

Suddenly, Collins saw something glint dully on the right, at the edge of the flashlight beam. He swung the light toward the wall. There was a tiny stone shoulder high, just on the point where the wall curved into the bend. It looked like silver, only it gleamed less, like opal. It was small enough so that unless the light hit it, a passerby wouldn't notice it. The young physicist moved toward it.

The ore wasn't embedded in the wall but was sitting on it. As he approached, he saw that it was not actually on the wall but was raised slightly. It cast a slight shadow underneath. And then he saw that there were holes in it.

No, not holes, he realized. *Gaps. Between a body and legs.*

"Man, oh man," he said. It wasn't ore at all. It was another statue.

Of a tarantula.

CHAPTER 13

THE OFFICE PHONE was resting between Tally's right ear and shoulder. She had just dug into a late lunch at her desk when the phone beeped. Greek salad, heavy on the grape leaves, shot through with black olives. Harold was on the other end, apologizing for interrupting. Tally forgave him. She was impressed that he knew what time it was and that he might be intruding.

"There is something really screwy here, and there's no one else I can discuss it with," Collins said.

"Why not?" she asked. "I would have assumed there are other investigators out there."

"There aren't," Collins told her. "The only other person within questioning range is a guy from the sheriff's office who's watching the place. He's pleasant but he's not terribly curious or well informed. Besides, even if someone else was here, what could they tell me?"

"What do you think I can tell you?" she asked, a little petulantly.

"You have objectivity."

That was honest. And true. Perhaps even semi-flattering. "Okay. Shoot."

"I was up in the cave and found a spider statue, also life-size."

"Life-size as in spider-life-size or big-as-a-person-life-size?"

"Spider life-size. It was on the wall, just stuck there."

"Did you leave it there?"

"Of course not," he said.

"Jeez, Harold—what if it's diseased?"

"I'll take that risk. Besides, I don't think spider diseases jump to humans."

"You don't know what's turning living tissue to stone."

"True which is why I had to have a close look at it."

"Still, you should have reported it—"

"Tal, you've got to trust me on this. They would have had to involve some whole new division, one that's responsible for the ecology or arachnids or some crap. They're very departmentalized. Bureaucracy writ small."

"Okay, I trust you."

"Anyway, that's not the only thing I found in the cave," Collins continued. "There's also some strange oil on the wall, like you'd find in a can of sardines. Only it smells like roasting nuts."

"That's odd."

"Why?"

"Water in caves usually interacts with the minerals to create particles of calcite, which is what makes stalac-

tites," Tally said. She felt guilty. After saying she would
be of no use, she was of use.

"Well, there were none of those here," Collins told her.

"Could it have been sap? Are there trees above the
cave entrance or on high ground anywhere?"

"No," Collins said. "Frankly, this reminded me of
snail slime, only there was a lot of it. And I didn't see
any snails."

"Tarantulas don't slime."

"I know," Collins said.

"Harold, was there any of this slime near the spider?"

"Beside it."

"Could it have been glue that someone might be using
or planning to use to stick little statues to the cave wall?"

"I don't think so," Collins said.

"Why not?"

"Because there's nothing sticky about it," he said.
"Just gloppy. Also, I'm not buying the idea that this is
some kind of art fair."

"Not per se, but it *could* be a Native American activity, something they don't want to tell people about except the people who are helping them. Wasn't the first
statue of an Apache?"

"So they say. I haven't gotten that far into the cave. I
stopped when I saw the tarantula."

"Did the tarantula come away from the wall easily?"

"It did not," Collins told her. "I think I left some of its
feet attached to the stone wall."

"So it broke before the rock did."

"Yes."

"What about a pattern?" she asked. "Was there one to
the goop?"

"None that I could tell. It was only on a narrow

stretch of one wall, though. As though someone had hit it with a hose."

"From which direction?"

"From the inside blasting out. Why, what are you thinking?"

Tally was silent as she popped and sipped a Diet Sprite.

"Tally?"

"Yes," she said.

"Why did you ask that?"

"Because when you said that about the hose, the image that flashed into my head was—did you ever see pictures of the shadows of atom-bomb victims charred into walls in Hiroshima and Nagasaki?"

"Yes."

"Those images were flat and solid black. These are dimensional and pure white. Almost like a negative version."

"Hmmm. Interesting. I don't know if the flash-images from Hiroshima are relevant, but the human remains left by the blast were black and charred—like a reverse of these statues."

"This is gruesome. Maybe we can wait till after I finish eating—"

"It's gruesome, I agree," Collins said. "But there's something very compelling about your thinking."

"What?" Tally asked.

"This spider statue is very dry *but* it's somewhat shiny. Like marble. Almost as if that oil got baked around it."

"Like glazed clay in a kiln."

"Exactly like that," Collins said.

"Still," Tally said, "it's a big leap from that to the idea that this thing was nuked somehow—"

"Ho. Ly. Crap."

"What?" Tally said.

"Remember what we were discussing yesterday morning with Dr. Jackson? About the possibility that there are black holes on one end of a wormhole and white holes on the other?"

"So?"

"Blackened remains on one side of the wormhole, ivoried remains on the other," Collins said.

"Meaning?"

"The energy could have come from the flip side of our universe, our dimension," Collins said.

"That presumes there is a wormhole in the cave," Tally said.

"It does. But we can't rule that out."

Tally ate an olive, wincing as she always did when she ate black olives. "Maybe we both ought to step back and give this a think."

"I agree. But this has been very helpful," Collins said. "I'll give you a call when I've had a—"

Collins was silent. Tally wondered if the phone had cut out. "Harold?"

Nothing.

"*Harold?* If you're there, I can't hear—"

"Whoa," he repeated softly.

"What is it?

"Whoaaaaa," he said louder.

"Harold?

"Whoaaaaaaa!" he shouted.

"Harold!"

And then the phone did cut out.

CHAPTER 14

JACUZZIS, ON-LINE service, and a leg.

If innkeeper Joe Wyndham had learned one thing in his seventy-something years, it was that life was all about change and the unexpected. A man had to be willing to accept new things. Unlike a lot of his contemporaries—a majority of whom were *former* contemporaries, since most of them were dead now—he felt richer for that. Younger. Not that he had much in common with the youth of today. They were pampered wimps. But he, at least, had an open mind.

Like when he converted this place. That also took something special, what he called the "two-fors": foresight and fortitude.

"Sergeant" Joe Wyndham and his wife Meg had opened the new Boots and Spurs bed-and-breakfast in

1983, about the time Sedona had become a destination rather than a place to stop en route to somewhere else. Until then, the idea of jetted, in-room tubs and, more recently, phones with data ports, had been about as alien to them as the actual aliens who supposedly buzzed into the town every now and then. The Wyndhams had gotten used to the upgrades, though, just as they'd gotten accustomed to having people smoke outside only, including themselves until they'd given it up when the doctors had taken one of Meg's lungs two years before. That had made her feel closer to her husband, not only because they'd beat cancer as a team but because now they were both missing something—she a lung, Joe a leg. But they still had what mattered most: each other.

The chalet-style Boots and Spurs was built on the site of the Wyndhams' original home, the ranch house where Joe was born in 1925. It was not a ranch house the way realtors refer to them: it really was a ranch with a house. Joe's dad raised cattle. When Joe enlisted in 1943 and went to fight in the European Theater, the newlywed Meg moved in with his sort-of widowed mom. Joe came back eighteen months later with his left leg still somewhere in the Ardennes, courtesy of a German mortar. The family used his disability pay to turn the place into the Boots and Spurs Motel. Meg did not stop making the "Flagstaff firefly" jewelry that had helped support the two women while Joe was gone—small pewter bodies with brilliant gemstone tails. She sold it in the gift shop and through catalogues and made a fair enough income. She always wore a piece or two and had been known to make a sale off her blouse or jacket.

Until the place went from "motel" to "bed-and-breakfast" nearly two-score years later, Joe was content to pin up his empty trouser-leg. Now he wore a prosthetic metal leg that allowed him to walk without crutches. Meg had been afraid that the missing limb would turn off some of the younger, wealthier Eastern and European guests. What a generation, to be so protected, so squeamish. It was as if men had lost their stones in the post-Vietnam world.

Still, Joe didn't have a problem with the request. He actually learned to like his "bionic left foot" as he called it. About the only thing he didn't like were German guests, whom he had trouble forgiving—not for the leg but for the buddies he'd lost. He was unrepentant about it. The 103-year-old Dorothy was unforgiving as well. Her husband George had left her shortly before Joe was born. He had gotten tired of ranching and had left to become a sailor. He'd never sent a nickel home, leaving Dorothy to sell off all but the ranch house to pay off debts. She still hoped "the rattlesnake" was alive and would show up one day. She wanted to spit on him and didn't expect to be going to Hell.

Joe wondered if he would help her; he often wondered about the father he never knew. His mom was enough to send any man to sea. Unfortunately, Dorothy never talked about the man and every trace of him—a few photographs, a few letters, even his books—had been burned while Joe was still a fetus. He also wondered if his love of smoking and barbecuing came from smelling that fire in the womb.

Maybe, Wyndham thought with a smile. *Weird things happened in Sedona, they say.*

Like the thing that happened when he went out front to fire up the big grill, the one on which he cooked the meat and poultry and toasted the sourdough rolls and bread they served for lunch, poolside. People liked to eat out there, at the very foot of the foothills, where the

Earth started its climb toward the sky. Even though it was off-season and they only had four guests, he enjoyed doing this. Besides, he and his wife and his mom had to eat.

What was strange was that a man came running up—unusual enough, since people around here tended to amble, shamble, or just plain stand wherever they happened to find themselves. But what made it stranger was that this fellow had his hands cupped and was shouting for something:

A bun.

CHAPTER 15

"I'VE GOT A POPPY kaiser roll," a big cowboy-looking guy shouted toward Collins. He reached into a plastic bag beside the grill. "What are you gonna do, trade me for a handful of magic beans?"

Collins was not in the mood for jokes or talk. "Can you hollow it out?" he asked as he ran.

"Are you a guest?"

"I'll be registering in a minute," he assured him.

"'Cause you got a reservation or 'cause you need a roll?"

"Collins. Reserved on-line early this morning."

"Okay," the grill master replied.

Whoever thought that layered gardens with a winding walk was a good idea had never been in a hurry. *Then again, most gardeners wouldn't choose that as an avocation if they were in a hurry,* Collins thought. The garden was the only way into Boots and Spurs and it was snuggled between two high split-face rock walls, one that hid the parking lot and one that hid the mini-strip-mall next door. The smell of the cooking burgers was nice, though.

Collins made it through the garden and its crunchy white gravel, then hurried across the poolside walk to the grill. The big man was standing there in his jeans and denim shirt holding the ends of the roll in his hands. His expression was distrustful and mildly irritated, like someone who'd just opened a bogus E-mail asking for his account information.

"Thank you," Collins said as he stopped beside the man. "Okay—now I'm going to put something in there. Something that isn't food."

"Go on, I'm listening," the man said. He paused to flip his burgers then picked up the roll again.

"When I do, I need you to close the bun quickly but gently."

"It's a roll," the man said.

"I'm sorry."

"What have you got there, a gecko?"

"No. A spider."

"Poisonous?"

Collins looked at him with poorly concealed alarm. "Are tarantulas poisonous?" he asked.

"No."

"Then—no," Collins said. "Are you ready?"

The cowboy-cook nodded once. Collins placed his cupped hands on the top of the roll bottom, pinkie-sides down. He parted his hands slowly as the man brought the other half of the roll over. The chef lowered the top and very carefully placed the two sides together.

"Thank you," Collins said.

"Is that for here or to go?" the man asked. "I got some aluminum foil—"

Collins grinned and looked at his hands. There was a crusty white residue on them. It was very odd. The man handed him the roll.

"You bringing this home for your girlfriend, or is there something special about your spider?" the man asked.

"Yes to the latter, not exactly to the former," Collins told him. "A half hour ago the spider was white, calcified, and stuck to a cave wall. Now he's alive. Ever hear anything like that?"

The man frowned and shook his head once. He was a dictionary of expressive economy.

"Me neither."

"May I?" the chef asked, indicating the roll.

"Go ahead."

The man raised the top and peeked inside. "Mind if I ask you something?"

"Shoot," Collins said. Remembering suddenly that he was out west, he wondered if he should have chosen another word.

"Were you chewin' mushrooms out in the wild?"

Collins frowned. "Why?"

Gingerly, the man lifted the top of the roll.

The spider was once again a stiff white figurine.

This was embarrassing as well as perplexing. Collins didn't linger. He took the roll and closed it again. Then he checked in, went to his room overlooking the pool, and set the kaiser roll on the desk. He checked to make sure the spider was still immobile. It was. He tapped it with a hotel pen. It was solid. Then he turned on the desk lamp, took out some of the room stationery, and put his palm over it. He used his fingernail to try and scrape off the white particles. They didn't want to come off. He scraped them harder. They seemed to be stuck to the balls of his hand. He picked at one of the flake-like particles.

It wasn't stuck to his hand. It *was* his hand.

"Okay. *That's* screwed up."

Maybe there was an explanation. The flakes were on his right hand. Collins had been holding the spider in that hand. That was when it came alive.

He picked up the roll, inverted it, and put it on the paper. He lifted the bottom with his left hand and held it there. The spider was on its back. He gently placed his right palm on top of the spider's extended legs with their broken tips. He held his hand there, slowly counting, starting with "One-Mississippi." He felt the chalky pressure of whatever a spider's feet were called.

After "Twelve-Mississippi" something tickled Collins's palm. He raised his hand and looked down.

The spider's legs were normal and moving slowly up as far as whatever a spider's knees were called. Since the arachnid was on its still-hard back, it wasn't able to move. Collins looked at his palm.

"Damn."

He saw eight tiny spots of white.

The scientist went to the bathroom. There were two plastic cups wrapped in plastic wrap sitting on the vanity. He expected something classier from a bed and breakfast, but he was glad to see these. He tore one open, filled it with water, and went back to the desk. He sat and dripped several drops of water on the tarantula's hard, white belly. He counted to twelve. Nothing happened. He dripped water on the legs. Maybe it had to be absorbed through them, like tree roots. He counted up to "Twelve-Mississippi" again. Again, nothing happened.

What was different?

"Me." He answered his own question.

Collins eased his thumb between the tarantula's legs and touched it to the same spot. He counted off the seconds. Once again, at "Twelve-Missisippi" the spider began to change. The bristles on the creature's belly began to darken and pop free of the calcified exterior.

"What's the difference between me and tap water?" he wondered aloud.

The answer was obvious. Oil. There was oil in his skin. There wasn't any in water. He looked at his thumb. The skin was slightly flaked.

"My bodily oil reconstituted the figurine, which means this isn't a statue but a temporarily petrified living thing."

He watched as the tarantula slowly returned to its solid, white state—legs first, from the outside in, followed by the belly.

"Sorry to be messing with your head, spider," Collins said.

At the same time Collins felt his right hand begin to feel slightly warm. He looked at it. The flakes were slowly shrinking. His own body, his natural oil, was causing them to heal.

"Something in the spider absorbed the secretion from my skin, and then something inside burned that up quickly and caused it to revert."

The physicist thought about the oily substance he had found on the wall of the cave. Had that come from the spider? Had something in the cave caused the creature to become desiccated? Apparently. A mineral perhaps. Or an oil-eating bacterium of some kind. There were microbes that ate all sorts of biological matter. Or maybe there was something that drained only bodily fluids, the way some insects do. Perhaps it left behind only the indigestible oil components.

Collins was sure the cause could be found. What puzzled him equally, however, was whether or not the other statues in the cave could be revived and why this whatever-it-was hadn't gone after him. Maybe it only happened at a certain time of day or night. Or else the living tissue had to be there at least x number of minutes before it became affected. Or both.

What about clothes or metal? What about the dog collars and license tags? What about aging? Was this a form of suspended animation? Did it have anything to do with the vortices?

The young man replaced the bottom of the kaiser roll and washed his hands. Just to see what happened, he also rubbed in body lotion. The flakes vanished. There was oil in it.

Collins decided to go outside, have a hamburger and a think. When he was done he would probably return to the cave and do a little more investigating. He would undoubtedly discover an insect or germ or plant, or one of those hibernating toads, something the opening of the cave may have liberated for the first time in a century. Something that was really hungry for potassium or protein, or something contained in animal tissue. Maybe it was even this spider or its kin that did a leech-thing on the people who entered the cave. Perhaps they were comatose, white like this one, when they were digesting or hibernating.

Note to self, he thought. *Don't touch the spider again.*

There were lazy bugs that injected acid into prey to dissolve internal organs so they could suck out a liquified meal. This could be something along those lines. Case probably closed.

Then he would do something else.

He would find a vortex so the trip would not be without something a little consciousness-expanding. . . .

CHAPTER 16

THOUGH TALLY RANDALL didn't spend the day thinking about statues, her head was like a city park; every once in a while she'd turn a corner, finish a thought, and there one was. Something about the Sedona statues nagged at her.

Logistics.

Tally had seen exhibits put up at the museum. These included a full-scale animatronic triceratops; a computer mouse the size of a phone booth with a clear plastic shell and talking parts, all voiced by Robin Williams; and something even more transparent, a totem pole that had been liberated from an Alaskan glacier and "presented" by the oil company that found it, an effort to show their commitment to the preservation of native cultures and, by inference, the environment. Getting all of those objects into the museum took teamsters, dollies, and the occasional forklift. The idea of someone sneaking a life-size statue into a cave was improbable. It would take people, trucks, and equipment. It was a covert operation conducted, in all likelihood, by amateurs. They would leave footprints, tire tracks, oil leaks, something. Pulling it off would take a conspiracy of silence not only among those people but among their friends and their families. And surely before all of this the statues would have been seen somewhere, mentioned, asked about. It isn't likely that a sculpture of the town vet would have been done by a gallery in New York or London. She had a vision of this being a variation of the fraternity prank in which someone opened a door and a bucket of water poured over them. Anyone who walked into this cave was drenched with plaster from a chute.

Shortly after four o'clock, when the weekly three-hour-long editorial lunch meeting ended—the one all editorial staff had to attend—Tally went back to her office. She tried to call Harold; he didn't answer. She checked her cell phone and office phone. Harold hadn't phoned, which surprised her. In the short time she had known him, he was the one who was usually in her ear with thoughts and theories. Either he hadn't found anything interesting or he'd been caught in the papier-mâché booby trap of Snake Mountain.

She realized that by calling him she was validating his quest for a unified theory of the unexplained. More than that, she was implicitly signing on for the rest of the ride. But after sitting in a slow, dry, almost *doloroso* meeting chaired by Dr. Armstrong, she did crave a pick-me-up.

Tally punched in the number. It beeped once. For some reason she counted it out. And doing that, a song from *A Chorus Line* played in her head.

One singular sensation . . .

It beeped again. This time to the tune of Meatloaf.

Two out of three ain't bad . . .

It beeped a third time. This time it wasn't a song that came to her but a wave of fairy-tale magic—three wishes, three bears, three billy goats gruff—

" 'Lo?" Collins answered.

"Hey, Harold—it's Tally."

"Hi."

'Lo followed by hi, Tally thought. *In a different context they meant opposites. Here, they meant the same thing. Such was the life and mind of an editor.*

"Just checking in," she said. "The way you jumped off the phone before had me a little worried."

"Yeah. Sorry."

Yeah, sorry? That was supernaturally laconic for Harold. "You sound down," she said.

"Well, I'm thinking you may have been right to stay home."

"Oh?"

"This looks like one phenomenon that may not be so phenomenal after all," Collins said.

"How so?" The young woman was both relieved and disappointed to hear him say that.

Collins explained what had happened.

"So you think something is leeching fluids from living things and putting them into a kind of hibernating state?" Tally asked.

"It's a rough working theory," he said.

"Harold, the human body is ninety percent water. It

would take a helluva lot of microbes to drain that much liquid."

"Is that unprecedented?" he asked. "Aren't there bugs with big appetites?"

"Certain species of ants can strip a cow of flesh in less than five minutes then lose themselves in the field," she replied.

"Okay. And what's the name of that flesh-eating bacteria that chews through muscles, tendons, and all the connective tissue?"

"*Streptococcus pyogenes,*" she replied. "They're the cause of necrotizing fasciitis. Until fairly recently immunologists didn't realize they were as widespread as they are."

"See? So there may have been something dormant in the cave that revived after getting a snootful of twenty-first-century air. Ironically, more of a story for your people than for me."

"I suppose," Tally said, though something bothered her about that explanation. "What are you going to do? It sounds like you're driving."

"I'm on my way back to the cave. I want to put some of that wall-gunk on one of the people statues, see what happens."

"Harold, when you were there, did you see the statues of the dogs or any of the people?"

"That's another reason I'm going back," he said. "I didn't really get a close look at any of them."

"You know," Tally went on, "I seem to recall from the news report that the first statue was holding a gun. A metal barrel doesn't have any enzymic juices that can be sucked from it."

"I know. I was thinking that before. Neither do belt

buckles and fillings in teeth and eyeglasses and a bunch
of other stuff," Collins said. "Do you have a theory about
that?"

"Well, thinking on the run I'd say that if those things
are affected then maybe they were covered, not drained.
Like something left out in the snow. Or—did you ever
see those figures that were buried in Pompeii?"

"Sure. Copies of the outside of people and dogs. The
insides were burned away by the volcanic ash."

"Exactly."

"But that wouldn't explain why the spider came back
to life when I touched it," Collins pointed out.

"What I'm suggesting is that it could be something
like volcanic ash that covers a thing and creates a shell.
Perhaps something in the oil dissolves the shell. There
could be some kind of vent in the cave, or a radiation
source, or who knows what, that creates this coat."

"Even a vortex," Collins said.

"Even a vortex, spitting out nastiness of some kind."

Collins said he would check for signs of burning on
the cave wall. He thanked Tally and hung up. The young
woman felt better now. It was like making up with a boy-
friend. All the old problems remained but what was good
had been restored. Instead of taking notes and listening
to a smart but ultratraditional man shoot down new if ec-
centric ideas for articles—like the role of animals in
black magic and a history of sea monsters—she'd made
herself a partner in something—a little side-business
that had the possibility of taking off.

That was a pretty good feeling, as long as she didn't
dwell on the fact that it was based on dinosaurs and re-
animated spider statues and, if it all tied together, somehow could undermine society as well as everything

humans thought they knew about the nature of existence.

The only thing that bothered her was the toasty-fuzzy
feeling the compliment that she may have been right had
given her. . . .

CHAPTER 17

DETECTIVE WOODWARD WAS not in his patrol car when Collins reached the base of Snake Mountain. There was another vehicle parked beside it, a Ford Explorer. That, too, was empty. Collins surmised that it belonged to the forensics detective and that the two had gone up the path to the cave.

Collins headed back up the dirt road. He heard two cracks that sounded like distant lightning. He didn't see any storm clouds and wondered if there might be a rockfall somewhere.

The early afternoon sun made the climb a lot more miserable than it had been before. Perspiration felt like a parade of bugs as it meandered through sensitive places high, low, and in between. His legs were unhappy having to carry the rest of him up the incline. Even the kaiser roll was getting soggy. He was holding it firmly in both hands with the tarantula safely inside. There was something he wanted to try and he needed the spider to do it.

The dirt rose in little puffs as he neared the cave. They could be puffs of smoke from his melting shoes. It was hot enough.

Suddenly, there was another muffled report from ahead. It could have been a tree branch breaking or it could have been a gunshot. Collins was not an NRA kind of guy. He wouldn't know the difference.

"Deputy Woodward?" he shouted. "Deputy, it's Harold Collins from the United Nations."

"Mr. Collins, do not come up here!" the deputy shouted back.

"Deputy, I won't get in your way. I'm a scientist. I know how to be careful. There's something I want to—"

"Mr. Collins, go *back* to your car and leave."

Collins stopped. That was pretty emphatic. "Deputy Woodward, is something wrong?"

The deputy did not reply.

"Deputy? Hellooo?"

No one answered. He listened. He didn't hear anything. No talking, no shouts, no movement, no pebbles being kicked or stepped on. Only his own strained breath. Collins looked ahead. The mouth of the cave was about fifty feet off, pointed slightly away from him. Maybe they had gone deeper and couldn't hear him. He went forward a few steps.

"Hellllooo!" Collins said.

Singing it didn't help. Collins moved closer. As he neared, the entrance to the mine turned toward him ominously—solid matte black against a sky of saturated blue, like the eye socket of a skull.

"Deputy?"

There was an oily smell in the air. Not gas-station oily but sardine-can oily. It seemed to be coming from the cave. Maybe they'd been examining the little blobs he'd found on the wall and had triggered some kind of chemical reaction.

Collins reached the mouth of the cave and peered in. The entrance was dark. The belly of the cave was even darker.

"Rats," Collins muttered. Walking around with the eight-legged kaiser, Collins had neglected to bring his flashlight. He considered going back for the penlight but decided against it. The spot he wanted to check was not very far off. He could make his way using the little bit of daylight that reached inside.

Collins didn't speak as he eased his way in. He listened. He didn't hear anything coming from the far end of the cave. Perhaps the law officer and forensics expert had found another passageway and had gone into it. They couldn't hear him. Maybe it was steep and treacherous and that was why the deputy had warned him off.

Collins breathed through his mouth so he wouldn't smell the oil. He went to the spot where he'd found the spider. The oil was still there, though there was slightly less than before. He opened the roll, put the top underneath the bottom, and gingerly placed the spider onto the greasy spot. He held it there for a moment. A moment was all it took. Even in the dark Collins could see the bristles began to darken and rise from the spider's legs. Then the legs themselves started to regain their natural color. The creature's natural hue—black with patches of brown—made its way up the tarantula's legs to its belly. Collins released the spider. It clung to the wall of the cave. He leaned toward the wall and looked closely at the oil slick: it was shrinking rapidly.

The spider was absorbing it.

It took less than thirty seconds for the spider to be revived. The tiny creature began to move up the wall, tentatively at first, then with more animation. Only a few bristles on top remained white. That made sense: if this oil had come from the spider, there would not be quite enough to "fill it up" again. Collins had taken a drop away when he touched it. Some of the liquid content may have evaporated, leaving solid residue that could not be reclaimed. But there was enough to revive it. There was one puzzle, though—why it had reverted after sucking the oil from Collins's palm. Perhaps it was a simple question of genetics or immunity. Maybe the creature's body had "rejected" material that had not come from it initially.

The scientist looked into the black interior of the cave. He listened. All he heard was the hollow echo of the gentle wind that moved across the mouth. He put the kaiser roll down and took a few steps forward. He listened again. The bend in the cave was twenty-odd feet ahead. He walked slowly toward it. He held his arms in front of him so he didn't walk into a statue or an outcropping of rock.

Suddenly Collins stopped. He couldn't see anything but he could feel something with the front of his shoe. He lifted his heel and touched his toe around the cave floor. Something gooey was there. He crouched and put the tip of his right pinkie into it. It had the same unctuous texture as the glop on the wall. He dragged his finger

along the cave floor. There was, he discovered, one difference between the stuff on the wall and the stuff on the
floor.

There was a lot of it, piled deep.

Enough to have come from a human being.

CHAPTER 18

A S THE END of the work day neared, Tally went on-line to fact-check something in an article about the Leonid meteor showers. She did—the annual display would be their most brilliant in 2099, as the author had written. That was the end of her paid-work day. She stayed on-line to look up statues of spiders. It was a pretty curious thing for any life-form to become entirely calcified; she was doubting her own explanation. Perhaps what Harold had found was an artifact of some ancient peoples who were into tarantula-worship.

She found a lot of Spider-Man statues and a few statues with spiderwebs, but nothing about spider statues. She checked spider sculptures and found a number of jewelers who did them in pewter and platinum, gold and silver, sometimes gem-encrusted. There was even a spider mobile for baby's crib, though she couldn't conceive of who would want that other than Morticia Addams.

She broadened the search to insects, with roughly the same results. Then she went on to religion. There was nothing about indigenous peoples who worshiped spiders. That surprised her. There were hawk, cougar, wolf, and snake worshipers among the Native Americans, very many of them in the Southwest, but nothing to do with arachnids or any other insects.

Duh, Tally thought suddenly. *The place Harold went to is called Snake Mountain.* Obviously, there was an animal component to whatever had happened there at some point—even if it were only snake sightings. She looked up the mountain to learn something about its history.

Tally discovered that the cave appeared to have been a silver mine at one point early in the twentieth century. There was no indication about who owned it or who worked it before a landslide closed it off. The only accounts were, oddly enough, an arrest warrant that a sheriff had issued for an individual who had been illegally squatting below and mining the cave. The warrant had ended up in the possession of an ephemera dealer in New Hampshire who was selling it on eBay. Prior to that the Apaches had used the mountain as a place to prove one's manhood and nocturnal hunting skills. Apparently it was rich with rattlesnakes. It was considered a rite of passage for a young man to climb to the cave at night, remain until just before sunup, then climb over the top and down the other side.

"So—snakes," she muttered. "The one animal that apparently has not been included in the statuary."

Which was pretty odd, if they were so populous and there was something in the cave that was causing a cross-species necrosis. Snakes didn't like the sun. They should be in the cave. Unless they were immune . . . ?

She wondered whether to pass the non-information along to Harold.

Why not, she decided. What you can eliminate could be as important as what you add.

CHAPTER 19

COLLINS STOOD IN the cave for several minutes simply listening. He was momentarily distracted by the distant rumble of aircraft. It was as if the gods disapproved of him being here.

Too late for that, he thought.

The thunder faded quickly. All Collins heard was the sound of his own labored breathing. He reasoned that hearing it was better than not hearing it.

Collins wanted to go forward but he wasn't sure it was a terrific idea. If the deputy and the forensics person had found another passage, perhaps a vertical one, he didn't want to go tumbling in after them. Visiting parts unknown didn't scare him. Hard landings did. Besides, it was dark as 1 a.m. in here. He didn't want to knock over the statues or slip on undetected puddles of oil.

The scientist called out to the deputy one more time. He touched the goop again with his toe. It had stopped crawling forward and was just sitting in a puddle. It extended back into the cave though he didn't know how far.

Collins considered his next move. He thought seriously about going back to town and finding out if there was a library or an assessor's office, someplace he might be able to find out more about the geology of this region. Maybe there was a history of petroleum percolation. Some kind of mineral or hydrocarbon oil coming up through porous rock. Maybe it contained a hitherto unknown species of paralytic virus or chemical compound. As Collins stood there in the whistling mouth of the cave his cell phone beeped. Collins yelped and his arms flew out like Ray Bolger's Scarecrow's. He snatched the phone from his belt. The greenish glow of the readout seemed eerie in here.

"Hello?"

"Harold, it's Tally. Where are you?"

"In the cave. Something weird just happened. I put Spidey back on the cave wall, in some of that ooze, and it was like adding hot water to oatmeal. He plumped up and came back to life."

"Given what happened before, that's not a huge surprise."

"No, it was just really strange to see. He walked off as though nothing had happened. The only memento of whatever happened were some white hairs."

"Were they still solid?"

"I think so," Collins told her.

"Probably from whatever amount you pulled away when you touched it," Tally suggested.

"Most likely."

"So what are you going to do?"

"I don't know," he admitted. He angled the phone so the light shined in toward the cave. He moved forward a few steps then crouched. "The deputy and a forensics person are up here. They told me to stay out but then they stopped saying anything. I think they may have gone deeper into the cave."

"Harold, from what I saw on the newscast last night the cave didn't look all that deep."

"Well, I'm sure the TV crew didn't get very far in," Collins said. "It would have been difficult lugging that stuff around in here. There are some pretty low ceilings. I'm thinking the deputy must have found a passage somewhere in back. Maybe an old volcanic vent or a well or something. Funny thing, though. I'm looking at a river of goop that wasn't here before."

"Like the spider juice?"

"Exactly like it," he told her. "Only there's a lot more of it on the floor than there was on the wall."

"Harold, maybe you ought to get out of there."

Collins rose and turned the glowing face of the cell phone toward the bend in the cave. It was less than ten yards away. He walked slowly toward it. "I was thinking of going to town and trying to get more information about the mountain," he said. He walked alongside the oil. He felt as if he were in Candyland, crossing a molasses river with a green gumdrop wall ahead.

"Harold, what are you doing?"

"Just looking."

"You're going in, aren't you?"

"A little," Collins confessed.

"Your job is to investigate, not to take blind risks."

"We don't know that there's a risk."

"We don't know that there's not."

He was going to say, "We don't know that there's not

not," but his heart was rising in his throat and his mouth was getting dry. He could do with some whistling past the graveyard but he didn't have the energy to be silly.

"Why did you call?" he asked. "Did you find something?"

"Actually, no. I wanted to tell you that I was doing some research on Snake Mountain. I didn't find much."

"I'm not surprised. No one knew it was here."

"It's more than that," she said. "I also didn't find anything about animal totemism, any reason for there to be a statue of a spider, or a spider ceremonially encased in plaster or pumice."

"Well, we know why. It wasn't a statue."

"Yes, we know *that,* which brings me to what we don't know. Something obviously cooked the fluids from a spider. It came back to life, apparently with no side effects. That needs to be studied."

"It's the reason I'm going forward."

"Which doesn't mean rushing in," she said.

Collins stopped. "Are you not telling me something?"

"No."

"You sound worried."

"I am," she said. "At least wait until the deputy comes out. Better yet, go back to the car. He may have found another way out and you could miss him, fall down that rabbit hole you were talking about."

Collins had to admit that made sense. He wasn't in a rush. And the cell phone light wasn't exactly making this the Great White Way.

"Harold?" Tally said sternly.

"All right," he said. "I'm going."

"Thank you," she replied. "Also when you leave, watch your step."

"Why?"

"Because it wasn't named 'Snake Mountain' for nothing."

"Good point," he said.

Collins hung up and turned to go. As he walked toward daylight he thought he heard a rattle.

Power of Tally suggestion, he thought.

He stopped, half-turned, and listened. He used the cell phone to light the area around his feet. Nothing was there, save for the outer reaches of the goop. He turned to go.

There was a throaty rasp behind him. He stopped and turned back. Waited. Listened. He thought he heard a faint rasp.

"Hello?" Collins said.

No answer, no sound.

"Is anyone back there? I'm with the United Nations. I won't hurt you. I can't. It's in our charter. Plus, we're wusses."

He waited. No one spoke. But something was back there. Maybe an animal. Maybe one of the snakes Tally feared.

Just a snake, he snickered to himself.

He had survived a trip through time and a tussle with a mosasaur, or whatever that monster was. He had to see this through. At least he had to see the statues, even if it was just in the light of a cell phone. Screw running. The answers weren't behind him, they were ahead. He wanted to scoop some of the oil onto them, just to see what would happen. He was a scientist and this is what scientists did. They explored the uncharted regions.

Pulling a long breath of greasy air into his lungs, he continued back toward the bend.

CHAPTER 20

AFTER HANGING UP with Collins, Tally sat at her desk. She sat there staring at nothing and chewing the inside of her cheek and wondering if Harold was really going to leave the cave.

Probably not, she told herself.

No, probably, she decided after a quick rethink.

Then, *probably not,* she concluded. Harold would have to go back in. Tally wanted to be impressed by his dedication, but she really didn't think it was the only thing that drove the guy. Harold was like a little boy. If someone told him "Don't touch" he had to touch, just to shake things up, just to keep himself or other people from becoming complacent, from buying everything they were told. She wondered if Harold's parents had discouraged or encouraged that.

Encouraged, she decided. He was just too uninhibited about getting in peoples's faces.

Tally also wondered why she should worry about it. If he wanted to go into a cave where it appeared that fluids were being squeezed from living tissue by some unknown agent, that was his business. She had tried to reason with him.

"Damn him." She was still worried.

She went back on-line to search organic, inorganic, petrologic, and metallurgic desiccants. There were certain kinds of clay, silica, activated carbon. Chemical desiccants were used to *kill* insects and vermin; she wondered if someone had placed those inside the cave.

You know how much you'd need to freeze-dry a person? she thought.

Anyway, there would also have to be a delivery system. Someone would have to consume it in massive quantities. Then there was diatomaceous earth, which was comprised of the fossilized remains of marine diatoms—spiny microscopic prehistoric life-forms. Their tiny spines could pierce the tissue of living things and drain them of fluids. But only of tiny living things like insects. Not people.

There was nothing to suggest a natural explanation. She went back to the idea that this was a joke or publicity stunt.

But what about the spider?

The phone beeped. Caller ID told her it was Harold. She snapped it up.

"Tally—"

"You're going in," she said.

"Just a little bit," Collins said. "I can't go too far too fast. I only have the cell phone for light."

"Can you say 'stupid'?"

"It's all right," he insisted. "I'm kind of sliding along, feeling my way."

"I repeat: this is not the way to do research."

"Tally, there's no such thing as 'a way.'"

"Also, you're breaking up."

"I know," Collins said. "The signal's not too good in here. Listen, Tally. I need you to do something. Please."

"What?"

"The deputy who was up here. His name is Woodward. Please call the Coconino County Sheriff's Department and ask them to call his radio or cell phone, whatever he has on him. They've probably got some kind of amped-up signal that will allow them to communicate."

"And if they do?"

"Tell them to give him a jingle. I want to know if he's receiving and, if so, where he is. If not, they need to know that."

"Why don't you just go back to the mouth of the cave and make the call yourself?" Tally asked.

"Because for one thing, they may tell me the same thing the deputy told me, which is not to go in."

"Which, I repeat, would be the smart thing to do."

"That's beside the point. More importantly, I don't want them to know that anyone is currently up here."

"Why?"

"I don't want the site polluted any more than it already is," Collins said. "If I go back, if they send more people up here, I may never have a chance to explore this cave. They'll bring in dust, dogs, corrupt the oil. Also, I want to investigate while whatever is active is still active."

That made some sense.

"Also, you're a journalist," Collins went on. "You know how to interview people. If you call you may get us new information. Maybe your credentials at *Natural History* will open them up, I don't know."

"I'll be surprised if they've heard of the magazine," Tally said.

"Deputy Woodward has a sister who works for the U.N.," Collins said. "Y'never know."

"All right. I'll do it," Tally agreed. "But I'm not going to pretend I think this is a good idea."

"For the first time we're in complete agreement," Collins replied. "But 'easy' isn't in any job description I've ever read."

"Neither is 'reckless.' Harold, are you talking because you're nervous?"

"Yeah. Why?"

"I just wanted to know," the young woman said. "It gives me a tiny level of comfort to think there's a little common-sense survival instinct lurking in that go-get-'em brain."

"It's there, insistently poking the rest of me in the ribs," Collins said. "I'll call back if I find anything—assuming I can."

"What do you mean?" she said with alarm. The remark didn't come packaged in his usual joking tone.

"The reception will be iffier the deeper I go," Collins told her.

"Oh. Right." He probably didn't realize there were two ways to interpret what he had just said.

"Also, if the same thing happens to me that happened to the spider, I want you to do me a favor."

"What?"

"Make sure you reconstitute me from the head down. I can live without my ankles if I have to."

"Not funny."

"I was being serious. I'll be in touch."

Collins hung up and Tally called information to get the number of the Coconino County Sheriff's Department. She got it and placed the call on her cell phone. She didn't want to have to explain this charge to the boss. She got the automated phone mail system, input #5 for "non-emergency," and was given over to a dispatcher. Tally told the woman that she was from *Natural History* magazine and asked to speak with the public information officer about Snake Mountain. They put her through. Either they were not terribly discriminating or caller ID verified that Tally was who she said she was. A sergeant named Tex McAllen took the call.

"Ma'am," he said when she finished her "I was wondering if you could help me with a sidebar about early twentieth-century silver mines" speech, "I would be delighted to E-mail you the press release I wrote on the situation this morning. There's nothing more current than that."

"Oh?" she said. "The news report I saw suggested that you were going to have people looking into this."

"We are," McAllen said. "We do."

"But—?"

"We haven't heard back from them yet."

"Is there any way you can reach them?" Tally asked. "I'm kind of working against a deadline."

"I suppose I could give Deputy Woodward a jingle right now," he said.

"Would you? I'd really appreciate it."

"All right. Would you call back in ten minutes or so?"

"I'd rather hold the line, if that's not a problem."

"It's not a problem for me," the sergeant said. "Hold on. I promise I won't forget you."

"Thanks."

Tally looked around her office as she waited. There were framed posters from the museum, her diplomas and honors—mandatory, not vanity—and favorite photographs from the magazine. In between were bookcases with bound back-issues, plants, and a small TV for watching promotional videotapes sent by authors, nations, institutions, and others who wanted to be part of the magazine. There should be more of her here, she thought. Of course to have that, she had to have more of a personal life. It was funny. She had first met Harold when he hit on her at a party. That had fizzled badly, but here they were, in a professional relationship that showed a few reflexive tics of her caring about him.

McAllen came back after just two minutes. He sounded a little rushed. "Ma'am, I'm going to have to ring you back in a little bit."

"Is something wrong?"

"Probably not," he said. "It's just that we can't raise either of the two people we have out there."

"Signal problems?" she suggested.

"That's our guess," he replied.

"Is that common out there? In caves, I mean?" She was trying to get every scrap of information she could.

"Sometimes. This is a little odd because they've got two radios and two cell phones between them and we can't raise any of them."

"Maybe they're just preoccupied—"

"Can I have your number, please?" McAllen interrupted. "I promise to call back as soon as I have something."

Tally gave her cell number, thanked Tex McAllen, then immediately called Collins. She couldn't raise him either.

Because he was a little too deep in the cave.

She hoped.

CHAPTER 21

COLLINS HARDLY NEEDED the dull green light of the cell phone to illuminate his next few steps. He wouldn't have needed the flashlight either. The nearer Collins came to the bend in the cave the brighter it got. It looked to him as if a flashlight were coming closer, in lock-step with his own progress.

"If that's you, deputy, don't shoot!" Collins said. He wasn't being facetious now. He didn't know whether sheriff's deputies out here would go Chuck Norris on an intruder. He didn't want to find out. "It's still just me, Harold Collins. From the United Nations."

There was no answer and he continued to approach cautiously. The white light grew. He slowed, it slowed. He stopped, it stopped. He didn't know how the other person knew to do that: they couldn't see him and the cell phone wasn't throwing off enough illumination to be seen around the turn. Perhaps they were listening to his footsteps. If so, why weren't they answering?

"Deputy Woodward? Forensics person?"

This was getting silly or scary, he couldn't decide which. It occurred to him that he may have caught whoever was behind this thing and they were trying to scare him away. Or maybe they heard the sheriff go by and thought it was safe to come out. Either way, they weren't going to want Collins to see them.

Too bad, he thought as reason took hold. He wasn't going to let a flashlight get in his way. This whole thing was going to turn out to be just a damn cave with some statues and petroleum-based muck, and a spider that got frosted somehow.

Collins started forward once again. The turn in the cave was just a few feet away. The light started moving again, expanding outward in all directions and growing in intensity. The whole thing was strange. He reached the bend and was about to go around when he saw it.

The small object was lying on the rugged floor of the cave, right where it turned inward. The thing was just beyond his feet, near its own very tiny puddle of oil. Collins bent and picked it up. He held it between his thumb and index finger and turned it over several times.

It was a shell casing. Or rather, it was the statue of a shell casing. Collins knew nothing about firearms and he didn't know whether this was old or new. He did wonder if gunfire could have made the loud pops he heard. The young scientist held the outside rim of the object and touched the open end into the oil. At once it started to become brassy again.

That's not biological activity, he thought.

It was becoming very clear that something had vampirically drained all the fluid from a spider and now a bullet casing, and probably from the other "statues" in the cave as well. Two questions were in the front of his brain: first, what did it; and second, if the perpetrator—whether sentient or mineral—was still somewhere in the cave, did the light have anything to do with that? Was there some strange, radioactive ore that was cooking people and things to hard ash?

The edge of the pure-white light was just two feet or so from the spot where Collins waited. He wasn't about to look around the bend to take a precise measurement. That would surely give his position away.

Collins was becoming increasingly convinced that he didn't belong here at this particular moment. But there was one thing he had to find out. Placing his back against the cave wall, he slowly, slowly edged the toe of his shoe toward the bend. The light moved with it. Compared to this, going into the Loch Ness wormhole was easy. He descended, he got sucked down. No thought required.

He took a moment to untie his Nike. It occurred to the physicist that if his shoe got welded to the cave floor he didn't want to be stuck inside of it. He wiggled his finger under the laces to make them as loose as possible. The light was just inches away. He kept moving the shoe forward until it was an inch away. Then less. Then the light touched the tip.

Nothing happened except that the tip of his shoe got a lot brighter. Collins almost laughed with relief. So the light wasn't the problem. Maybe what *caused* the light was. Maybe one of those wraparound wormholes Dr. Jackson had theorized had come unglued and was spritzing around the cave like a water hose, spraying anti-time over anything that got in its way.

But Collins's relief was short-lived. He remembered, suddenly, that the tarantula was found much closer to the cave entrance than where he was now. Whatever was causing the light could move.

It was definitely time to go.

Suddenly there was a sound like the release of steam from an Old West locomotive. Only it was a very faint and echoing hiss, almost like a chorus of very distant steam engines—

Or snakes.

There were probably a variety of indigenous snakes. But what if there were some that were not "local"? At least, not to this time period. Collins had escaped his last reptilian encounter, in the past, just barely. What if there was a wormhole here that went to the same past and there was a tiny dinosaur around the bend? One with a strange kind of night vision. Or a tail light, like modern-day fireflies.

Meg Wyndham makes fireflies. This may be where those totemistic images came from.

There were too many "ifs" and not enough "ah-has." Collins paused to tie his shoe and then started to back away. As he turned, the young scientist realized he was still holding the bullet casing. He decided to try something: he flicked it back into the cave, around the bend and into the light. Just to see what happened. As it clinked on the cave floor the hiss grew louder. Even before the small metal cylinder stopped rolling, the area around it flared brilliantly, like a photo flash. The brightness lasted even less time than that, however, and when it was gone the casing was entirely white again with oily glop rolling off and behind it.

Collins no longer backed away. He left, quickly.

CHAPTER 22

HER EYES AND the eyes of her children returned to their natural yellow color. The glow around her receded, then died, as the other creature moved away. There was no longer a need for the light because there was no longer a threat.

At the moment.

This one was different than the others. His comings and goings were tentative and he had tested her before going away. She sensed that he would not warn others to stay away. She sensed that he would return and that could not be. There was the Law, and the Law was her burden.

He and the others would have to be stopped. There were so many of them now, more than at any time in the past.

She waited, her long, slender legs bent outward from her side. They were useful for propping herself upright, but useless for walking. When she moved, she folded them alongside her tail, which was coiled behind her now and supporting the bulk of her lengthy torso. Her small arms were cocked at the elbows, hovering at her side, their sharp talons at the ready. Sometimes the ignorant creatures tried to defend themselves and it was necessary to stop them with force or fire. That, too, was her burden. To have been made a fighter.

She dropped to her belly and moved low, like her kind, following and watching him. She observed his passage down the hill and into his conveyance. She watched the object move off, followed it with her keen eyes.

This being was different from the others. She had to preserve the Law, but perhaps she could do it another way.

A way that was far more permanent.

CHAPTER 23

IT WAS A mystified and frightened Harold Collins who hurried down the path to Deputy Woodward's patrol car. He wanted to use the radio to call for help. He pulled on the driver's-side door but it was locked. So was the door on the passenger's side. He considered smashing the window to use the radio but decided just to call 911 on his cell phone. He slipped it out and punched the first two numbers.

Then he stopped.

Call and tell them what? That the deputy told him to stay outside and he went in anyway? That he worked some alchemy on a tarantula and a bullet casing? That he saw a bright light and couldn't find the law officers who he wasn't supposed to be with in the first place?

No, he told himself. *Just tell them you're at the car*

*and you've been waiting a while and the deputy is miss-
ing and you're concerned.*

He did. He called and, after providing his name and
location, told the dispatcher exactly that.

And she told him, "The sheriff's office reports that
they are not getting any kind of signal from the radio. It
could be the cave."

"My cell phone worked," Collins said.

"Were you near the mouth?"

"Yes."

"That's the reason," she said confidently. "May I ask
what you are doing at the site, sir?" Her tone was official. A half-note rise in "sir" kept it from being downright unfriendly.

"I saw it on the news and wanted to see it in person,"
he replied. "I work for the United Nations," he added.

"Sir, they have no jurisdiction here."

He couldn't tell whether or not she was being serious.
So he resisted saying anything.

"Please stay away from the site until the investigation
is completed," the woman added.

"This is all pretty strange, isn't it?" he said. "Are
there any theories?"

"The Sedona Police Department is not investigating
this directly. If you wish to call the Coconino County
Sheriff's Department they may be able to answer your
questions. You can also check their website for any public information." Then she thanked him for calling and
disconnected him.

"And a very merry unbirthday to you," Collins said as
he folded away his phone. Either she had fielded too
many calls on the subject or didn't want to be handling
CCSD business, or both.

Collins looked back at the cave. The entrance seemed darker than it had before, possibly because the sun was now behind it. Or maybe it was because he had raised more questions than he had answered, deepening the mystery.

The Mystery of Snake Mountain. It sounded like one of the Hardy Boys novels his dad used to read to him. With Frank and Joe Hardy, though, the culprits would have been smugglers or saboteurs or counterfeiters or buried-treasure seekers working their evil mischief in and around Bayport. Somehow, Collins did not think any of those were responsible for any of this.

He walked to his own car and stood leaning on the door, looking up at the mountain.

"I need to think about you before I come back," he said. Either there was a big picture he couldn't see or something small and obvious he was missing. Either way, he needed more information.

Collins got in his car and drove back to the Boots and Spurs. A shower, a hang in the lobby, a chat with the locals—that would give him a fresh perspective and possibly relevant information. He wished Tally were here. He'd have to put on an uncharacteristic social face to do that. She would enjoy his suffering.

Joe and Meg Wyndham were outgoing hosts. They were in the lobby when he arrived, talking to two of the other guests, Pat and Gary Seawall, an early twenties newlywed couple of school teachers that were hon-econo-mooning by driving cross-country from Silver Springs, Maryland to the Pacific Ocean and back. The bed-and-breakfasts, they said, were their big splurge, as opposed to motels. Well, they were happy and that was all that mattered. Collins watched Meg oh-so-gently try to push some of her homemade jewelry, but though the Seawalls were polite they weren't buying.

When they left, Collins went over to the display case, a chrome and glass cream filling between the staid, solid oak brochure stand and matching reception counter. The case was well-stocked with silver and pewter works that ranged from bugs to faux Native American designs. Sitting well behind the counter was a third member of the family, Joe's centenarian mother, Dorothy. The lean, pale woman was sitting three or so feet from a television set, watching CNN and sipping ice tea from a movie tie-in cup with a plastic straw.

"Mother's a news junkie," Joe said, limping from behind the counter. "She has been ever since the war."

"Which one?" Collins asked as a way of getting into the conversation.

"The 'great' one, double-u double-u one," Joe replied. "She's still mad at President Wilson for having kept us out of the war so long."

"I'm mad at him too," Collins said.

Joe frowned at him. "Forgive me—you're a guest and all—but just because something's from another time, that doesn't make it unimportant."

"I wasn't implying that," Collins said. "If he had worked harder and smarter on the League of Nations, maybe I'd be working for a more effective world body than the bureaucratic compost heap I work for now."

"You work for the United Nations?" Meg said.

"I do."

"How interesting!"

"It's not dull, no," Collins agreed. "And I happen to agree with your mother, Mr. Wyndham. Wilson kept us out of that war far too long. So did Franklin Roosevelt with the Second World War, according to my mom who's from Hawaii and was raised around Pearl Harbor. Truman and Nixon kept us *in* wars too long. There's never a way of knowing something for certain at the time, only when we look back."

The proprieter's frown turned into a smirk. "Well. I do apologize, Mr. Collins."

"No need," Collins said.

"Yes, there is," Meg said. "He can't get used to young people having opinions *or* money."

"It's really all right, Mrs. Wyndham," Collins assured her. "My dad gives me the same thing all the time."

"Then let's get back to the present," Joe said.

"Something I always enjoy doing," Collins said.

"Did you get your spider back to your room all right?"

"I did, thank you."

"What?" Meg asked.

Collins looked at her. "I found a spider with a kind of atrophy, Mrs. Wyndham. It was white and stiff one second, then normal after I touched it. Have either of you ever heard of anything like that?"

"Not from anyone sober," Joe said.

"You've heard it from drunks?" Collins asked.

"No. Just a figure of speech."

"Do you have a girlfriend?" Meg asked.

"Uh—no. Not really," Collins replied. This was becoming non sequitur central.

"Too bad. They like my jewelry," she said. "Mothers too. Grandmothers. Aunts. Piano teachers."

"It's very lovely," he said. He turned back to the counter and looked down. "Is there any significance to the insects?"

"When I was waiting for my husband to return from the war—Mr. Roosevelt's war," she added with a smile,

"I was looking for hope in the blackness. Fireflies gave that to me."

"Very sweet," he said sincerely. "What about the materials?"

"The silver and pewter I used because of local legends," she went on.

"Oh? Legends about what?"

"They were considered talismans against evil." She frowned. "Or would the plural be talismen?"

" 'Talismans' is correct," Dorothy said.

"Thank you, mums," Meg shouted. She leaned forward and whispered, "Became a schoolteacher after the old ranch failed. She watches the news all day, talks to the newscasters as though they were students. Hates their grammar, their cliches. Every time someone says, 'hail of bullets' or 'torrential rain,' she yells at them."

"I'll watch my language," Collins said. "Tell me, Meg, are you sure it was silver and pewter?"

"Yes!" Dorothy said.

"Against what kind of evil did the talismans offer protection? Was it something specific?"

"It was the burning!" Dorothy rasped from the other room. She muted the sound of the television but didn't turn away from it. Sitting in silhouette, in the whitish glow of the picture tube, she seemed almost like a statue herself. Her eyeglasses glowed slightly, giving her an additional otherwordly component.

"What was the burning?" Collins asked.

"It was a legend among the Apaches," Meg answered. "I don't know much about it. It was a fire that killed all those who saw it."

"*Saw* it?"

Meg nodded.

"How did it kill them?" Collins asked.

OPERATION MEDUSA   149

"The way fires are supposed to kill!" Dorothy said from the other room. "It turned them to ash."

"To ash," Collins said.

"Yes. White ash."

CHAPTER 24

"SILVER," TALLY SAID into her cell phone as she walked. "Do you think that's really significant?"

"Yes, but I'm wondering if it was the metal or the color that was important to the Apaches," he replied.

Color happened to be very much on Tally's mind when he asked that question. She had just come from the subway when Collins called. She crossed Greenwich Avenue as she talked, heading west to the apartment. It was a glorious twilight, the air sweet, with a hint of coolness, the kind of sunset that bounced off the countless windows and metal facades and lit a big golden sign over New York that screamed "Life!" as, uptown, Broadway came to life, and the after-work bars and restaurants and clubs of the West Village came to life, and the commuters left the city by car and train, and the wide-eyed, map-reading tourists left the

streets to sit down, and the native New Yorkers retook possession of their priceless bauble in the bay, cherishing its
countless facets and deep and varied riches. Centuries
merged on virtually every block, old brick townhouses beside fitness centers beside taverns in which the end of the
Civil War had been—toasted—all without one of Harold's
white dwarf particles to make the connection.

"I would think the color," Tally said. "How else can
you explain both silver and pewter being used as talismans? Pewter is what? Mostly tin and lead, right?"

"Right," Collins replied. "Silver shows up in the lore
of the supernatural, used to slay vampires and were-
wolves, flowing through the bodies of certain dragons—"

"It's also the Lone Ranger's horse."

"Not the same thing," Collins said.

"You don't know what the character's creator may
have heard or learned," Tally said.

"That's true. The point is, pewter is never mentioned
anywhere else in supernatural lore," Collins went on.

"That's because it isn't pure," Tally said. "Isn't silver
supposed to represent the purity of Christ?"

"I think so, which is why it kills vampires and were-
wolves," Collins replied.

"I knew all those years of mass would pay off," Tally
said. "So maybe your hotelier is wrong. Maybe only silver is an evil repellent."

"No. Meg's mother-in-law was adamant about that."

"Well, that ices it."

"You don't know her. These people *are* Sedona."

"Then what do they think about the statues in the
cave?" Tally asked.

"The husband thinks it's a prank, the wife has no
idea, and the mother thinks it's restless spirits."

"Sedona is divided."

"On this they are," Collins said. "But I'm with Mom. Not necessarily that it's spirits, but something restless. I saw that light—"

"A dropped flashlight."

"No. It moved when I moved."

"Vibrations? Air currents?"

"The floor was solid, Tal, and there was no wind that deep—except for my very heavy breathing. There was also the noise."

"Running water somewhere. Your own breath. Caves make noises and noises echo through caves."

"All possible, but I'm telling you there was something eerie about this," Collins said.

"An hour ago you were telling me how you thought this trip had been a big fat bust," Tally said. "I think your words were, 'This is one phenomenon that may not be so phenomenal.'"

"I was discouraged, stymied," Collins said. "But the stuff about the silver and pewter could be part of the solution. I mean, we have a cave hasn't been open since this land belonged to the Apaches. It's a former silver mine. There is an Apache legend that includes both silver and white ash. There are legends of animal spirits. Y'know, I've been thinking of the statues as chalk or pumice or something like that. But what if that's exactly what they are, compacted ash?"

"That still doesn't explain your pet tarantula coming back to life," Tally pointed out.

"True, and there may not be a neat, unified theory. But the ash idea is as good a starting point as any. I mean, you've seen charcoal in a barbecue and wood in a fireplace, right?"

"Yes."

"Both of them get all white and cakey after a fire.

Maybe we're dealing with an enzymic blotter of some kind—or a sponge. Or maybe it turns living tissue *into* a sponge, something that draws fluids out, and then you just soak it back in by touching object to liquid. Sponges are living things."

"Yes. And most of them are attached to rocks and coral."

"So these could be microscopic sponges," Collins suggested. "Or ambulatory sponges."

Tally grinned. "A house cleaner's delight, just mop and scatter."

"Tally—"

"I'm sorry," she said. "Editorial meeting days always leave me feeling like I've been released from prison. I get a little giddy. Also, it's a stunning day. I want problems to be solved and gone."

"Me too. Except that, as you just said, every time I try to put this one aside it teases me back in."

Tally stopped at a small Middle Eastern restaurant. While Collins thought out loud she ordered a lamb gyro on an onion pita, hold the tahini. As she waited at the counter she noticed something.

"Hey, Harold—there's one thing you may not have considered."

"I know. Silver foil as an aphrodisiac?"

"Not the one I was thinking of, but that's true. Indians—the India kind—use finely pounded silver leaf for that."

"Great, as long as you don't have fillings."

"Another thing silver is used for, but not pewter," Tally pointed out.

"True. Silver as purity and silver as sex. There's a contradiction for you," Collins said.

"Yes, but what I was thinking of is something else

that silver and pewter have in common," Tally told him. The young woman bent closer to the chrome frame of the display counter. She looked at her distorted facial features. "Both of those metals reflect, like a mirror."

"Reflectivity," Collins said thoughtfully. "I don't see how that would help protect you from danger."

"Reflected sunlight, for one thing," Tally said. "Ancient armies such as the Persians and the Babylonians used highly polished shields to bounce the sun into the eyes of their enemies, blinding them."

"But brass could do that. Brass would probably be *better* for that. Silver or pewter wouldn't stop a sword or lance. In any case, that wouldn't have been a concern for the Apaches."

"Brass would color the light, dull it," Tally said. "Maybe the Apaches didn't want that to happen."

"But the color of light wouldn't impact its capacity to blind an opponent," Collins said. "Focus and intensity would do that."

"Well—it was a sudden thought."

"And a good one. I'll have to think about it. Assuming that the metal and the events in the cave are related, the Apaches could have realized a prophylactic value in these metals if the siccative element in the cave is light-based."

"That expression was *way* more complicated than it needed to be," Tally said as she paid for her meal.

"Sorry."

"I'll be back at the apartment in a few minutes," she said. "I'll go on-line and do a word search on 'silver siccative prophylactic.' I'm kind of dying to know what comes up."

"You know, I just thought of something," he said.

"What?"

"The vortices."

"What about them?"

"By definition they draw things down. *Away*."

"Okay—"

"What if . . . *yes*."

" 'Yes' what? What if what?"

"What if we have a situation similar to Loch Ness? What if there is an intense gravity center here that's doing the sucking?" Collins paused. "Was that uncomplicated enough?"

"Yes. Touché," she said.

"In Loch Ness I was wearing headgear. I had earphones under that. I might not have heard it. It's possible the sound I heard in here, a hissing, could be the compressing of material."

"Or snakes who didn't want you hanging around."

"I would have seen at least one, don't you think?" Collins asked.

"Not necessarily," Tally told him. "They're pretty shy unless you step on them or their nests."

"I didn't know that. Nests, huh?"

"Getting back to the vortices," Tally said, "you're thinking that the central processing station for the Sedona vortices could be inside the cave, covered up until recently, and now exerting some kind of petrifying or de-synoviating force on any living thing that comes near."

"De-synoviating?" Collins said.

"Yeah. Synovia. It's a lubricating fluid secreted by membranes in joint cavities, sheaths of tendons, and bursae," she said. "Okay, Harold. I won't criticize your language anymore."

"Thanks. What I'm thinking is, maybe the light I saw was being drawn *to* the wormhole and not being emitted by it. The visible spectrum could be undergoing a compacting of some kind."

"Wouldn't that be black instead of white?" Tally asked. "Absorption instead of reflection?"

"It would be black once it got past the event horizon, yes," Collins told her. "Not before."

"Then why isn't this sucking happening to the cave itself or the stuff that's in it? The walls, the statues, everything?"

"I don't know," Collins admitted. "Why didn't it happen to Loch Ness?"

"Good point."

"Maybe it only attracts energy of a certain wavelength. Maybe it solidifies the light around things in a way we can't begin to comprehend."

"A lot of maybes."

"I was thinking the same thing earlier," Collins said. "Screw this. I know one way to get rid of them."

"You're going back."

"First thing in the morning," he said. "There are two things I have to do first."

"What?"

"Get detailed maps of the vortices," he said, "and buy some pewter fireflies."

CHAPTER 25

PROPPED IN BED, laptop and TV on, Collins reflected on how Tally was a good sounding board, and then some. Once in a while she hit a valuable carom shot, and sometimes she tagged the sweet spot so confidently that Collins was dazzled, delighted, and a little angry. Dazzled because she had a good eye; delighted because it helped him; angry because he didn't think of whatever it was that she had seen.

Mirrors. Reflectivity.

That was a little of both, carom and a bull's-eye. All Collins had to do to see whatever was in the cave was do a periscope routine—use a mirror to look around a corner. In this case, he would use one of Meg Wyndham's larger pieces of jewelry. It wasn't as good as a regular old mirror, but if pewter or silver were some kind of charm he wanted that protection.

He bought a firefly broach that had big, spread wings and a glass taillight. It was relatively inexpensive and would suit his needs. Then he went back to his room to do his own on-line research. Tally was also on-line and instant messaged him about her findings on silver siccative prophylactic.

There were none.

He read more about the Sedona vortices—learning that here they were ungrammatically called "vortexes" for some reason no one could explain, and which would probably tick Dorothy Wyndham off mightily—and learned that some of them had masculine natures and some of them feminine. Those nearest Snake Mountain were feminine, which meant the energy there strengthened qualities such as kindness, compassion, generosity of spirit, and patience.

And squeezing the life essence out of you, he thought.

That was a cheap shot at Rose Coronado and Collins mentally slapped himself for taking it.

The five vortexes formed a pentagon: Boynton Canyon Vortex to the northwest, the Airport Vortex to the northeast, the Red Rock Crossing–Cathedral Canyon Vortex to the southwest, the Bell Rock Vortex to the southeast, and Snake Mountain to the east, between but apart from the line formed by the Airport and Bell Rock Vortexes. Collins did not think there was any significance to that, though it was ironic. Some force appeared to be at war with them.

"People are supposed to feel energy at these places, and light is energy, so maybe this is what's supposed to be happening. Only *more*," he thought aloud.

More, Collins thought. *Hell, we're talking about*

enough energy to flash-fry living creatures. And then allow them to be revived. Collins hadn't learned about energy like that at MIT. The white dwarf as a funnel for some seriously strange or vacillating wavelength radiation was seeming more and more likely.

Hours had passed since he'd left the cave. It was dark now, and Collins didn't think he should go back there. Instead, he slipped off his shoes, dropped onto the bed, and checked the local evening news on KPNX channel twelve, which had provided local coverage to CNN the night before.

The tone of the reporters at the NBC affiliate was considerably different than the night before. The anchorwoman reported that shortly before 5 P.M.—nearly an hour before—local and county law enforcement had gone to the cave to find out what had happened to a deputy and a county forensics specialist who had visited the site early that afternoon.

"What we found were three more statues, deeper in the cave," said Sheriff Donal Birdsong, who had gone to Snake Mountain himself. "One of a police officer who came here after his shift and two of our people. There are no traces of the individuals themselves, nor evidence of criminal assault, I would like to add."

Collins sat up in the bed. "I knew something went wrong in there," the young man muttered. *And that's an interesting combination,* he thought a moment later. *An Irish Native American.*

"Did you find anything else in the cave?" asked the on-site reporter, Evelyn Van Buren, a young raven-haired woman who looked as if she were fresh out of high school. Maybe she was.

"Nothing that we can comment on at this time," the sheriff replied.

The goop, Collins thought. *And the calcified bullet casings.* He had to have seen them but he wasn't talking about them.

"We understand you found the Corvette belonging to the missing assistant police chief," the reporter said.

"Yes. It was parked behind the slope. The Sedona police department have gone over it and found no evidence of anything unusual."

"Turning to the statues, sheriff, do you have any indication yet of who may have brought them over or why?" the reporter asked.

"Again, that's something on which I don't really want to comment right now," the sheriff said.

"Could one of your people, Deputy Woodward, be involved in this mystery?" the reporter pressed.

"We have no indication of that, and our research will move in other directions," the sheriff concluded. "We hope to know more when it's light and we can have a better look around the perimeter."

Translation: I'm stonewalling because I haven't a clue, Collins thought.

"And a final question, sir. Your forensics expert, Dr. Joliet, is a woman. Do you know of any sort of relationship between her and the deputy?"

"Yes."

"You do?"

"Yes. She is his colleague."

The sheriff walked off-camera then and a grinning Evelyn Van Buren turned the story back to the anchor.

Collins wanted to talk to that guy. Sheriff Birdsong had to know more than he was telling. The young man got off the bed and put his shoes back on. He pulled a blue windbreaker from his carry-on and put the firefly talisman in the pocket. Then he slapped his pockets and then the bed to find the car keys before finally locating them on the desk, beside the phone. Not having a car in New York meant not having a regular place where he put car keys.

Collins shut the main light in the room's small entranceway. He made sure he had his room key, a big, old-fashioned brass job, and was about to leave the room when he noticed something. The shades were not drawn and he saw lights outside, beyond the pool. There was a thickly treed hill there with underbrush to prevent erosion. The lights were just beyond the two picnic tables, just beyond the amber lights that lit the pool. They looked like yellow fireflies, only they weren't flitting about nor flashing off and on. They just hung in the new darkness like Christmas lights. He wondered if they were coyotes and coyote babies out for a meal of half-eaten hamburgers and kaiser rolls. Or maybe they were owls. He always thought, though, that nocturnal predators were somewhat more hidden.

Collins also had the odd feeling that they were looking at him. Which was absurd, since he was larger and far less accessible than a field mouse. Part of him wanted to ignore it but it was a mystery, albeit a small one, and part of him wanted to shoot over and have a look. Since he had to go out anyway the "have a look" part won. This time he remembered his flashlight.

Holding the small light in his left hand, he slipped his right hand into his pocket and let his fingers play around the sharp-edged firefly as he left the room and headed outside.

CHAPTER 26

"**M**R. COLLINS?"

Collins turned as he headed down the hall at the bottom of the stairs. Joe Wyndham was limping quickly toward him.

"Yes, Joe?"

"I was just going out to close the pool area, if that's where you're going," Joe said.

"Well, I *was* going to go out there—"

"Thought so. It's a peaceful spot. But we get too many drowned animals at night so we just close 'er up. People don't like waking up to bloated wildlife floating belly-down."

"I don't blame them," Collins replied. "Actually, I was just going out to check the lights back there."

"What lights?"

"Well, I don't know. They're like little fireflies."

Joe reached Collins's side. "I didn't notice them. Mind if I come with?"

"Not at all."

The men walked down the short hallway. It was decorated with ornately framed Western oils by a local artist, someone Meg had met at a local craft fair. Joe wasn't overly fond of them but he liked art that was realistic, not abstract. A green splash on a tawny background wasn't "Desert Cactus" to him.

They reached the door that led to the pool. Joe opened it and gestured for his guest to go outside. Collins stepped out and Joe followed him. He looked out across the walled-in pool.

"Funny. I don't see them now," the young man said.

"Where were they?"

"Back by the picnic tables," Collins told him.

"You know, it could have been bats hanging upside down from the oak tree. They do that sometimes. You wouldn't be able to tell them apart from branches during the daylight. Same color."

"Do they have yellow eyes?"

"They do when they're around yellow light," Joe said. He pointed to the hooded spotlights around the pool.

"Hmmmm," Collins said. He walked along the perimeter of the pool and shined his small but powerful flashlight on the picnic area. There was nothing there. "I didn't imagine it," Collins said.

"Didn't say you did," Joe told him. "Maybe it was bats or it could've been a mountain lion. Ever since people started building their homes higher in the mountains the cats've been forced to come down looking for food. Had one track a jogger couple of weeks back, up on one of the hiking trails. Guy got lucky when a chopper happened to scare the cat off."

The young man walked several steps closer to that area, turning his flashlight here and there. The grounds were vacant. He shined the light on the ground for a moment then snapped it off.

"Hold on," Joe said.

"What?"

"Turn the light back on."

Collins obliged.

"See over there?" Joe said, pointing. "Back by the far left table. The grass is presssed down."

"I see it now," Collins said. "Looks like a big fat hose was laying on it."

"Right."

Collins tracked the depression with the flashlight. Now that Joe thought about it the width of the depression was more like a drainage pipe, about two, two-and-a-half feet in diameter.

"It trails off behind the house," Collins observed. "Do you have any idea what could have made it?"

"Not a one," Joe said.

A gate through the wall led to the back. Joe made his way toward it. Collins followed, lighting the way. The ground was depressed to where the lawn ended, at the back wall of the house. There were no markings to the left or right. Collins shined the flashlight up to an open window. The room was dark, save for the glow of a TV.

"That's mother's room," Joe said. "She doesn't like living on the first floor. She's afraid of someone slipping in her window." He looked down the wall. "Bring that light over to the right," he said.

Collins moved it closer. Joe studied the aluminum siding. He didn't like aluminum, but this side took a baking during the day and it held up better against the sun. There were gashes in the wall, as though a big bird had pecked at it. They went all the way up, in two rows about a yard apart.

"Now that ain't right," Joe said.

"I take it those are new?" Collins asked.

"Yeah. I'm going upstairs," he said urgently.

Collins went with him. They went through a side door that led directly to a staircase. The guests all stayed downstairs. Upstairs was for the family. Meg was in the kitchen, cleaning up the dinner plates. Mother always went upstairs for the evening network news.

Joe moved as fast as he could. Even though his artificial leg had a joint it was still difficult to make it up stairs with anything approaching speed. In case of a fire, they had a chute that deployed to the ground. Joe had been meaning to look into an ultralight prosthetic with battery-driven myoelectric controls, but change was not something that appealed to him. He still wrote letters and owned a manual typewriter and had no idea what the Internet looked like. That was his wife's deal.

They reached the upstairs corridor. Collins had shut his flashlight and tucked it in his windbreaker. His hand was in his pocket.

"What have you got in there, a pistol?" Joe asked.

"Huh?"

"In your pocket," he said as they neared the room.

"No. It's your wife's broach."

"Why? You think the boogie man's up here?"

"Do you know for sure that he isn't?" Collins asked.

"You can't be serious," Joe replied.

"I am. What if we were right and our parents were wrong when we were kids?" Collins asked him.

"Mother wrong?" Joe was making light of this because he was scared. What Collins was saying was ridiculous. It had to be.

"What if there *was* something in the closet or under the bed?" Collins asked, his voice a whisper now.

"You're like my wife," Joe whispered back. "She says that about religion too, that it's just as easy to believe as it is not to believe."

"She's right."

"That's just mental gymnastics," Joe replied. "It's like the kid who says, 'I know you are but what am I?' If I didn't find God on the battlefield, I'm not going to find him here."

"How do you know you he didn't find you?" Collins asked.

Wordplay, that's all this was. If God had been with Joe Wyndham he wouldn't have lost his leg. Hell, there never would have been a war in which to lose his leg. There wouldn't have been a Hitler. It was all buffalo chips.

The men reached the door. It was closed. Light from the TV was flashing under the door. Joe knocked. "Mother?"

"What?"

"Is everything all right?"

"We should be bombing China," she said. "I don't trust them."

"I mean with you," Joe clarified.

"Yes. Why wouldn't it be?"

"Did you hear anything outside?"

"An airplane."

"Anything unusual, I mean," Joe said.

"No."

"Which way is she facing?" Collins asked.

"Why?"

"If her back is to the window she might have missed something. We know her hearing is good, but—"

Joe rapped on the door again. "Mother, would you mind if I came in for a moment?"

She didn't answer.

Joe knocked again. "Mother?"

Still nothing.

"Cave déjà vu," Collins said.

Joe had no idea what he was talking about and didn't care. He turned the handle and opened the door.

"Holy Christmas," Joe said.

There was someone else in the room, someone who was not his mother.

Seated a few feet from the television, Dorothy Wyndham was awash with its changing glow. Her eyes seemed to be shut though she was sitting upright. Joe wasn't close enough to examine her. And there wasn't time. The other someone was lying on the floor on—his? her?—back. The intruder was under his mother's chair looking up at the old woman. Her eyes were yellow. Smaller yellow lights framed her face and what appeared to be a python was stretched toward the window.

"Mr. Collins," Joe said, "I think I know what your lights—"

A ball of white light rolled forward swiftly, like an oncoming locomotive; it didn't so much strike Joe as envelope him.

And that was all he saw, all he knew, all there was.

CHAPTER 27

TALLY WAS TAKING a walk through the Village when the phone beeped. The caller ID said it was Harold. Tally was on the south side of Washington Square Park, heading toward NYU, and sat on a bench to take the call. There were skateboarders, musicians, chess players, and crack dealers all out enjoying the balmy night. Tally could even smell the ocean here, blowing through the man-made canyons. She looked at the Empire State Building framed by the arch at the northern end of the park. It was all so rich and textured, and she felt lucky to be a part of it.

She answered the phone.

"I think I know what's doing this," Collins said even before her "hello" was finished. He sounded out of breath. Either he was running or scared or both.

"Harold, are you okay?" Tally asked.

"It's Medusa," Collins said.

Ooooooookay, she thought. That answered that question. He was nuts. "Harold, what are you talking about?"

"Medusa! The Gorgon of Greek mythology. She's here, now, in this hotel, turning people to stone."

"Harold—"

"Before you tell me she wasn't real, neither was the Loch Ness Monster till we found it."

"Yes, but what you found was a dinosaur that was being called a monster," Tally said. "This is different."

"That doesn't make it any less plausible."

"Sure it does."

"Look, I'm not imagining this. I tell you I just saw the hotel proprietor get turned to stone by the same kind of white light I saw in the cave. Not only that but goop is all over the floor and wall behind him."

"Did it come out of him?"

"I couldn't tell," Collins told her. "The light coming from Medusa was so bright I had to look away."

"Why didn't it affect you?"

"Because I wasn't looking into her eyes, I suspect."

"Where are you now?" Tally asked.

"On the second floor of the hotel. I'm going down the stairs to see if Joe's wife is all right and then I'm going to get in my car."

"Why don't you call the police?"

"And tell them what I just told you? So they can do what, exactly, when they get here? They'll all get turned to stone, just like Joe."

If he was right about what he was seeing, he had a point.

"Oh, shit," Collins said suddenly.

"What?"

"I hear hissing outside. Medusa must have gone back out the window in the old lady's room."

"Harold, listen to me. You're making a big leap here. You didn't see her."

"Joe did," Collins said in an emphatic whisper. "He saw something that startled him."

Tally couldn't believe they were having this conversation about a lady with snakes for hair, whose gaze reportedly turned people to stone. And then something occurred to her. Something that, as bizarre as it sounded, fit.

"I wonder," she said.

"What?" Collins asked.

"The reflectivity of silver and pewter. Remember the myth? You could only look at her in a polished surface."

"The broach," Collins said. "The amulet properties— not in the possession but in the use of the thing. Good one, Tal."

"Can you get one?"

"I have one, but it's small," Collins said. "Listen, Tally, thanks. You may have just been a lifesafer."

"What are you going to do?"

"I'm going back upstairs to look for a mirror."

"I still think you should call the police. They've seen the statues. They may believe you."

"You want to place bets on that?"

She did not.

"Tally, before I do anything I want to see her. I *have* to see her. Scientists need proof before they make claims. Especially claims like this."

Tally got up and started walking back to her apartment. Quickly. "Harold, I'm not ready to buy this yet but I'm going to look Medusa up on the Net, see what I can find out about her defenses, possible weaknesses. I'll call you back."

"Thanks. If anything happens to me, tell the police about the goop."

"Sure."

Tally hung up, picked up the pace, and couldn't decide whether she hoped Harold was way off base on this or not. Meeting two classic monsters in two outings—that was too much. She was right about this much, though: he would need harder evidence this time, and she didn't think calcified people qualified. They were hard, but evidence of what? On the other hand, if he was right and this was Medusa, if she was somehow a part of the wormhole theory Collins and Dr. Jackson had been discussing—that was amazing.

Tally felt very lucky and very concerned as she raced across Sixth Avenue. Despite her resistance to all she heard, the world suddenly seemed much larger than New York, Planet Earth.

CHAPTER 28

COLLINS WISHED HE knew more about mythology. He wished he knew more about Native American spirits. He wished he knew what the link between them might be. But more than anything he wished he knew whether the uninvited guest downstairs had any defenses other than her deadly gaze. She had obviously climbed the aluminum siding, up *and* down, so she probably had fingers or toes or claws. He seemed to recall somewhere in the legend that she had bronze talons. That would trump aluminum.

He also wondered if she could climb stairs. Given the size of the depression in the grass, that was a lot of snake carcass to haul around. He didn't know if snakes could climb steps like a reverse Slinky.

Yet there is one good thing, Collins thought as he

moved toward what looked like a master bedroom. *She didn't attack me in the cave. Maybe she doesn't attack unless she feels threatened.*

Except that she zapped Mrs. Wyndham and her son and they didn't do a damn thing. Maybe this creature thought the TV was a weapon. Maybe she thought the light would paralyze *her.*

Maybe she knew something the televiewing public did not.

The bedroom door was open and Collins swung in. Meg Wyndham wasn't there. He hoped she was still in the kitchen and stayed there. He hoped the other guests were out and about. He would go down and warn them as soon as he was armed. He ran into the bathroom; in addition to the large mirror there was a hand-mirror on the vanity. Collins picked it up and went back to the bedroom door. He rested the flashlight on his shoulder and pointed it behind him. He didn't want to miss anything in the subdued light of the corridor. The young man felt a little foolish backing into the corridor, looking into the mirror like Annie Oakley about to do a shootin' trick. But he didn't want to end up like Joe, whose chalk-white butt was bent slightly toward the hall, reflected in a viscous pool of oil. Collins had not seen it.

Medusa, he thought. What the hell was a mythological Greek monster doing alive—and in Arizona?

He listened as he moon-walked toward the stairs. The hissing was definitely closer. It occurred to him that if the creature were climbing the stairs there might not be a way for him to get past her. He stepped backward over the glop and stepped beside Joe. The man looked just like the statues in the cave. Collins waited by the door. Should that thing come up the stairs he could always go out the window if he had to.

He wished he had a free hand. He would put the ooze on Joe to see if it brought him back. If it did revive him, Collins wondered if Joe would have all his marbles or if he would be a zombie, functional but without will. He wondered if the man was alert and aware even now, only frozen.

Stop the wondering, Collins warned himself. *You can't afford to be distracted.* That thought aside, he did consider something else, something that could save him. He wondered if the thing on the stairs could speak, whether she was intelligent or a mindless killer.

Whether there were some way to communicate with her.

Collins waited while the hissing grew. As close as he was to a really nasty death right now, it chilled him to think how much closer he was just a few hours ago when this thing was around the bend in the cave and he had no idea what he was facing. That thought comforted him, in an odd way. He felt safer now, a little more in control. He had his little reflective surface and he had a couple of ways out. If only he could convince his hard-tripping heart of that, he'd be a lot happier.

It was difficult to keep the flashlight steady. Collins was trembling too much. He finally had to put his left shoulder against the wall, the one with the flashlight resting on it. His mirror arm was getting tired but he didn't dare rest it for more than a second or two at a time.

At last, Collins saw a claw appear from behind the wall. It entered the upstairs corridor low, just a foot or so off the floor. It was a left hand, pinky finger first. Long bronze talons glistened in the glow of the flashlight. His heart traveled upward, chest to throat to chin. The palm turned toward him, the claws digging into the wall. They sparked as they struck a pipe or wire inside. She was

bracing herself for the final climb. The right hand did the
same, cutting deep notches into the far wall. The claws
sparked again. Obviously, she could do that at will.
Maybe it was a form of venom or just the flint-like
claws. His eyes moved to her skin, which was grayish-
white and smooth. The palm was a patch of greenish skin
with large scales like snakeskin. The patch traveled
down her wrist to her forearm.

This is Medusa, the *Medusa, and those are just her
hands,* he thought, more terrified than he had been when
he had fallen into the past. There, at least, he had no time
to think. Now—

The hissing, muffled before, became sickeningly
clear when Medusa's head rose past the top step. It was
as if someone had turned up the treble on an amplifier.
Turned it way up. Her face was also grayish-white,
hollow-cheeked and slightly elongated. There was more
snakeskin along her tight throat and even tighter cheeks;
it ran up to her forehead and down the bridge of her nose.
Her eyes were long, flattened ovals, yellow with a fat
black iris. She had no lips and a human-like tongue that
was split in the middle. Strange as she appeared, her
most arresting and unnerving feature was her hair. Four
or five large, fat serpents moved in all directions on top
of her head and down her neck. They were green with
white streaks; unlike their host, they had wholly serpentine features. They were watching and hissing, their
forked tongues spitting. The ones on the far side were lying along the back of her neck, looking in his direction
and also checking ahead and behind.

The creature's two hands tensed and pulled the rest of
her toward the corridor. She had a human neck and that
was it: the rest of her was snake. Her arms were like dry
tree branches set high on her thick serpent's body. Only

the stumps, the equivalent of upper arms, were knotted with muscle. As he watched, two other sets of claws appeared. Feet. They speared from behind the wall and then the claws splayed and dug down. It reminded him of an eagle snatching a mouse, the way they opened and grabbed. Once they had a hold on the floor she moved into the corridor. Her snake-body was about four feet long. It ended in a tail that split into three parts, each with a bony projection. It looked like a bolo-whip combination. He would not want to get struck with it. As soon as she was in the corridor her legs folded up and in, hugging tight against her side. Her arms did the same, all four limbs pointing toward her tail.

She moved forward purposefully, but without expression on her half-snake face. There was a kind of sensuousness to her undulations. It was not turning Collins on, but he noticed it.

His cell phone beeped.

"Shitjesus!" he screamed. He didn't have a free hand so he turned off the flashlight and set it down.

The creature stopped. *That* was interesting.

Collins took his phone from his windbreaker. He looked at the number. It was Tally. He was glad it wasn't his mother.

"Tal, she's here," he said. "Down the hall."

"Seriously."

"Yes! It's Medusa. I'm looking at her in a mirror."

"God, I wish you had one of those photo phones."

"I wish I had an automatic weapon."

"What's she doing?"

"Nothing at the moment. She was coming toward me till I turned off the flashlight."

"I wonder why," Tally said. "Do you have a way out of there?"

"Several," he said. "I'll take one if I have to."

"I'm thinking if it's her light that turns people to stone she may have seen your turning it off as a submissive gesture."

Suddenly, all of the snakes turned front. Their eyes, and those of Medusa, focused on the same thing: Collins.

"Tal, she's looking at me. She and all her snake hairs. I gotta go."

"Harold, call back—"

"I will." He clicked off, scared beyond scared. He totally understood the concept of "marking one's laundry." He was shaking from the knees up. He put the phone away and bent very slowly to pick up the light. He kept the mirror on Medusa, watching for any sign that she was going to start moving again. Give or take, ten feet separated them. He wondered whether the creature could lurch or spring or somehow cover that distance faster than he could get away.

If she can, running probably won't do me much good, he decided.

Instead, Collins rested the light on his shoulder, pointing toward her. He waited. For fifteen or so seconds neither the mini-snakes nor the big snake moved. Then, as one, their eyes began to shine, Medusa's glow larger and brighter than the rest. They were individual lights but just for a moment. They quickly merged and slammed forward. Collins held the mirror in his megatrembling hand.

As long as you look in the mirror you'll be okay, he reminded himself. *Light has no punch. It can't knock you over.*

Especially when it doesn't hit you. The light stopped halfway to Collins. It dissipated like a popped balloon

and, an instant later, started up again. Collins didn't have
to start shaking from fear again since he was still aflutter
from the last glow-attack. Once more, the light stopped
and vanished.

Collins turned on his flashlight once, just for a moment, then shut it. He turned it on again, then clicked off.
He didn't know why he had done that, other than that it
seemed like the right thing to do. Actually, it was the
only thing to do short of running—and flight wasn't why
he was here. If Medusa used light as a weapon, she
might see his action as a threat and retreat. Conversely,
seeing that the light didn't affect her, she might be encouraged to attack.

She did neither. She and her head-buddies rolled two
more balls of light at Collins. They matched the intensity
and duration of his flashes pretty closely. He decided to
click one more time. Medusa did the same.

Okay, he thought with sudden excitement. *We're talking!*

Though he didn't think he could be hurt unless the
light flashed, Collins continued to look in the mirror. He
used the flashlight to point from the goop to Joe Wyndham back to the goop. Medusa did not respond. He repeated the pattern. The creature didn't move. It was as if
she and her brood had turned to stone. Except for moving the light, Collins also remained as still and unthreatening as possible. And in a day of wildly unexpected
events, the most unexpected thing of all suddenly occurred. Joe Wyndham began to radiate white light. An instant later he flashed and returned to normal. The puddle
of ooze was gone. Nor was there anything on the hard-
wood floor to indicate that it had ever been there. No
dampness, no discoloration. Nothing.

A moment after that there was a flash from Dorothy

Wyndham's bedroom and a second later there was a third flash from somewhere downstairs. That had to be Meg Wyndham. Presumably, the other guests were out.

Wyndham jerked forward, then back, as though he were suffering muscle spasms. Collins dropped the flashlight, stepped backward—and so moving forward—and literally pushed Wyndham into his mother's bedroom. The veteran stumbled on his bad leg and had to grab the footboard of the bed to keep from falling. Beyond him, the old woman was looking around as though she had no idea where she was. Perhaps she didn't. Collins had no evidence that their minds had returned. He dropped the mirror, went over to Joe Wyndham, and turned the man toward him. Joe's eyes were moving around anxiously. From outside the room they heard a woman shrieking.

"Meg!" Joe yelled.

"Probably, yes," Collins said. That was good. Wyndham remembered who she was, how to speak. The proprietor could see. Whatever had happened to him created no apparent permanent damage. The young man stood between Wyndham and the door. He put his hands on the man's shoulders. "I'll go downstairs and make sure your wife is all right. What about you? Are you okay?"

"Yes—how did this happen?"

"I'm not sure. Tell me: what do you *think* happened?" Collins asked. He wanted to know what Wyndham's perceptions of the experience had been.

"Everything shifted."

"What do you mean?"

"You saw," Wyndham said, looking at him. There was a touch of wildness in his eyes. "I was looking into the room and then it all changed, shifted. Like a bomb went off but nothing was destroyed. What happened?"

"Do you know where you are?"

"What do you mean?"

"What building, what floor?"

"Of course. We're at home. We're in my mother's room."

"What's the last thing you remember?" Collins asked.

"I saw a light from the window and then it was gone."

"That's all?"

"No," Wyndham added quickly. "There was someone in there, under her chair. Someone hideous, deformed. Or maybe the light of the television made them look that way, I don't know."

"Whoever it was, it's gone," Collins said. "But after I check on your wife I want to try and find her."

"Maybe you shouldn't do that," Wyndham said.

"You're probably right, but I'm doing it anyway," Collins said. "You just stay here with your mother, keep the door closed, and everything will be okay."

Wyndham turned and went over to his mother. He still seemed disoriented but that would probably pass. Collins ran to the corridor, quickly applying the brakes when he realized he needed the mirror. He got on his knees to pick it up where he'd dropped it. He had to keep saying to himself, "Don't turn around don't turn around . . ." while he reached out for it. It was one of those things he might do without thinking, not that he thought Medusa would harm him. She had restored the Wyndhams, after all. The trick was going to be to build on the slight, slight trust he felt he'd built. She was obviously intelligent. They had to figure out how to communicate further.

The mirror had broken when Collins dropped it. He fingered through the shards, picked up the largest, and used it instead. He didn't bother with the flashlight. He shut the bedroom door and rose, looking backward in the broken glass. He was surprised by what he saw.

Nothing.

Medusa was gone.

CHAPTER 29

"TALLY, THE PROCESS can be reversed!"

Collins was shouting into the phone, hyperventilating excitement in his voice. Tally was glad to hear that he had new information, good information. Hell, she was glad to hear from Harold at all.

"That's great news but back up a sec," Tally said. "Where are you and are you all right?"

"Oh yeah. I'm at the inn and I'm fine, everyone's fine. I just checked on Mrs. Wyndham, sent her upstairs to be with her husband. She was turned to stone too."

"No aftereffects?"

"None that I could see. Listen, Tal—I communicated with her."

"With Medusa?"

"No, Mrs. Wyndham. Yes, Medusa!"

"Okay, then, one more time," Tally said. "You're absolutely sure it was her? Not someone in a costume, or just a big snake?"

"I'm sure. This thing had moving snakes for hair, a snake body, bronze claws, and she was turning people to stone."

"That's the checklist," Tally admitted. Actually, there was a lot more. Scaly skin, yellow eyes, countless other details she had picked up on her quick Internet scan. "And you're saying she spoke?"

"No. I used light to communicate with Medusa, kind of like a heliograph or semaphore, whatever you want to call it."

"You flashed her."

"Yes, and she flashed back. I used the light to indicate that I wanted her to restore Joe, who got zapped, and she did it. She depetrified him. Then she left."

"Where did she go?" Tally asked.

"I don't know. More important is where she came from. What I saw is an entirely new species. To us, anyway."

"To this dimension, possibly?" Tally asked. She couldn't believe she'd just said that.

"If the wormhole has an outlet in this region, yeah," Collins said. "It doesn't make sense that there was just one of these creatures hibernating in a single cave."

"Well, according to my research there was more than one of her. More than one Gorgon, I mean. She has— had, I mean—two sisters. Stheno and Euryale."

"Who were their parents?"

"Harold, do you really want to know this now?"

"Absolutely! I have *zero* information."

"Okay," Tally said as she read. "Medusa is the daughter of Phorcys and Ceto and the aunt of the hunter Orion."

"Were the parents gods or demigods?"

"Mortals. Medusa is also mortal. She was a beautiful woman until she offended the goddess Athena, who turned her most striking feature, her hair, into snakes. She was supposedly slain by the hero Perseus and upon her death her blood mingled with the earth to bring forth the flying horse Pegasus. Other legends say that she bore the horse after mating with the sea god Poseidon."

"Jeez."

"Yeah, that must've smarted."

"What?" Collins said.

"Foaling a winged horse."

"No," Collins said. "I meant that's a helluva story. I wonder if her blood was actually the goop."

"Interesting idea," Tally said. "I'm wondering if the creature who was up there is one of her sisters. Not that it matters, I guess."

"Does it say where these sisters came from?"

"It says here their father was Pontus, the personification of the sea, and their mother is the earth goddess Gaia."

"Then how did they become sisters?"

"By living together, not by blood," she said. "Like when girlfriends call each other 'sister' I guess. They lived in Oceanus, at the end of the world."

"Interesting. All kinds of symbolic possibilities there. Maybe they are three different facets of the same creature, like the id, ego, and superego."

"Or maybe the creature you encountered is a scout or a guardian for a whole bunch of them," Tally said, once again not quite believing she'd said that. "Maybe they live underground."

"That's not so far out," Collins suggested. "Medusa does have self-generated lights."

"Where are you now?" Tally asked.

"I'm just about to leave the lobby and go outside. It's not easy because I'm walking backward with a mirror, negotiating with the outdoor lights, and talking to you. I don't think there's a danger, though. I just saw Joe's wife Meg and she was okay. If screaming and hysterical is 'okay.' I sent her upstairs to stay with her husband."

"I can't imagine Medusa would stick around," Tally said. "Too many people have seen her."

"I agree. I'm guessing she went back to the cave. But Tally, you know what the most astonishing thing is from a pure physics point of view?"

"What?"

"I was clobbered by the same light as the others, but nothing happened to me," Collins said.

"You had the mirror, you said—"

"Why should it matter whether I was looking directly at Medusa or not?" Collins asked. "Light is light, and re-flected light is simply redirected light. It doesn't change the essence of the photons. I mean, if you're sitting on the beach, your skin gets burned whether you look at the sun or not."

"Not me. I use sunblock," Tally said. She didn't know why she'd said that, other than that cracking wise was like a spoonful of sugar. It helped her take the edge off what she was being forced to swallow.

"I don't believe that the mirror or talisman had any magic power that protected me," Collins went on as if she hadn't spoken.

"Why not?"

"Meg Wyndham wears her own silver jewelry and it didn't help her. There is something about our eyes that makes us vulnerable.

"A lens effect?" Tally suggested.

"That's one possibity," Collins agreed. "The other possible x factor is the vitreous substance. The glop."

"What effect could that have?" Tally asked.

"Maybe there's something about the chemical composition, maybe it conducts whatever light Medusa throws out. Catches us in the middle—I don't know."

"Hold on. What if we've got that backward?"

"What do you mean?" Collins asked.

"What if she's actually producing that stuff?"

"Interesting," Collins said.

"It's not as if you've actually seen her when she's paralyzing someone," Tally went on. "Maybe that appears an instant before."

"You're saying she could spit that out like venom?"

"Some snakes do, albeit not from their eyes," Tally said.

"Maybe that's the paralytic agent," Collins said. "Maybe the light is just to distract us."

"Deer in headlights, venom over body," Tally said.

"I guess that's possible, but how would it work?" Collins asked. "What kind of chemical interaction would cause that?"

"I don't know the answer to that but I'm going to get it," Collins said. "Look, I'm outside now and I don't see her. Just a depression in the grass where it looks like she went slithering. I'm guessing coily-locks did, in fact, head back to the cave. I'm going to drive up there rather than try to follow her through the foothills."

"I needn't tell you, Harold—"

"I know. I'll be careful."

"Actually, I was going to say I don't think you should drive backward."

"Cute."

"Thanks."

"I won't," Collins said. "Anyway, I'm sure Medusa has a secret entrance or something. Otherwise she couldn't have gotten here so fast."

"Those mountains probably have a lot of hidden passages," Tally said. "Or maybe she used a mini-wormhole."

Collins was silent for a moment. "Wow."

"What?"

"You know, that isn't so crazy," Collins said. "In fact—" His voice trailed off.

"In fact what?"

"I'm just wondering if she somehow creates her own event horizon," Collins told her. "Scoops it out of the cosmos and leaves the goop behind."

"You're talking way over my head and you didn't even use three-syllable words," Tally said.

"I'm not sure I understand it," Collins admitted. "Anyway, I'm at my car. I'm going up to the cave. I'll call you when I know more." He paused briefly. "Damn, Tally, that was a really good get."

"Thanks, but I'm not sure what I 'got.'"

"Neither am I. But it's got me thinking that there may be more to this than I was imagining. Listen, I'm going to get off before my battery croaks. I'll talk to you later."

Collins punched off.

Tally sat looking at an image of Medusa on the computer monitor. Everywhere Harold Collins walked there were new discoveries. Time travel. Dinosaurs. Earth-based wormholes. Now a possible new species. She didn't know which was stranger: all of that or the fact that Harold Collins kept tripping over these things, a one-man Renaissance, a da Vinci in Dockers.

Either way, the whole thing made her dizzy.

And she was on the sidelines.

CHAPTER 30

IT WAS STRANGE to be driving at all, let alone to be driving at night. Most New Yorkers cabbed or subwayed or bused or walked wherever they needed to go. They didn't drive. Even if and when they did, to Collins's knowledge, very few of them headed out for a hoped-for rendezvous with a mythological monster. Blind dates could be bad, but not that bad. Usually.

Collins wasn't at home behind the wheel, nor was he accustomed to riding forward momentum in his thought process. He was a step-by-step kind of guy, only now his brain was not on what he had to do next or what might happen to him. There was no way of predicting and he would deal with events as they happened. He was trying to figure out the larger picture, and what Tally had said made sense.

Mini-wormholes. Or rather, portable wormhole entrances. Maybe the vitreous humor connection was a model, not a medium. The eyes were windows to the soul. What if the goop—he really had to come up with a better name than "goop," or "glop," or "ooze"; maybe "grease" was the word—what if the "grease" was a window to a wormhole? What if people weren't impacted by Medusa per se. What if the eyes were just a means of transfixing them for a moment while the wormhole itself opened behind them and did something? It would be like holding still for a photograph, only this photograph did more than record your image. It froze you somehow. That made sense, at least in a quantum physics context.

What did it mean to the world, to science, when mythological monsters started making sense? he asked himself. It was scary, for one thing. One plus one still equaled two, but if the Collins-Jackson unified theory of wormholes and fantastic creatures proved to be correct, the blackboard for the equations had suddenly become exponentially larger while he felt as though his capacity to process information had shrunk in the same proportion.

Portable wormholes, Collins thought. It was like something from a cartoon: Bugs Bunny drops a black circle on the ground and dives in. But there could be something to it, something in what Tally had told him. The Gorgons lived at "the end of the world." Translations were unreliable. Suppose that was "the edge of the world" in the original tale. And suppose that was the edge of *a* world . . . or the edge of a *strange* world . . . or the edge of a *shimmering wormhole.* "Oceanus" did suggest liquid. Maybe it wasn't water but the grease.

He wondered, suddenly, if that was how Medusa got away. Probably not. She certainly hadn't come through the grease. Which, now that he thought of it, wasn't much of an improvement over goop.

There wasn't enough evidence to support that theory now, so he turned to imagining what possible reason the creature would have for coming here, for venturing from the cave, for turning people to stone. Animals and people attacked when they felt threatened. What could possibly be threatening Medusa? What was in the cave that she was protecting?

The only answer he could think of was a wormhole entrance to her world. A world of snake people or a world where the Greek myths are real. A wormhole that was the nexus for the vortexes in Sedona.

That fit. It seemed to explain almost everything, at least most of the big issues. What it failed to address was why Medusa or whichever Gorgon this was felt threatened. What possible danger could humans or tarantulas or any living or material thing present when she could immobilize them with a glance? Maybe she and her kind were perfecting a means by which they could conquer the Earth by paralyzing all living things. In that case, she might be in for a surprise. He thought of H. G. Wells's *War of the Worlds,* wherein terrestrial germs attacked the unprotected Martian immune system. Germs didn't have eyes. They would be impervious to the Gorgon's attack, possibly deadly to her kind. And if that wasn't the scenario, why all this fuss? Why not just reseal the cave to prevent humans from approaching her vortex?

To teach us a lesson? To add to the lore about her kind so we would fear her? Perhaps the Gorgons feared an invasion of Gorgon-world and she was point-creature for the defense.

There was only one way he'd get those answers, plus the answers he wanted about the possibility of wormholes. And so he drove on through the dark and out to the mountain road, finally stopping at the foot of the dirt path. This time he had his flashlight. He turned it on and started up the slope on tired legs.

A warm wind was rolling in from the north. The night air tasted dusty, of airborne desert. He wondered what "her" world smelled like—what it felt like on the skin, on the inside of the mouth and nose, along the back of the neck. Whether it was another time, perhaps the far future, or another place. Another world. Another dimension.

One thing was relatively certain: he would soon find out. This time, Harold Collins would have to go around the bend.

CHAPTER 31

TALLY'S STOMACH WAS gurgling more than just a little when she said, "Dr. Jackson, this is Tally Randall. I'm sorry to call you at home, and so late, but we've had a new development."

Tally wasn't exactly sure how to say what she was about to say. She had just shut her computer for the night, frustrated that she had no answers. She turned on the news, saw nothing about Sedona, and decided she needed another point of view. So she called Dr. Jackson. She was interested to hear what was about to come from her mouth, almost as interested as she was to hear Dr. Jackson's assessment. His wife had answered the phone in their Westchester home and did not seem pleased to have their already-late dinner delayed. Jackson taught a college-credit class in celestial mechanics at the Planetarium three nights each week so she knew he wouldn't be asleep.

"Tell me about it," he said patiently. "Just the facts."

"Harold flew to Sedona to investigate these statues that have been appearing in a cave—"

"I read about those," he interrupted. "A prank?"

"We can't rule that out," Tally admitted. "But if so, it was apparently not created in this dimension."

"Go on," Jackson said.

"Dr. Jackson, Harold encountered a creature that petrifies people with light. He believes that this creature is the classic Medusa. He has managed to communicate with her and is en route to meet her—he hopes for further discourse—at the cave where she lives. He is going to call when he gets there."

That was it. Concise, frank.

And ridiculous-sounding.

"This woman Mr. Collins encountered," Jackson said. "She also resembled the classic Medusa?"

"She did."

"And what did they say to each other?"

Oh boy. "Harold used light signals to convince her to reverse the calcification process on several human beings."

"Did he?"

"Yes, doctor."

"Interdimensional detente."

"Something like that, I guess," Tally answered. She wanted to hang up and send him an E-mail saying that her phone had died.

"It's a compelling yarn and not entirely out of character for Mr. Collins. But it's a little off my astronomical beat—"

"Except that what I wanted to ask was—what *about*

other dimensions, doctor? You mentioned it—*them*—at breakfast, about gods originating there, and I thought—well, this creature doesn't sound like anything that ever existed on this planet. Could those theoretical wormholes you talked about do a kind of chutes-and-ladders through time, space, *and* parallel universes?"

"It is all conceivable, though at this point we don't have enough evidence to do more than speculate. No, I take that back," he said. "Unless I've missed something, we have *no* evidence whatsoever to support anything you've just told me. Is that accurate, Ms. Randall?"

"The proof *is* skimpy," she admitted. Tally felt as though she were back in grade school.

"Just Mr. Collins's report. No visual support either?"

"That is correct."

"Ms. Randall, did you ever hear of the Shaver Mystery?"

"No, doctor, I haven't." *Here it comes,* she thought. *He's calling me "Ms. Randall" now. I'm about to get the tutorial.*

"The Shaver Mystery was one of the things that first got me interested in science," Jackson said. "Of course, I was seven years old at the time and it excited my sense of wonder. There was a series of stories written by Mr. Richard Shaver and published in *Amazing Stories* magazine from 1945 to 1947. Mr. Shaver wrote what were reportedly fact-based tales about the world of Lemuria, an underground civilization populated by "deros," or "detrimental robots" that controlled human beings and their destiny through ESP. The editor, Mr. Ray Palmer, is said to have believed the stories. Mr. Shaver did as well. So did thousands of readers, who sent the circulation of *Amazing Stories* through the stratosphere. But it was all eyewash, Ms. Randall. It was done for profit, not science. You do not work for *Amazing Stories*. You work for *Natural History*. You do not enjoy the wiggle room Mr. Palmer had. I would caution you about buying into the things Mr. Collins is telling you, not because they aren't possible but because it's possible they aren't. Do you understand what I'm saying?"

"I do, Dr. Jackson," she replied, though it bothered her that his phrasing was so smug.

"Good," Jackson said. "Science is full of flimflams like the Shaver Mystery, full of men like Immanuel Velikovsky, who speculated that Jupiter gave birth to Venus and sent it pinballing around the solar system in 3200 B.C., or Erich von Däniken, who decided that extraterrestrials came to Earth in celestial chariots and taught us how to build things. None of it's true. None of it. I don't say that Mr. Collins is intentionally trying to mislead you or anyone. His ideas should be researched. But carefully and thoroughly. He wants very badly to believe the things he's researching. That causes even good scientists to lose their objectivity. If that is the case here, you must retain yours."

"I understand that, Dr. Jackson," Tally said defensively. "But Harold was talking as he was looking right at this thing, and it sounds as if there are several witnesses in this encounter—"

"And like eyewitnesses to the Kennedy assassination they will change their story with each telling, usually getting farther from the facts," Jackson said. "I repeat what I said to you both yesterday morning, and then I am going to finish my dinner. Mr. Collins is a scientist who experienced something out of the ordinary. That isn't the same as "He traveled through time." All possible theories merit critical, devil's advocate, hard-nosed questioning. I do not mean to discourage, only to caution."

"I understand."

"Good science is like the American legal system, Ms. Randall. Theories are false until proven true."

Tally thanked him, apologized again, then hung up before he had finished telling her to have a good evening. She was mortified. Maybe that was the reason she had called: to be subjected to a reality check. Unlike Loch Ness, where at least she'd had a seat on the sidelines, seen video Collins had sent from the past—albeit crude and indecisive and ultimately unconvincing—she was nowhere near the events that Collins was describing. For all she knew it was someone in a Halloween costume looking to whip up business for the Wyndhams' bed-and-breakfast. This whole thing could be a well-orchestrated scam, right down to the tarantula. Maybe someone had covered it with baking soda or confectioner's sugar or plaster or flour. Maybe Harold's sweat caused it to get mushy and release the spider. Maybe the glop was shampoo or canola oil, something to help the perpetrators slide the statues from one place to another. Or to create the illusion of a snake-lady gliding across the floor.

How's that *for devil's advocacy?* she asked herself.

Uncompromising, she decided. She didn't want to get down on what Harold was doing, especially since he *was* heading back to Snake Mountain to visit with an individual—or a species—unknown. And he'd be climbing around there in the dark. But she did want to stay grounded and objective, as Dr. Jackson had suggested. As he shouldn't have had to remind her. As her own instincts had told her even before she and Harold had flown off to Loch Ness.

The sounds of horns, sirens, and barking dogs no longer seemed so foreign. She cherished what once more seemed down-to-earth and familiar.

CHAPTER 32

COLLINS REMOVED THE visor-mirror from his car, made sure he had his penlight, then started out.

The dirt road leading up Snake Mountain was far, far different at night than it was during the day. For one thing, the walk up was quite chilly. For another thing it was very dark. There was a full moon, too low behind a hill to cast much light, and the plentiful stars provided no more illumination than the spilled salt they resembled. All the young physicist had was his flashlight, and that gave him a circle of light about a yard in diameter. The light was intense but it stopped at the edges like a cut-out from white construction paper. It was also extremely quiet up here, save for the occasional wailing of coyotes or the hoot of a night bird. Even the winds were asleep.

Collins himself was not quite so peaceful. Anxiety

and curiosity fought for control in him, finally deciding to share power equally. He felt like one of those plastic bags he often saw blowing around the city—moving about with apparent gusto but having no control over what was happening to them.

As he reached the entrance to the cave a new sensation took over. Relief. In a few moments, he hoped, he would have some answers—not just to the mystery of Medusa but to the whole question of wormholes. In a way, that would be fitting. So many discoveries and inventions were made by men working alone, unsure, feeling their way through new technology or new geography. Maybe that was how it was supposed to be, it *had* to be. The gods of human advancement demanded the vision and courage of one to pull along the many. Speaking of myths, maybe that was what the story of Prometheus was supposed to tell us. That the fire-bringer had to go it alone.

Or maybe I'm just all full of wind, like those plastic bags, he thought.

Collins raised the visor now, reversed the flashlight, and stepped over yellow "crime scene" tape that was now stretched low across the mouth of the cave. He entered backward. It felt sillier now, as a planned maneuver, than when he had done it spontaneously in the upstairs hallway. He walked slowly and cautiously through the cave, the flashlight trained down so that he wouldn't step on any of the grease he had seen there earlier. The cave was downright chilly, which caused him to shiver and the light to flutter like a projector shutter. He hoped Medusa or whichever sister this was didn't take that as a sign of weakness or aggression or confusion. Maybe it was the equivalent of Gorgon stuttering. He relaxed and also took slower, longer, deeper breaths in an effort to stop the trembling.

The grease was exactly where he had seen it before. It appeared unchanged, neither separated nor solidified. He wondered if it might even be alive. He moved around it to the bend in the cave. His fail-safe point. This time, though, the light was not on the other side. He wondered if Medusa would be.

Suddenly, he heard a scratching sound. It was coming from in front of him which was actually behind him, toward the mouth of the cave. Still looking in the mirror, Collins turned and stepped back around the bend toward the darkened entranceway. He shined his light around the rough edges, along the boulders that had fallen inside and out when the cave was reopened. He saw nothing. He turned the light toward the cave floor. Nothing was moving there. Then he shined it along the wall to the north, his right. He saw bronze talons. Coming through the rock. Still watching through the mirror, he saw the talons being withdrawn and pencil-thin stalks of light come shooting through the holes. The beams widened into cones and quickly became a circle of light. Medusa appeared in the center of it, rolling out with her head and shoulders, her tiny arms cocked at her sides, her legs and serpentine body following.

The light vanished. The cave wall was solid. There was grease along the base of it. And it occurred to him, then, what the grease was. Not part of the targets but part of the process. If Medusa came through a wormhole, the grease could be a bookmark, or an IOU, for that much matter. In which case the light probably wasn't turning people to stone. Not really.

"I am totally confused," he said.

The creature moved toward him. His back was facing her, the flashlight on the Gorgon's gaunt face. The glare didn't seem to bother her. She crept toward him on her small legs, her body swaying like a cobra rising from a basket in some Third-World bazaar. The snakes on her head hovered low along her jawbone and throat, facing him. Tiny tongues flicked in his direction. Medusa's mouth was still, her eyes steady. She was less than three yards away. Unless he went deeper into the cave they were going to meet, to touch.

That's what you came for, buddy, he reminded himself.

Nonetheless, Collins could barely breathe. His heart felt as if it were a balloon that had been inflated in his chest. His body was telling him something that his mind refused to acknowledge: that this was dangerous, reckless, quite possibly extremely stupid. He had communicated with her but not *communicated*. For all he knew she had restored the Wyndhams to gain his trust to lure him here and—

And what? Do to me here what she could have done to me there? That makes no sense.

Still, the young scientist was damn near hyperventilating and that wasn't going to make for a happy meeting. He reversed the light so it was shining into the cave, lowered the mirror, and took several steps forward. He saw the other statues. The veterinarian, the antiques lady, the two dogs. If Collins went further he was pretty sure he'd find the deputy and that forensics person, Dr. Joliet. He wondered if he could get Medusa to reanimate these people. Perhaps that could be the trade-off for his cooperation, assuming that's what she wanted.

Behind him, in the distance, Collins heard tires crunching on rock. And voices.

". . . check on the tags of that car. I'll go up, see if I can get further inside."

"On it."

That sounded like police or the sheriff or both coming to check on their missing persons. Perhaps Sheriff Birdsong had decided not to wait till daylight before looking for his missing team.

There was a flash behind Collins, from somewhere inside the cave. His instinct was to turn and he began to, then stopped. If that was Medusa—and who or what else would it be?—he wondered if she was leaving or if she was simply turning her gaze on the newcomers. He raised the mirror, turned the flashlight around, and walked back. She was gone. He wondered, suddenly, if the light was part of that process or if she was simply saying good-bye.

"Crap," he muttered. He'd been so close.

There was a moment of silence. Then, from just outside the cave, "Who's in there?"

"It's Dr. Harold Collins," he said.

"Say again?" the newcomer yelled.

"Dr. Harold Collins. I'm the director of the United Nations Institute of Technology."

"Are you the same fella who was up here this morning, talking to Deputy Woodward?"

"Yes."

"He told me about you," the officer said.

"Are you Sheriff Birdsong?"

"I am," the man replied. "Stay where you are. I want to talk to you."

"Not moving," Collins said. "I saw you on TV." He decided not to say anything about having heard Deputy Woodward in the cave. He didn't want to end up a suspect in his disappearance.

"If you saw that broadcast, then you are not unaware that this is a restricted area," the sheriff said. "Yes? No?"

"Yes, sir," Collins answered.

There was no further conversation until the man had

reached the cave. His super-bright flashlight rivaled the light of Medusa, though her glow was not as harsh. Collins looked away.

"Do you have any weapons, Mr. Collins?"

"Dr. Collins, and no." Ordinarily, Collins wouldn't have played and replayed the "title" card but he was hoping it would help him here.

"Why did you cross the police tape?"

"I'm a qualified investigator—"

"I didn't ask what you are. I asked why?"

"To investigate." So it was going to be one of *those* kinds of "I'm King Kamehameha and you're not" conversations. Collins had enjoyed a richer conversation with Medusa using a flashlight.

The sheriff sighed disgustedly. "Dr. Director, 'cute' may play in New York City and your international forums. It doesn't here. It causes 'oops.' Do you know what that is?"

"I can't say I do."

"It's 'Oops, he tripped over a rock and fell one hundred feet down a dirt road because he wasn't cooperating.' " The light moved forward. "Is there some reason the United Nations is interested in these statues, some reason I haven't been told about? You folks lose a briefcase full of uranium or something?"

"No—"

"Then what?"

"Before we continue, Sheriff, would you mind turning that light away?" Collins asked.

The sheriff moved the light down to the area between Collins and the officer. "The cave floor is yours."

"I'm doing scientific research," Collins said. "I'm not sure you would understand if I described the nature of that work."

"I took science in school."

"I'm sorry, I didn't mean to imply—"

"The reason you're here, Dr. Director?"

Obviously, Collins needed to spill and take his chances. "Sheriff Birdsong, there is a creature in this cave that paralyzes people using a form of energy." "Energy" sounded better than "light," he had decided. "This creature was responsible for turning people and animals into statues, I believe. I tracked it here from the Boots and Spurs bed-and-breakfast, where the same energy that calcified the proprietor and his family was used to revive them. I was trying to communicate with the creature when you arrived."

"The creature is here?"

"Was. I'm not sure about now."

"And you were communicating using a flashlight and a mirror?"

"Yes. But then there was a flash and the creature was gone, though I don't know if she's *gone*-gone."

"A 'flash.' Is it the same kind of flash she uses to turn people to stone?" the sheriff asked.

"It may be. I only saw her leave once."

"Can you describe this creature?"

"I can, though I'm not sure you'd believe me."

"It can't be stranger than what you've already told me."

"I believe it can be, sheriff," Collins said. "It—she—resembles the Medusa of mythology. She has snakes for hair, a serpentine body, the works."

"I see." There was another short silence. "My people used to communicate with mirrors hundreds of years ago."

"The heliograph," Collins said. The sheriff did not seem surprised to hear about Medusa. "The Ancient Hebrews used it too. A formidable way to signal." That was an odd segue. But it wasn't like Deputy Woodward was talking about his sister working for the United Nations. There was something different about this man.

"There are legends about this cave," the sheriff went on. "Are you familiar with them?"

"A few, sir," Collins said. "The Wyndhams, at the inn, told me about some of them."

"My Apache ancestors believed that this was a place where snake-spirits lived," the sheriff informed him. "My Irish ancestors claimed that these spirits were related to the banshees of the Old Country. They heard sibilant wailing." He came forward. "That was how my great-great-grandparents met, when their fathers got to exchanging legends over a bottle of whiskey."

Birdsong stopped in front of Collins. His wide, dark face was visible in the beam of Collins's own down-turned flashlight. It was a serene face that belonged to a man in his late thirties or early forties. He stood about six-foot two and had a heavy rope coiled around his shoulder, and a backpack.

"Sheriff, if you knew about the legends, why did you send people up here?" Collins asked.

"I didn't say I believed them," Birdsong replied. "We've got a lot of baying looneys in this county. Do you have some ID?"

Collins produced his wallet and flipped out his UN card. The sheriff stepped over and turned his light on it.

"Thank you. Dr. Collins, until my deputy vanished I believed someone was using the legends to attract tourism. Now I'm not so certain." He shined the flashlight beyond Collins. "Deputy Woodward reported that this cave goes back a way, then drops. I mean to have a look. You say you were going to try and communicate with this thing. Is there something that makes you think you could do that?"

"Yes," Collins said. "She paralyzed the Wyndhams with light. A few minutes later I shined my light back and forth between the statues and the grease behind them, and her eyes, to indicate that she undo it."

"Impressive. Well, if you'd like to come with me you're welcome. But I don't want you doing anything without asking me first."

"Sheriff, before you go any further I suggest you get a mirror. That seems to neutralize her energy."

"Why? How?"

"I'm not sure."

"A guess?"

"I suspect the beam only works when it's traveling in a straight line."

"I remember from that schooling I spoke of that light only travels in a straight line."

"You're correct. But I'm thinking there may be something to this grease that appears behind the individuals," Collins said.

"I noticed that earlier. We took a sample for evaluation."

"And?" Collins asked eagerly.

"Unfortunately, Dr. Joliet, our chemist, is missing," the sheriff reminded him. "Do you have any thoughts?"

"Well, it appears that the beam causes this grease to appear. Whether it's driven from the target or is used to complete a connection of some sort, I'm just not certain," Collins told him.

"Interesting. What kind of doctor are you?"

"Physicist."

"So you don't have any thoughts about what the 'grease,' as you call it, is made of?"

"I do not. It has a metallic quality, though."

"It reminded me of liquid gold," the sheriff said.

"Which, if it were, would give our guest a very good electrical conductor with a relatively low melting point, as metals go," Collins said. "I'm not sure what it means, but the liquidity is obviously significant."

"Perhaps the blood of your Medusa is gold."

"That is possible," Collins agreed.

"You know, Dr. Collins, you're a lucky man."

"I agree. Dangerous work, but fascinating—"

"I mean you're lucky that I am the one who came up here instead of Police Chief Jensen," Birdsong said. "She would already have sent you to the county bed-and-breakfast for psychiatric evaluation."

"I see. What does she think of her missing officer?"

"They're treating it as a standard missing-person case, though no one believes it is that."

"Why not?"

"Because from what I understand, only something grave would have torn him from his Corvette."

While he had been speaking, the sheriff had raised his light toward the bend. He seemed eager to proceed, though his manner was cautious. "I'll tell you what. Since you've got the mirror, why don't you lead the way. I'll watch your back in case there's anything on the ground to trip you up."

"All right," Collins said. "If we see her though, sheriff, please let me make any advances."

"No promises," the sheriff said. "But I'll be reasonable."

Birdsong got on the portable radio and advised Deputy Misoula about his plans. The deputy confirmed that the car was rented to Harold Collins of New York. Misoula asked if the sheriff needed him to check anything else.

Birdsong said no, that all he had to do for now was stay on the other end of the radio. When the sheriff was finished, Collins hoisted the flashlight to his shoulder, raised the mirror, and once again began moving into the cave.

CHAPTER 33

*G*LOP.
   Ooze.
  Goop.
  Grease.

It was very late but Tally couldn't shut her brain. She was thinking about the substance Collins had described as she took a shower. New York grime was unkind to her skin and hair and she liked the idea of getting into bed clean. If only she could clean out her skull as well.

Tally was accustomed to dealing with absolutes. Fully researched articles about fungi or glaciers or the Serengeti. Grammar. Deadlines. This was new to her and she didn't like it. Her imagination and enthusiasm took her one way. Reason brought her back and then doubt and new questions and inconsistencies swung her in the

other direction. It was maddening and she couldn't let it
go. There was always a, 'Yeah, but . . .' to move her off
wherever she found herself.

Like now.

Even if Harold's hopes or terror were fuzzing his
logic, that didn't automatically negate everything he had
said. A writer once pitched her an article on UFOs. She
declined, saying it wasn't really a *Natural History* topic.
The writer asked if she believed in flying saucers. She
said she had an open mind.

"Remember," the caller said. "All it takes is one
bonafide extraterrestrial craft to make the notion real."

In this case, all it took was one thing not to fit somewhere into a logical framework to make the entire framework invalid. For example, tracks in the road. If someone
brought statues up the dirt path there would be tracks from
the wagon or dolly or whatever they used. The police
would have noticed. That was a long stretch to clean with
a whisk broom, especially at night. Or the thing Harold
saw. Even if it was a gag perpetrated by the hoteliers or
the town council or just some deranged locals, how sophisticated would a costume have to be to fool Harold?
Even if he was scared, he was still a scientist. He would
have spotted a flaw, a seam, something. Then there was
the glop-ooze-goop-or-grease, whatever Harold finally
decided to call it. Why would someone add another element to a hoax that didn't need it? Just a few days before,
Tally had read an article in the *New York Times* about people who forged signatures on baseball and movie memorabilia. The more words the counterfeiters added, the
easier it was for handwriting experts to spot a fake.

Maybe she was overthinking this, but what else was
there to do in a shower?

The shower was extremely tiny, and all Tally's gels

and soaps were kept in a plastic rack that hung from the shower rod. Maybe the substance Harold had found was a lubricant. Someone might have used it to slide the statues along the rock. Her cousin Nicole had once greased the sides of a dresser in order to get it through a really small doorway.

Maybe it isn't the statues that need oil.

What if it was Medusa? She might need oil to move through the cave, or through the wormhole. Maybe that was her "diving suit." A number of snakes and other reptiles secreted watery solutions to help them move through rocky terrain and stay moist in dry climates. Some snakes, such as pythons, produced an oily fluid that helped them shuck their skin. Maybe Medusa was shedding. She could even be shedding hair-snakes. That might be where the mountain got its snake population.

Or not. Tally was losing her footing in reality. Snakes came from mother snakes, not other-dimensional monsters. Though Medusa *was* a female. . . .

Tally wasn't going to call Harold with these theories about what was itself a theory. Especially now, when he was on-site and probably preoccupied with more urgent matters.

Other dimensions, Tally thought. *Maybe this is just a bizarre creation from our own.* There was no UFO crash at Roswell in 1947. It was probably an experimental military vessel that went down. What if Medusa is a military experiment, a genetic creation designed to be dropped into other countries to hunt down leaders and turn them to radioactive powder? What better creature than a snake to make its way through a desert or a jungle, feeding on vermin or buzzards or whatever it encountered while slithering toward its target. She wondered—because it was late and her brain was softening—what the compensation package would be for someone who agreed to be genetically engineered into a half-snake. Were they paid in dollars or white mice? And, most importantly, was the process reversible?

The idea seemed ridiculous but, in truth, it was no more or less implausible than anything else. The "yeah, but . . ." here was that gene splicing didn't fit with the long-buried cave idea. Unless that was a cover story. But then, why would the military release a mutation in Arizona? As a test? To see how well she could conceal herself under somewhat controlled circumstances?

Or maybe she's a different kind of mutation, Tally thought, continuing her stream-of-consciousness musings. Maybe Medusa is a hybrid created by all the above-ground nuclear tests in the fifties.

Or perhaps, just perhaps, it's time for bed.

She finished up in the shower then got into bed with a stack of magazines. *Rolling Stone. Philadelphia. Pallium,* the magazine of her high school alma mater Canterbury in New Milford, Connecticut. There was a picture of a student on the field-hockey bench text-messaging on her cell phone.

"Teachers can't even stop you from passing notes anymore," she thought. In her day, which wasn't so long ago, that was a write-on-the-blackboard-one-hundred-times offense.

And then it hit her. The lightning-strike "duh." The missing piece she had been looking for. The one that was worth calling Harold for, wherever he was and whatever he was doing.

Medusa's light. What it might be and what it *really* did. A wireless phone. . . .

CHAPTER 34

COLLINS FELT HIS phone vibrate against his hip. He had turned off the ringer and the flashing light because he didn't want to be distracted when he met Medusa or alarm her with sudden light or noise. He didn't answer for the same reason: if she was around, talking might bother her. Besides, the reception in here would be intermittent at best. And Collins had gotten into a groove walking backward through the cave. He didn't want to stop.

Sheriff Birdsong was following a few paces behind. He was looking forward, flashlight bouncing where Collins's light wasn't. It looked like awards night at Bedlam Asylum. They had passed the other statues but didn't stop to examine them. They walked to the rear of the cave, where the ceiling sloped down. They followed the wall to the

west, where the cave formed the tail end of a funnel. This
was where Collins had heard the deputy shouting at him
earlier. Woodward and the forensics woman were still
here, statues crouched in the dead-end corner.

The sheriff walked over and touched the deputy's
drawn gun. "Now if that don't beat all," he said.

Collins continued to look around in the mirror. He
saw the grease on the cave floor and told the sheriff to
look out.

"I saw it," Birdsong replied. "Now if I were to chip
something off one of the statues, what would happen?
Would it remain broken when they were 'brought back,'
or whatever it is that takes place."

"That's correct," Collins said. "It happened to a tarantula earlier."

The cave brightened suddenly near the entranceway.

"Sheriff, look away!" Collins shouted.

The sheriff heard but he took a moment too long to
process the order. He started to move but was then swallowed in the glow. Collins was facing in the direction of
the flash but he was looking behind him, away from the
light, into the mirror. He swung his face toward the back
of the cave and shut his eyes as the white light burst toward them like a magnesium flare. Even looking away,
Collins's eyelids went from rust to bright red. He saw his
own veins clear and sharp. The light died quickly.

A moment later the sheriff cried out. Reluctantly,
Collins cracked an eye and looked in the mirror. The
sheriff *had* managed to look away in time, dropping his
flashlight when he bumped into the northern wall of the
cave. In the glow along the cave floor he saw Medusa sitting on her long, coiled tail, her clawed feet raking
painfully at the outsides of Birdsong's thighs. The sheriff
was trying to swat her legs away but they were too fast,

the claws splayed too wide to grab in a bunch. At the same time, in the beam of his own flashlight, Collins saw that the Gorgon had pushed her talons into the flesh along the sheriff's jawline. She was turning his face toward her. He couldn't see the Gorgon's face but he could hear a low hiss coming from her mouth. It sounded like bacon hitting a hot skillet.

"Let me *go!*" the sheriff said. It came out as "*lemmeho*" because of the way his jaw was being squeezed.

"Don't hurt him—" Collins muttered. He tried to speak in an unthreatening voice that probably came out as terrified.

Medusa ignored them both.

"Jesus," Collins said as he watched the dark tableau. He was not too frightened to move. He was simply resigned.

A moment later two of the hair-snakes shot out and bit the sheriff's cheeks. He screamed and opened his eyes. In that moment the Medusa removed her claws from his flesh and flash-froze him into a gargoyle-like monstrosity, his eyes squinted, mouth open and contorted, neck-muscles taut and ugly. A pool of grease had formed beside him. It appeared to Collins, who had been watching, that it collected there an instant before Sheriff Birdsong had been transformed.

Collins didn't move. What was the point? If Medusa wanted him, she'd take him. If he ran, he'd never get to communicate with her or reverse what had happened to the others.

Collins remembered, then, about the phone call. What the hell? He decided to find out who it was. While Medusa uncoiled her thick tail from beneath her and put her legs back on the ground, Collins put down his flashlight. He accessed the single message. It would have been funny if it was his mother checking to see how he was. It wasn't. It was Tally.

"Harold, it's me. I hope you're okay."

Just great, he thought.

"I've been doing some serious thinking about this and I'm kind of back on the 'we are probably not getting scammed here' idea."

I'm so with you on that—

"In line with that, there's a thought that I wanted to pass along. If there really is a Medusa and she is using light for something, mightn't it be some form of communication medium? Like the ethernet, something that connects her from this world to whatever place she's from. She could be getting information or power or who-knows-what through the light. Maybe the grease even acts like some sort of a—lens or amplifier, which we were kind of kicking around earlier. I don't know if that makes any sense but I figured I'd throw it out."

I like it . . .

"Anyway, sorry to ramble. I hope to talk to you as soon as possible. Give me a call and be careful up there in the dark. Bye."

The dark is the least of it, Collins thought as he folded the phone and put it away. He watched Medusa in the mirror as she realigned herself from the sheriff to him.

"I thought we had a relationship," he said quietly, his voice cracking as he waited for her to strike.

It didn't happen. The Gorgon stayed where she was, hovering high on her serpentine tail, her slender torso undulating slowly, her legs extended to the sides, her arms drawn back, claws hanging down, falling just within the glow of the sheriff's flashlight. The blood from his jaw glistened on the tips of her claws. It was as if she were waiting for *Collins* to do something.

"What do you want?" he wondered aloud, quiet and thoughtful.

Medusa's eyes glowed dully, but only for a moment. Collins watched in the mirror, stunned.

"I'll be damned," Collins said quietly. He had just whispered and she had 'whispered' back. If he interpreted correctly, she didn't want to harm him. Or maybe she just didn't want to *hurt* him. Maybe she was trying to talk him into paralysis rather than force him, the way she had the sheriff.

Why bother? he asked himself. She hadn't had trouble with a larger, stronger man. Why seduce *him?*

Maybe she wanted to gain his trust, get him to turn around. He wondered if that small-time eye-light would have paralyzed him. And if it had, whether Medusa would turn him back the way she had the Wyndhams.

The Wyndhams, Collins thought. Something had happened to Joe when he was paralyzed. The man's mind had gone to strange places. His brain wasn't getting oxygen for a time. That could have caused hallucinations. Or maybe Wyndham had been dreaming, or acting out the shock.

Medusa flashed softly again. She wanted something. Probably for him to trust her. Thinking about the impact of the paralysis on Wyndham, and wanting to spare the sheriff any ill effects—including possible death—Collins reached down and very slowly retrieved his flashlight. He shined it on the sheriff for a moment, clicked it off, then shined it again.

Medusa flashed once in Collins's mirror. Her light was stronger than before. He took that to be a "no." Sheepishly, the young man placed the flashlight back on the ground. He wanted to let her know that the discussion was over.

Obviously, there was only one way to continue this get-to-know-you process. Medusa had lured Collins here for a reason. He was going to have to give the lady his trust. He wished he could call Rose Coronado and tell her that. The things one thought of when terror poured ice into the brain pan. . . .

Collins was already bent low in the back of the cave. He crouched and put the mirror beside the flashlight. He regretted that he couldn't call Tally, but reception wasn't happening from in here. What he needed was a cell phone that had been designed for South African diamond mines, not the veldt.

Next field trip, he thought.

Collins was no longer shivering. He had gone beyond that to perspiring. It was running down his sides, along the backs of his legs, and tickling the backs of his ears. He pivoted in his crouching position, aware that these could be the last moments of his life but also aware that he was about to experience something unique in the annals of human history.

Again.

CHAPTER 35

SHE DID NOT like this place and never had. She came here whenever they tried to return, whenever they found the way, whenever they became aggressive. But it was an ordeal for her. It was difficult to adjust to the air, the temperature variations, the roughness of the terrain, and the misery that these beings had made of their world. They were hideous creatures, violent and out-of-synchronicity with the universe.

That was not a surprise to her. No, it was not.

Yet this one—he was the most disturbing of all. He could not be dealt with in the same way as the others. He appeared to have some understanding. He could be useful in stopping others. She had to explain, to show.

And if she failed, she could always stop him as she had the last creature.

She moved toward the wall at the back of the cave. The creature watched her, circling warily to the side as she came forward. Her children watched him, and she remained close enough so that she could strike with her tail if he tried to flee. But she didn't think he would. He came, after all, when she restored the others at the structure.

She raised her arms and stretched her fingers and put her claws against the rock wall in the back of the cave. Then she withdrew them and stepped back. The creature regarded her for a moment. She could see his features plainly; the lights they carried were quite blinding.

There was a noise behind her. She turned to look, though her children remained on the creature.

Her eyes glared.

CHAPTER 36

"WHAT'S HAPPENING IN there?"

Collins shot an alarmed glance toward the mouth of the cave. He raised hand to cheek to block the light from Medusa's eyes. He was still looking at the wall. She had just dug through it as though it were lard. He forced himself to address the more immediate problem.

"Whoever it is, don't come in!" Collins yelled. That was pretty much what Deputy Woodward had told *him*. He hoped this guy listened.

"I heard a shout! The boss's radio is dead."

"But your boss isn't, deputy, and that's the impor—"

Collins bit off the rest of what he was about to say when Medusa suddenly vanished into the light of her eyes. She was gone. He stood where he was, looking

around, and suddenly saw her. Or rather, he saw her
shadow on the wall of the cave. Her eyes must have
flashed again. He briefly saw her tail wrapped around
the throat of a human figure. His hands were raised and
she pulled him to his knees. The light died.

A moment later, Medusa was back beside him.

This time, though, he had been watching her in the
glow of the two flashlights on the cave floor. She had not
used wormhole science to move from place to place;
there was no spatial warping involved. He had seen a
blur of motion, as though she were a time-exposure photograph.

*She used the blinding light to cover her rapid move-
ment,* he realized. Why? More important, why hadn't
she attacked him back at the bed-and-breakfast? She
could have moved fast enough to knock the mirror away,
choke him, and turn him around. *She wants me to see
something,* Collins suspected. Yet there was something
about what Medusa had just done that troubled him. Her
movement against the deputy was not passive, like the
light attacks. It was aggressive, impatient.

The creature reached for the wall again. She put her
bronze talons against the rock and dug them through it,
and downward. She looked at him, her head rolling toward the wall in an exaggerated movement. She apparently wanted Collins to do the same, and quickly.

Fast-motion Medusa. Frozen people. The contrasts
were startling. What did it mean?

She rolled her head again, less slowly, ending with
her forehead pointing toward the wall. Now Collins noticed something else. The Gorgon's skin, the human
part, was changing color. It was going from ivory to
greenish. Two possibilities occurred to him. Either her
mood was changing or she was running out of time.

For what?

And if he delayed any longer, would she grab him with her tail and fling him through? Possibly. But he was scared, big-time, and wanted to know more before he went ahead. He held up his hands as if to say, "Hold on," and took a step away from Medusa, toward the entrance. He took the precaution of looking away as he did. His eyes were downturned, toward the flashlights. He wished he could just pick one up and leave. But he couldn't. In a flash of light they were turned to white stone. That was communication too.

"So . . . it's not just animate objects that tick you off," the young physicist murmured fearfully.

It was very dark now. Collins couldn't see a thing but he was betting Medusa could. After all, she had made her way to the Wyndham place in the dark. He turned very slowly toward the back of the cave and raised his shaking hands, palm out. He moved toward the rock—if it was, in fact, rock. He was beginning to think it might be a solid or at least upright form of the grease covering an entrance to a vortex, also known as a wormhole, also known as a passage to wherever she was from. And if that was the case, he was guessing that it appeared next to solidified people—and flashlights—because of the basic displacement of matter rule: two objects could not occupy the same space at the same time. Whatever happened to the individuals caused that much grease to be displaced from somewhere else.

He started as his palms touched the rock. It felt like rock, but only for a moment. His body heat—radiant energy, like light—caused it to soften and liquefy. He felt it run down his wrists and drip to the floor of the cave.

If I'm displacing grease just like the frozen people, why didn't she just zap me? he asked himself.

Collins had a feeling he would not like the answer.

His hands grew warm as they went deeper. He suspected that was the containment of his own body heat by the grease. He wondered if he should take a breath and hold it. He assumed he was going to emerge somewhere else and that Medusa was going to follow him in. He hoped so. The prospect of being trapped in solidified grease, or being on his own in a new world—again—did not please him.

Somewhere, somehow, he had crossed from being a scientist to becoming someone from one of the H. Rider Haggard adventures he'd read as a kid. *King Solomon's Mines, She, Allan Quatermain.*

Where did they find it? Collins asked himself. The Magellans and the Columbuses and the Shackletons. The people who hurled their bodies into the unknown. Where did they find their courage? The overpowering drive to explore? The thrill of being the first to do something?

Their guns?

All but the last of those were not rhetorical questions. The physicist needed to know. He needed that strength now. At Loch Ness he had been sucked into the past. There'd been no time to consider what was happening. Here, he had gotten a lot curious and a little confident and had the time, now, to consider how imprudent a combination that had been.

The rock was nearly to the elbows of his extended arms. He felt a little better when his fingers emerged on the other side. The trip was finite. The only thing he did not yet know as his chin reached the wall was the trip to *where?*

He did in fact hold his breath and shut his eyes as he pushed himself through the wall.

CHAPTER 37

"SO YOU HAVEN'T heard from any of them?" Tally said into the phone. "And you're okay with that?"

Patient Sgt. Tex McAllen was on the other end of her phone as she lay in bed. McAllen was the dispatcher for the Coconino County Sheriff's Department, the one who had not called Tally back as he had promised to do. Things always looked weirder and more dangerous at night and she had decided that Harold should not be playing Edmund Hillary on Snake Mountain in the dark, with a possible Gorgon or more-probable screwball New-Ager-gone-bad slithering around up there. It seemed, though, that the CCSD was a little short of personnel.

"Ma'am," said McAllen, "we have sent up a sheriff, two deputies, and Dr. Joliet. An assistant police chief from Sedona went there. I do not know the status of any of these individuals and I cannot reach them by radio. Until I hear from one of them, or get a distress call from someone at the site, I am not authorized, nor do I have cause, to send additional personnel to the cave."

"Cause? You just said that you can't reach them!"

"That is correct. The cave is not a good place for wireless communication."

"When was the last time you heard from any of them?" Tally asked.

"Deputy Misoula checked in fifteen minutes ago," McAllen informed her.

"To say what?"

"Ma'am, I can't—"

"Please, Tex," Tally told him. "I sent a reporter up there and I'm worried about him."

"You did?"

"Yes. Why?"

"Deputy Misoula said there was a gentleman in the cave with whom the sheriff had a conversation," McAllen informed her. "Would that be the individual you sent to the site?"

"It would be," Tally told him. "He's a local reporter I call on for help now and then."

"A stringer."

"Yes. Exactly. So what did the deputy say?"

"He had finished his perimeter check and was going up to see if he could help the sheriff explore the cave."

"Did the sheriff give you any indication of what might have happened to the other deputy?"

"He had not found him as of our last conversation, but that is not for publication," McAllen said.

"Of course not."

"Now, ma'am, did *your* friend give you any indication of what might be going on at the mountain?"

If she told him "no," this whole thing was just going to sit. If she told him "yes," she was going to have to tell him "what," in which case he would laugh, hang up, and cease to be a source of information. For the first time in her brief career she wished she had a little tabloid journalism in her veins, something that would inspire her to come up with a compelling lie-slash-cover story, something dangerous but credible.

"He didn't know what was going on," Tally said. "That's why he was going out there."

"Well, that stands to reason—"

"Hold on," Tally said. "This may be him on my other line."

There was no other line. Tally plopped her arm to her side and stared at the mirror on the opposite wall. Four people were strangely silent, statues had come from nowhere, and then there was Harold and his wild stories. There might not be a Gorgon on the loose, but there was definitely something going on. Something to which McAllen was underreacting.

She had to do it.

"Sgt. McAllen, my friend said there's some kind of wild animal running around up there."

"An animal?"

"Yes, a snake of some kind."

"Can you describe it?"

"It's big. About seven feet."

"They don't grow them that big out here," McAllen said. "Is he sure?"

"Yes," Tally said. "He thinks it's part of the whole statue thing, some kind of cult activity."

"Is your friend still on the other line?"

"No."

"Did he see specific evidence of a cult?"

"He said there were pelts, and paintings with blood from dead animals." Lord God, was she bad at this.

"Is that all?"

"Yes," Tally said.

"And you're sure about this information?"

"I'm sure he told it to me, yes."

"If that's true, and if there is a large animal of some kind—possibly a cult member wearing a costume—then this comes under the initial jurisdiction of the Arizona Wildlife Federation, Trail and Desert Division," Sgt. McAllen told her. "They don't have evening hours."

"Jeez. What about *you* guys? Or the highway patrol or the Sedona police department?"

"Not their jurisdiction," McAllen said.

"Sgt. McAllen, I'm a little confused here. Aren't you the tiniest bit concerned about these people?"

"Ma'am, I'm concerned every time one of our people gets in his car," McAllen said. "That doesn't change what we're permitted to do. We have strict regulations and protocols. Unless there is a category four situation or higher I can't call them in."

"Category four being—?"

"Fire, sniper, terrorist activity, things where what we call LOS-con, loss of situation control, is imminent."

Well, gee. If the dispatcher had said that earlier Tally would have said it was a snake with an AK-47.

"This is also not New York City, Ms. Randall," McAllen went on. "We don't have the kind of resources you're accustomed to. People watch after themselves out here. But I'll look into this through channels and I'll make a deal with you. If I can't find anything out I'll go out there myself as soon as it's light. That's when my shift ends. Is that acceptable to you?

"More than acceptable," she said. "Thanks."

"I have your telephone number. I'll call if I hear anything before then."

Tally thanked him again and hung up feeling helpless. She was also deeply concerned. Never mind what was behind this, whether supernatural or not: disappearing deputies was not a good thing. She went back to her dwindling stack of magazines, her cell phone close by in case Harold called.

Paranormal, she thought as she paged through *Mad.* *The supernatural.* If Gorgons truly lived then what did that word mean anymore? Nothing. They were simply aspects of the universe that science hadn't yet explained. In which case anything could be real. Ghosts. The afterlife. Heaven and hell.

She fell asleep no longer thinking about Gorgons but about gods and souls. . . .

CHAPTER 38

APPARENTLY, NOT ALL wormholes were alike.

Assuming that it was a wormhole Collins had slipped through in Loch Ness, he had been pulled and pained and distorted on that journey. This one was slightly different. It offered a somewhat easier passage, as though he were going through an airlock of some kind. There was a great deal of pressure against his sides; he thought he felt a rib or two crack. But it was definitely less painful, and slower, than the Loch Ness experience. The grease had to be the reason for that. What Collins didn't know was whether the grease was used to facilitate passage or whether it was here to stabilize the wormhole. They had no knowledge of exactly where the entrance was in Loch Ness, whether it stayed put or roamed around or opened and closed like an iris. If the grease was a way of keeping the wormhole door open, so to speak, perhaps Medusa and others like her were responsible. They might be more scientifically advanced than the creature's naked, snaky appearance suggested. That was certainly one of the questions he hoped to answer by making this passage.

First contact with extradimensional beings, he thought excitedly as the grease pressed in around him. What a great job he had. Assuming he didn't run out of held breath before he got to the other side.

The grease did not slime him. His eyes and mouth closed, he pushed his face against the grease which stretched like Saran Wrap as he emerged. Collins popped through and before opening his eyes felt the sleeve of his jacket. It was dry. So was his hair. Pretty amazing. He reached into his pocket and withdrew his handkerchief, which was also perfectly dry. He wiped his eyes as he emerged. There was nothing on them. He savored the anticipation of opening them and tried not to contemplate the terrifying possibility that he could be millions of years in one direction or another, and billions of miles, from where he had started.

Or maybe not, he reflected as he opened his eyes.

Collins looked out at the cave—at what appeared to be the cave in Sedona. But it wasn't. The statues were not here, nor was Medusa. Otherwise, it was exactly the same. He thought back, tried to remember if he had hit his head at some point. That was one of the oft-cited explanations for the Loch Ness wormhole, that maybe he had imagined the whole thing.

"No, you didn't hit your head," Collins said. "It would hurt if you had."

He stood there, looking out into the near-blackness. There was pale, thin light coming from somewhere beyond, probably the moon. It would have risen above the hill by now. Only the upper region of the cave received any of the light.

Something moved to his right. He felt it touch his leg. He jumped and looked down as Medusa finished her own passage through the grease. Now she was moving low along the ground. He felt the pressure of her thick, serpentine torso against his shin as she moved by. It was the same as when a dolphin had moved past him in the water once, only this was not a sweet Flipper-like creature. He listened carefully as she continued to move forward among the low shadows.

There was a scratching sound to his right and he looked in that direction. Medusa was dragging her talons across the stone, creating sparks along the wall. They cast a faint light in the cave, burning for a moment and then dying, like jet contrails fading in the sky. She was communicating, again, using light—albeit a different kind. She wanted him to follow. Collins did, touching the rock wall as he passed. It was covered with grease. He moved forward as though he were walking on ice. The cave floor felt as though it had a coating of grease as well. There was a slight spring to it.

This *definitely* wasn't the cave in Sedona.

Collins let his feet slide along. He was tired. Maybe that was good. The experience was flowing into his brain without analysis. What sense would it make even if he thought about it? None. Not without knowing what was outside the cave, anyway. He imagined the Arizona countryside populated by Gorgons. Fanciful land vehicles and possibly airships, other life-forms, maybe a golden or yellow sky with three moons, lakes the color of wheat or wheat the color of lakes. Maybe, because they were snakes, they kept giant field mice as cattle. Or field mice with human bodies.

They neared the bend in the cave. Only Medusa's tail was visible in the firelight as she moved around it. Obviously, it was night here just as it was in "his" world. Or maybe it was always night here. That could be the reason the Gorgon had glowing eyes. They just had the added benefit of turning people to stone. Or maybe they only worked that way in his world. The combinations were too vast and varied, and information was still too scarce.

He stepped around the turn, glancing at the spot where the spider had been. The entrance was ahead, the hint of firelit grease framing darkness. Medusa was almost at the cave mouth. She stopped and turned toward him in an undulating sweep, as though her body were following her head. He stopped and half-looked away, but she didn't zap him. She pulled back, toward the wall to the right. She seemed to be inviting him to come forward.

He walked ahead several paces then stopped. His right side hurt from the passage but he ignored that. He touched his mouth. "Do you—*can you* speak?" he asked gently, then touched his lips again.

Her head moved slowly on her shoulders, from side to side, as though she were a belly dancer. There was something very seductive about her movement; not sexual but sensual.

"Is that a no?" he asked, shaking his head in emphasis.

Her forked tongue licked forward. Collins saw it in the dying firelight on the cave wall. He guessed that was a "no." Medusa moved her spindly right arm outward and raised her long index talon toward the cave mouth.

He moved several steps ahead, planting each foot carefully on rock that felt like hard rubber. There was something different here than in the Sedona cave, something he couldn't quite define. This place had a depressing quality; not like a tomb but like the hospital where his grandmother had died. Just this sense of death, of loss, of emptiness.

He reached the mouth of the cave and stopped. He saw stars and a full moon, just as they looked on the other side of the wormhole. The sweetest breeze was coming from outside. Very warm and caressing, with a variety of floral smells, like a mountainside in Hawaii. There, it was from the rich volcanic soil, and happy buds of all kinds. He did not know what it was from here. He also did not go outside. He had followed Medusa to this point. He would let her lead.

The creature stayed where she was. Collins stayed where he was. He watched the moon relative to Venus. They changed relative to one another as he watched, so they were moving in the sky. That aspect of "here" was the same as well. But he still didn't know where "here" was, or *when* it was.

Or why. Why did she want him to follow her here?

"I don't suppose you have any food," he thought aloud.

Medusa did not make a sound.

He was hungry and he was also tired. He also wondered about something. Instead of standing by the mouth of the cave, he turned toward the back. He took several cautious steps toward the greasy airlock between his world and hers.

Medusa and her snake-hair hissed. Collins heard her nails click. She must have raised her arms in preparation of grabbing him. He stopped.

"Returning to the cave mouth now," Collins said as he retraced his steps backward.

The sudden tension dissipated. All that remained was that very strange, pervasive despair.

"On the off-chance that you have some idea what I'm saying, I'm going to sit," he told her. "I'm guessing if that's not okay you'll flash or give yourself a manicure on my throat-flesh." He crouched slowly. "Bending knees," he said.

The Gorgon did not seem to object. When he reached a squatting position he held it for several moments before lowering his butt to the rubbery floor. Again, Medusa did not show disapproval.

"So you obviously want me to wait," he remarked. "Otherwise you'd be going out the front door and I'd be tagging behind you like a walking Flying Monkey. Are we waiting for someone or maybe for some*thing* to happen? Is this like *Wheel of Fortune* where you don't tell me anything unless I guess right?"

He heard Medusa move. He looked away, into the cave, and listened carefully. She did not seem to be coming toward him.

"So . . . maybe you're gonna rest too? Take a nap?" he asked.

He wished he had a flashlight, a match, flints, anything. It occurred to him that he might be able to use his belt-buckle flange the way she used her claws and strike a fire on the grease but he decided against it. If she wanted him to know, to see, it would have happened by now.

"Of course, I could be sitting here like one of the world's great losers," he said. "For all I know you can't leave the cave because of some curse or barrier or invisible leash, and there's an army of whatevers on their way

ready to haul me off and hook me to some machine
that's going to read my brain. Then they'll use that intel
to invade my world."

Medusa's hair hissed very slightly. He could tell the
difference now. The hair snakes made a higher, more
sibilant sound. Medusa's own hiss was more guttural,
like an unhappy lion on helium. He was guessing that his
chatter bothered the little serpents. Maybe they were trying to take a nap.

"Too bad, little dudes," Collins muttered. He looked
back out the front of the cave. "I'm missing something,"
he said softly, after a long moment's reflection. "What is
it? We're in what appears to be a parallel dimension.
God, how easily I said that. I am in. Another. Dimension.
Or else hallucinating, like Dr. Jackson said. Which is it?"
He dug a fingernail into the floor of the cave. It was like
chalk. It was real. He was not imagining this.

A cave sealed for a century. Medusa inside—waiting?
Guarding it? Why? What was so important that no one
could come through?

Collins couldn't begin to guess but had a suspicion he
wouldn't have to. The moon was moving and the sun
would rise and then he'd be able to see what was out
there. Unless his other fears were correct, in which case
it wouldn't matter. Either way, his body told him this
was a good time to shut his eyes and rest.

Five minutes later he was asleep.

CHAPTER 39

TALLY THREW OFF the covers and sat up. She couldn't sleep. In fact, her mind was more active than it had been when she'd turned off the light at midnight. And not all of it was about Harold and his Mystery.

"One-thirty," she said, sitting on the edge of the bed, looking at the digital clock, and grumping. She was out of magazines, out of Internet sites, and had no interest in turning on the TV. She had never been a sitcom or soap-opera watcher. The Randall life was that, and more. Instead, she got dressed, slipped her cell phone into its holder, and went for a walk. She needed to think about the other thing that was keeping her awake. Tally and her Future.

The West Village at this hour was pretty deserted. The warm breeze carried the hint of saltwater from the bay and urine from dogs that had gone on walls instead of in the street. There was a little downtown traffic on Seventh Avenue, a little uptown traffic on Hudson. Most of that consisted of cabs taking young people home from bars or jazz clubs, late night sushi or a late night spat with a lover. She always liked stumbling on those. It was like being invisible because couples had nowhere to hide in the city. They simply ignored you. The only spats she ever had were with her mother. She really needed to get a lover, share the wealth.

She wished she felt that way about Harold. The lover part, not the spat part. She truly did. He was smart, he was not uncute—but he just didn't hang the moon for her. No one did. Not since Professor Whiting. James Whiting, Elizabethan Drama. Oxford, tweed, accent— the works. Smart and funny and married and what a *bad* idea all that had been. But when you're crazy about someone you're crazy and, not unexpectedly, the whole thing ended quickly and badly for her after a single semester. It was funny how a guy could read the same play over and over and find new subtexts or interpretations, but got bored of a lady after just a few months. Well— she had gone to college to get an education, and she got one. She didn't regret it, however many tears and undigested meals she'd spilled over him. Once, even, *on* him. That was her last memory of him, scooting off to the rest room to wipe his trousers.

But Harold . . .

Tally found herself on Christopher Street, heading toward Bleecker. The bars were still rockin' here. There was no point going in one, though. For one thing, she didn't drink. For another, the patrons were all gay.

She didn't want to settle for a relationship that had to grow on her. That was what fungus and barnacles did.

She knew. She had done articles on both. She was fond of Harold, but "fond" didn't become "love." It became affection or deep friendship or all kinds of things that skirted what she was looking for. The weird thing was, until Harold had stirred up some of that stuff it wasn't in her face that she was missing any of that, or maybe even needing it.

Maybe she needed to live on a commune or kibbutz, somewhere she could be herself and do her job and take from others what she needed: conversation, fellowship, sex. Different people for different wants. Because finding them in one person was just not happening for her. Not at the museum, where everyone was either married or silver-haired, and not in the Village where "straight" was a minority.

She turned north on Bleecker and headed back to the apartment. She looked at the antiques in the windows of the darkened shops. The streetlights caused her reflection to be superimposed over old armchairs, paintings with ill-fitting frames, and Tiffany lamps. She felt ghost-like, drifting through time. Quite a change from the early evening, when Sixth Avenue had been alive and she had felt a part of it. Right now she didn't feel as though she belonged to anything.

A lot of this was tiredness talking. Defenses down, mind on pause, heart taking a stroll like an emotion-vampire eager to feed. Things wouldn't seem so lonely in the morning. And resting would be easier if she knew that Harold was okay. He was still a new friend, one who both exasperated and challenged her. She wasn't ready to see him turned into a fountain decoration.

She reached the apartment and walked back upstairs. Now it was after two. Coupledom had come to Tally—at least on the clock.

She was only a little less awake than when she had left so she found a magazine with a crossword puzzle and got back into bed, cell phone on the nighttable. She worked on that until her tired eyes shut, her head rolled onto her shoulder, and her conscious mind turned over the truth-seeking to the subconscious.

If a dream about a windy desert, a blind camel, and her mother hunting for a chest containing a lost manuscript by Erma Bombeck had any truth in it, Tally's subconscious failed to locate it. . . .

CHAPTER 40

HAROLD WOKE WITH a half-start: his left shoulder twitched and took the rest of him with it. He sucked sweet air through his nose, opened his eyes, and saw that it was still dark out. But it was not the same under-the-covers-at-night darkness that it had been before. There was a hint of apple-red on a far horizon. He blinked the shards of sleep from his eyes, put his palms on the cave floor, and pushed himself up from a slumping position. He looked at his watch. He had slept for about six hours. He felt refreshed. There was something about the grease-rock that had been surprisingly comfortable. As if it had conformed, slightly, to his contours. It was very strange but Collins felt like Alice in Wonderland. The unreal was becoming the norm. It would take something pretty considerable to surprise him now.

He squinted across the cave. He couldn't see Medusa but he could feel her presence. If she was awake she was being extremely quiet, like a good roomie rather than a dog. Not that he expected her to come over and lick his hand. At least other Gorgons hadn't come by in the night to take him away. Presumably, Medusa was waiting for the sunrise as well.

Collins did not rise. He stretched his fingers without allowing the knuckles to crack and looked out at the new day. The physicist tried to imagine what the sunlight would reveal. With some grasp of the rules—don't move unless bidden and don't disagree with the lady—and a clearer head, he was feeling somewhat more confident than he had the night before. The prospect of being able to see soon probably had something to do with that. Still, the only frames of reference he had to imagine the next hour or so were what he had seen before: a starry night. That didn't give him any kind of clue what might be out there. Only the quiet. He hadn't heard mechanical devices of any kind. Perhaps there weren't any; or perhaps they were so sophisticated they didn't make any noise.

As the horizon brightened Collins began to hear birds. Their songs were all over the musical scale, serenading the sun as it started to form perfect yellow-orange rays. He half-expected to hear the *Pastoral Symphony* piped through hidden speakers. Because of the cave's height it was light enough to see inside now, and Collins was surprised to find no Medusa. He looked behind him as dawn spread into the cave. He did not see his guardian there either. He stood and yawned and stretched and yawned again loudly and waited to see if she came running. She did not, so he went around the bend. The cave was empty.

"What did you do, go back through the grease?"

Maybe. Which was when the words "scam" and "hallucinating" slipped from the back to the front of his
mind.

He turned and went back to the mouth of the cave.
The air was mild, with nothing of an early-morning chill.
The sky went from ultramarine to cobalt blue and sunlight began to drop along the terrain. Collins watched,
half-expecting to see the dusty desert, the two-lane road,
his car, and the various police vehicles parked alongside
it, cacti and other now-familiar flora, and the distant
hills. Maybe even a group of Sedonans hauling statues
out to U-hauls.

That was not, in fact, what Harold Collins saw. What
was out there puzzled him. He didn't know what he was
supposed to *do*.

Below was a valley. It was not the kind of home he
imagined a Gorgon would have. There was no morning
mist, no low clouds blocking the sun. The sun itself was
warm and sharp-edged, the sky a rich blue, like a child's
construction-paper cutout. The trees were thickly
canopied, a healthy green, with birds moving to and
from them. Some of the birds were white, some black,
some multicolored. There was a slow-moving river in
the center of the valley and, through breaks in the trees,
he saw deer and what looked like a family of bears. Pur-
ple and orange flowers spotted the walls of the valley to
the top, which was about fifteen hundred feet up. He
could picture the bees moving from bloom to bloom.
Though there was no road below the cave mouth the hill
was not very steep. He could walk it if he wanted to, or
had to. He didn't see why he would, though. There were
no hints of campfires or huts or tire tracks or wagon-
wheel ruts. There was no indication of human habitation
whatsoever. Moreover, he had nothing with which to

trap an animal and didn't see fruit of any kind. When it was time to eat, Collins would have to go back through the wormhole.

"All right, Gorgons and gentlemen. It's mega-beautiful," Collins said. "Now what?"

He waited for an answer, not really expecting one. So what did he do now? Go back or go out? If he went back—assuming the door was still open—he would return with no knowledge, no information, no way to help the other "statues." If he remained, he could make a fatal misstep. Something innocent that just happened to be against the local laws. Maybe this was a test, like the Lady or the Tiger. Bring a human through the grease and see what he'll do: chicken out or go ahead.

If that was the case, why were they being tested? To see how cautious they were or how inquisitive? "Which" was an important question.

"Well, Harold, why do scientists like me put mice— like me—in mazes?" he asked himself. "Not to see if they'd rather leave the way they came and not to let them sit there and stare at their whiskers. We do it to see if they're smart enough to figure the way out. Then we make them smoke cigarettes and wear makeup and give them all kinds of diseases."

If Collins was going to screw up, he wanted to do so searching for answers, not running from risk. Emboldened by that, the young man moved slowly toward the mouth of the cave.

Collins looked around as he moved forward. Up, ahead, side-to-side. The scenery didn't change, there was simply more of it. The slope of the cliff still did not have even the hint of a trail. Not even deer tracks. There were no bird droppings on any of the rocks that lay half-buried among the flowers, suggesting that they didn't come this way. He exited the cave and looked to the right. The slope continued gently toward the south. He saw a few wild hares and chipmunks racing through a clearing of sienna-dark earth to his right. He looked to his left.

There was something down there, about two hundred feet away. He couldn't quite see it from where he was standing; the rise of the slope gave him only glimpses of what looked like brittle white bones reaching into the sky. Big ones. The flowers were slightly crushed leading toward it. Perhaps Medusa had moved off in that direction. He decided to go and see.

"I'm coming out," Collins said, just short of a shout. "If I'm not supposed to, someone better say so now."

The young scientist left the cave. The toasty sunlight felt extraordinary on his face and hands. He removed his jacket and tied it around his waist. His neck felt as though it were absorbing vitamins right from the air. Wherever this was, it would make a hell of a resort.

"Is that why you brought me here?" Collins said, only half in jest. "You need a front man for Medusaland tours? 'Come to our cave! Leave your worries *and* your dimension behind!'"

The earth was extremely soft and spongy. Jokes aside, it was the kind of place where he would ordinarily remove his shoes and socks and let the damp soil and cool grass caress his toes.

The object was easing into view. He looked at it, the sun behind him brightening the hill and everything on it with new day.

Except that.

He stopped. A cold wind swept from the south and rode under his sleeves and up his pant legs, chilling him.

"Oh, no," he said in a cracked whisper. "No. No."

He turned and looked back into the valley. He was wincing, his heart was picking up speed, his breath was coming in uneasy gulps.

"No . . ."

He looked ahead at Medusa. His brain felt as though it had run into a rock wall. A hard one, not one made of grease. She was looking back at him. The snakes in her hair hung low and there was a sadness in her eyes; he could see it even at this considerable distance.

"No," he said again, backing away.

The Gorgon moved toward Collins as he turned and walked back toward the cave. The cool wind clung to him like oily vapors. His brain felt as though it had hit a boulder with a big splat, then dropped. It wasn't working, wasn't processing data. It was stuck on one thought, one short sentence, one idea that he couldn't fit into the scheme of things:

"It is. It *is*."

Collins looked around. He felt heartbroken and small. He understood now, in his brain and soul, the feeling of depression that inhabited the cave. He had wanted to know stuff and now he did. And the world and everything in it was forever changed. Physically, he could go home, just as he did at Loch Ness. He would be back in a safe place. But he would never be the same. He had just acquired knowledge that made Einstein and Newton, Columbus and Balboa all seem like blind, groping monkeys.

He had acquired certainty.

Collins felt nauseous. He felt as though he were taking the worst hike in the history of humankind. Because he was. He *was*.

He didn't remember entering the miserable darkness of the cave and moving toward the back. He was barely aware of the flash of white light that lit his back and the area around him, and followed him through the grease. The grease that wasn't grease, to the statues that weren't statues, to a home that was no longer a home. To the entrance that in all likelihood would never again be an entrance once he passed through it. He had trouble convincing Tally and Dr. Jackson of what he had seen in Loch Ness. Compared to this, that was easy sell. Compared to this, that was a walk to the corner market. Lord, he hadn't been ready for this. The only consolation he took was that in all probability, no one on Earth could have been ready for it.

As he emerged into a harsh new day in a cave in Sedona, Harold Collins, the man who was afraid of letting Medusa make him a coward, of embarrassing his species of naked gorillas, wondered if he would ever be able to think of anything other than what he had just seen.

CHAPTER 41

"A HA! I TOLD her there was nothing to worry about."
Short, beefy Sgt. Tex McAllen was just entering
the cave, huffing from the climb, when Harold Collins
came toward him. The eleven-year CCSD veteran was
happy to be right; he was also very happy to see his fellow officers. Behind the scientist were Sheriff Birdsong,
Deputy Woodward, and the other listed-as-missing resi-
dents of Sedona. Birdsong was helping a short Native
American man who had a windbreaker tied around
his waist and the sheriff's jacket across his shoulders.
He was trembling. Save for the lost and befuddled look
he was wearing, the swarthy man was quite naked.

"Sergeant, call the Sedona Medical Clinic and the
Sedona Fire Department EMTs and tell them we've

got—people," Birdsong said. "A half-dozen, dehydrated, possibly hypothermic."

"Right away," McAllen said.

"And get a vet for the dogs," the sheriff added. "Dr. Fox is not feeling up to caregiving."

"Yes, sir."

McAllen stepped outside. He didn't bother routing the call through the station but used his cell phone. He looked back inside as the others approached. The nearly naked man recoiled from the light, almost like a vampire. It was strange.

The sergeant made the calls and was told to keep everyone where they were at the entrance to the cave. A chopper would come to get the worst-impacted individuals. McAllen wasn't sure how they'd make that determination. They all looked pretty beat-up. Wobbly legs, shaking arms, heads hanging, stop-and-start gait with more stop than start. Even the two dogs had to be carried. They were lying across an arm each as Deputy Woodward slouched his way out.

It was *very* strange.

But strangest of all was the look on the man McAllen took to be the stringer Ms. Randall had been calling about. He didn't have the outdoorsy Western tan the others had. He also didn't seem like he was alive from the chin up. As soon as the sergeant had made the calls he walked over to him.

"Mr. Collins?" he asked.

The man looked at him with a sad expression.

"Are you Harold Collins?"

Collins nodded vacantly.

"Your employer has been calling about you."

"Sam called?"

"No, a Ms. Tally Randall."

"Tally." Collins didn't say anything else.

"If you'd like to call her you can use my phone," McAllen said. "I have the number if you need it."

"Not just yet," Collins said.

"Do you want to sit down?" McAllen asked. "You look kinda beat. There's a rock over there—"

"I'll be okay," he said. His voice was flat, mechanical. "Thanks."

"Sure," McAllen told him. "If you want, I'll call the lady and tell her you're okay."

"If you would," Collins said.

"I'll take care of it in a couple of minutes." He regarded Collins suspiciously for a moment. The man didn't have a notebook, tape recorder, or camera. "Are you really a reporter?"

"I'm sorry?"

"A journalist. A stringer."

"No. I'm with the United Nations."

"The same fellow Deputy Woodward saw?"

"Yes," Collins said.

McAllen's mouth twisted unhappily. He felt used and confused as he turned to help the others.

There wasn't a lot of room on the ledge so he suggested the move down about two hundred yards, to a turn in the dirt road that was next to a large, flat, grassy area where a helicopter could land. It was located just to the south of the road. The sheriff agreed and asked McAllen to give him a hand with the Native American.

"What's your name?" McAllen asked the youth.

"N-name," the man said. His voice was low and raw and the word came out with more cracks than it had letters. He was looking down, away from the sun, and still squinting.

"Yes. Who are you?" McAllen asked, pointing to him.

"His name is Jonah Monday," Birdsong said. "That's all I got from him. I'm not sure he understands anything else."

"I see. How are the others?"

"Pretty much as you see them," Birdsong replied. "We're all kind of shell-shocked."

"Why, sheriff? What happened in there? Why was everyone out of touch for so long?"

"Sergeant, I have no idea," the sheriff said. "Last night—at least, I think it was just last night—"

"It was."

"—I was attacked by something," Birdsong said. "I don't know what exactly, but it was very strong."

"A seven-foot snake?" McAllen asked.

Birdsong was taken by surprise. "Why do you ask?"

"This guy's friend," he said, nodding at Collins. "Ms. Randall. She said that's what was moving around out there. I didn't believe it."

"I was there and I'm not sure I believe it," Birdsong said. "Whatever this thing was, it grabbed my throat, did this." The sheriff lifted his head and displayed the marks along his jaw.

"Those don't look like snake bites," McAllen said. "They seem like talon marks from a hawk or falcon."

"It was dark, but I know the difference between feathers and scales," the sheriff said. "Or maybe there was something in the cave that caused me to imagine it. Methane gas or some other kind of leak. Anyway, there was a flash and the next thing I knew I was waking up."

"What about the statues?"

"MIA," the sheriff said.

"Any idea where they went?"

"None. They were inside the cave when I got here and gone when I woke up. Did you see anything?"

"No, but I only just arrived. This guy's friend in New York was concerned so I decided to have a look," McAllen explained. "Maybe a chopper came and got the statues?"

"It's possible, though it seems like a lot of effort. For what?"

"A ruse for the hell of it, like crop circles. Just to see if they can slip one past the experts."

"That might explain the statues but it doesn't explain this gentleman," Birdsong replied, indicating the Apache. "Look at him. He has self-healed scars on arms and legs that have never seen a doctor. He is comfortable saying words that I haven't heard since my great-grandfather died. And there are seeds in his hair from plants that aren't in season."

"Oh."

"And back there in the cave?" Birdsong went on. "He had a mint 44-40 carbine that hasn't been manufactured in nearly a century. That woman, the antiques dealer, confirmed it after I shook her a little."

McAllen looked back at her. She held the weapon cradled to her bosom. She seemed as dazed as the others.

"I removed the shot," Birdsong assured him. He opened his hand and showed it to the sergeant. "Silver. Handmade. I tell you, there is something very strange about this man. About this entire situation. And the only guy who seems to have some insight isn't talking."

"Collins?"

Birdsong nodded. "Which is unusual, because he was all mouth before we were assaulted."

McAllen shook his head. "Sheriff, are you seriously suggesting that we've got some kind of Rip Van Winkle scenario going here?"

"I don't know, sergeant," the sheriff admitted.

"I wonder if that's why the United Nations was looking into this," McAllen said. "Maybe he was investigating some kind of global abnormality or treaty violations,
possibly buried canisters of toxic gas."

"I can't rule that out," the sheriff said. "I'm hoping a
thorough medical evaluation will tell us more about Mr.
Monday and what happened to the rest of us."

"A psych evaluation probably wouldn't be out of line
for him," the sergeant suggested.

"It will be," Birdsong said. "Assuming one thing."

"What?"

"That we can find someone who still speaks collo-
quial Apache," Birdsong told him.

The men reached the flat section of hillside and
stopped. They sat Jonah Monday down and the others
pretty much dropped where they were. Sitting, lying,
sprawling. Even the dogs dropped on their sides and
didn't move. All except Collins, who stopped well short
of the clearing. McAllen watched him for a moment.
The young man was just standing there looking out at
them, at the clearing, as if it were the field where he had
just lost the Super Bowl.

"If you'll excuse me, Sheriff, I'm going to call this
man's friend. Let her know that he's okay."

Birdsong nodded and McAllen stood. He took out his
cell phone and walked away. He punched in Tally Randall's number, eager to give her the good news—and to
find out why she had lied to him about Harold Collins.

CHAPTER 42

TALLY WAS AT her desk, listening to a phone-pitch about a history of housepaint, when her cell phone beeped. She told the writer she would call back after lunch and took the call. It was Sgt. McAllen.

"Yes, Sergeant?"

"Ms. Randall, we have your friend."

"How is he?"

"He's all right," McAllen told her.

"Thank God," Tally gushed. "And thank you—very, very much. May I talk to him?"

"I don't think so," McAllen replied. "He's acting a little weird."

"Harold's always weird." Though she said it dismissively, Tally was genuinely concerned. Wormhole trips could be like drug use. Too many could damage the brain. "What's he doing that's so unusual?"

"We'll get into that in a second," McAllen said. "First, Ms. Randall, I want to know why you lied to me."

"I did?" Boy—she was really, *really* bad at this.

"Ma'am, that may be how you get by in New York, but not here. Mr. Collins works for the United Nations. Why did you tell me he's a reporter?"

"Because I'm a magazine editor and he *is* researching a mystery, the appearance of those statues," she replied. It was a fudge, but not a bad one. "Did you see them? The statues, I mean?"

"No, and they're gone," McAllen replied.

"Excuse me?"

"They're gone."

"What about the missing persons?"

"They're back," he replied.

What had Medusa done, reversed everyone?

"And that other thing," Tally asked. "That crazy big snake thing that Harold mentioned?"

"Off the record?"

Ouch. "Okay," she said. *For now.*

"The sheriff may have seen it too. He did not mention the other things—the blood, the pelts, the fire."

"Maybe he didn't see them," Tally suggested.

"Ms. Randall, I've got to go," McAllen said, "but I do wish you had been more up front with me about Mr. Collins. It wouldn't have made any difference in our determination to help find him."

"I'm sorry, Sergeant," Tally replied. "I wasn't at liberty to reveal sensitive international research to which I was privileged." That too was a fudge. But it probably

256   Jim Grand

sounded better than, "Harold was in your backyard looking for a big, fat hole in time and space."

"I wondered about that when I heard the United Nations was involved, and I need to ask as a matter of
course and record—are there public-safety issues we
need to discuss with Mr. Collins?"

"I honestly don't know," she answered. "That's something you'll have to take up with Mr. Collins." Finally,
the truth. Tally had no idea what, if anything, Harold had
discovered in the cave. The fact that the statues had all
been restored suggested that any threat had been neutral-
ized.

"I'm sure the sheriff will want to do that," McAllen
said.

"Before you go, Sergeant—do you happen to know if
Mr. Collins still has his cell phone?"

"I didn't notice," McAllen said. "Ms. Randall, our
chopper is arriving—I've got to go."

"Where are you taking everyone?"

"Sedona Medical Center," the sergeant replied.
"They'll probably want to keep your friend and the others until tomorrow."

"Thanks. I'll try him there. And thanks again for all
your help."

"You're welcome."

Tally hung up and tried Collins's cell phone. He
didn't answer. That wasn't surprising, what with a helicopter about to land. What surprised Tally was that
Collins hadn't phoned her when he got out of the cave.
She was more interested than ever to find out what had
happened in there. He was talkative when he came back
from his tilt with a dinosaur. For him to be silent now
was inexplicable. Above all, Tally hoped that Harold was
all right.

She went to lunch—if grabbing a turkey wrap at a deli on Amsterdam, eating it on the way back, then going directly to her office could be called going to lunch— then got the number of the hospital and called. She was connected to Harold Collins's room. He did not pick up. Nor answer his cell phone. She called the duty nurse and said she was his sister, and asked if he was all right.

"All I can tell you is that he cracked one of the floating ribs on the right side," the nurse told her. "Other than that, he appears to be fine."

"Do you know how he cracked it?"

"I'm sorry but I don't have that information," the nurse replied.

"Will you be keeping him overnight?"

"That is my understanding."

"I see. Is his doctor available, by any chance?"

"I'm sorry, but she's treating the others who were brought in."

"Are they okay?"

"I don't have that information either," the nurse told her with a rockier voice that communicated, *"Even if I did, I couldn't tell you."*

"Great," Tally said. "Thanks for your help."

Now Tally was really frustrated. She hung up, checked her messages, then called back the archaeologist who wanted to write about house-painting in Pompeii. Tally tried not to think of Harold Collins. She promised herself she would not call him again, though it was clear that something significant had happened: either he had found another wormhole or he hadn't and was too humiliated to tell her.

Whichever it was, Tally was putting the matter from her mind. She didn't even phone back Dr. Kathryn Castle, the scientist they had met at Loch Ness. Tally didn't want to think about wormholes right now. Or how angry and hurt she was. Or the real warping of time-and-space reality: how this felt just like being dumped, though it was by someone she wasn't even going out with.

The day moved marginally faster than one of the taxidermied animals in the museum's mammal wing. Tally was dying to know what was "up" with Collins but she refused to call again. She kept her cell phone plugged in, to make sure the batteries were fully juiced and she didn't miss his call. She checked her voice mail once every half hour or so to make sure she hadn't. She checked her answering machine at home. She checked her E-mail.

Nothing.

By quitting time, Tally's anger had turned to concern. It wasn't like Harold to be quiet at all, nevermind this long, or to shut her out of anything—let alone something that could be important to the work they were doing. Work they were supposed to be doing *together*.

Tally took the subway instead of walking. She wanted to get home and see if there was anything on the news about Sedona. There was nothing. She called the sheriff's office and was told by the desk sergeant that someone would have to get back to her. It was all too strange.

Strange enough to get her to call the airlines and find out who had a nighttime flight to Phoenix.

CHAPTER 43

SHERIFF BIRDSONG WAS the only member of the Snake Mountain group who did not stay in the hospital overnight. He had Sgt. McAllen take him to the M.D. who looked after his department and was told that except for the gouges along his jaw and extremely dry skin he was fine. Which he knew. Petrification tended to do that. The claw marks were taken care of with peroxide and bandages.

Birdsong had gone directly back to the cave. He was met by officers from the Sedona Police Department who had become involved at the request of the assistant police chief, who claimed he was assaulted by an "unknown individual" who had been hiding in the cave. Although doctors did not find any marks on his head, he insisted he must have been struck because he'd seen one hell of a flash in there.

The two officers and Birdsong had a cursory look around the cave. They did not find evidence of a fight, or bloodshed—or any of the statues, and there wasn't even a clue as to who might have removed them, or how. Birdsong was not surprised. He told the two officers that he would fold all of that into his investigation of what had transpired up here. Since no one had apparently suffered any serious injury, and the only thing missing were statues that did not technically belong to anyone, the police officers were happy to leave things in Birdsong's hands.

What the sheriff wanted most right now was to take control of the site and have a temporary barrier erected at the front of the cave until a permanent one could be put up. Something with bars, a gate, and a key, like what the Department of Native American Affairs put up whenever cemeteries or paintings were discovered in caves. Whatever had happened up here was intended to discourage intrusion and investigation. He intended to make sure the warning was obeyed. As quickly as possible.

Birdsong knew what he thought he had seen in the cave but he did not know how to explain it. He was not prepared to rule out an environmentally caused delusion, an assault by a spirit-guardian of the site, or any other explanation. The first thing he needed to pin down was whether Mr. Collins had shared in the same delusion. The second question he wanted answered was whether Collins knew something that he did not. Birdsong did not believe it was simply an unusual news report that had brought the young man to Sedona.

The sheriff decided to give Collins—and himself— the night to rest. Birdsong went home to Flagstaff and then, early in the morning, went to the Sedona Medical Center. He asked for Harold Collins. The woman at reception told him where to find the patient, and added that he was not the only one waiting for him. There was a young woman, also from New York. She was alone in the small lobby waiting for visiting hours to begin. The young woman was curled across two seats, dozing, a backpack for her pillow. Her shoes were side by side on the floor and her blazer was across her like a blanket. Birdsong went over and leaned close to her ear.

"Tally Randall?" he asked.

The young woman's eyes opened slowly. "That's me."

"I'm Sheriff Birdsong," he told her. "I understand you're waiting to see Harold Collins."

She sat up on the plastic bucket seat and looked at the speaker. "Yes. I got in early this morning from New York City. I was just waiting for the opening bell of visiting hours."

"No need for that," he said. "I was just about to go and see him. You can come with."

"Thank you," she said. "God, I must look spectacular."

"You do."

The woman smiled a half-smile. "In New York, that would be a line."

"It would be a line here too if it weren't true," the sheriff admitted.

Tally thanked him as she reached for her Nikes. "Is everything all right, Sheriff Birdsong? Harold didn't break any laws or anything, did he?"

"None of ours, that I'm aware of," Birdsong replied.

Tally regarded him suspiciously. "That's an odd way of putting it."

"It's been an odd twenty-four hours. Have you spoken to your friend since he's been here?"

She shook her head. "The last time we spoke was right before Harold went back to Snake Mountain. That's why I flew out here. He wasn't returning my calls and I became concerned." She bent to tie her Nikes. "Tell me, Sheriff. Were you with Harold in the cave?"

"Briefly, yes."

"Did anything unusual happen there? Something—" she hesitated. "Something that might have had its own laws?"

He smiled back. "Yes. There was a creature inside, one that resembled a serpent of some kind."

Tally stopped tying her shoe and looked up. "You saw it too?"

"I did more than that," he said, pointing to his bandaged jaw.

"It attacked you."

"Not exactly," he said. "It held me and forced me to look at it. The last thing I remember thinking was that it had a grip like a wolf jaw."

"The last thing before—?"

"There was a flash of light and then good night."

"It's real, then," Tally said.

"Real enough. If it was a costume or a vision, it was very persuasive. Ms. Randall, Sergeant McAllen told me what little he knew about you. May I ask what your interest is in this investigation?"

"As I said, it's kind of complicated, and the parts that aren't are completely bizarre," Tally said.

"I'd like to try and understand," Birdsong insisted, forceful without being pushy. "We can talk as we walk."

"All right." Tally grabbed her backpack and walked alongside him, toward the elevators. "I'm on the editorial staff of a science magazine and Harold's a scientist who works for the UN. He's been investigating unusual phenomena and I've been watching to see if there's enough science in this to write about it."

"Has something like this occurred elsewhere?" Birdsong asked.

"I won't know what exactly 'occurred' here until I talk to Harold," Tally said. "But when we were in Europe he found a strange reptilian creature under similar circumstances."

"Were there statues involved there as well?"

"No," Tally said. "That's a new twist."

"Do you believe the two encounters are related?"

"I don't know," she said. "Only Harold can answer that."

They entered the elevator, took it to the second floor, and walked over to the nurse's station. Birdsong asked for two rooms, those of Jonah Monday and Harold Collins. He stopped at Monday's room first. The patient was asleep and heavily medicated. His doctor was not yet in. Birdsong removed the medical chart from the slot on the door.

"Who is he?" Tally asked as they stood outside.

"The original statue," Birdsong replied.

"He was inside when the cave was opened?"

"Yes," the sheriff said. He was shaking his head slowly. "And unless the lab reports are in error, Mr. Monday was also inside when the cave was sealed. Nearly a century ago."

CHAPTER 44

TALLY AND SHERIFF Birdsong walked down the hall to Collins's room. Neither of them spoke. What was there to say? They had just been to the room of a centenarian who looked like a Gen-X Tarzan. Stunned silence said more than words could possibly express. So it was on to Harold who, they hoped, could tell them something about how Medusa worked her magic.

The door to the room was closed and the TV was on. The sheriff knocked on the door once. "Mr. Collins?"

"Hmmmm."

"It's Sheriff Birdsong. May I come in?"

"Yes."

"Your friend Ms. Randall is with me. She'd like to see you."

"Okay."

Okay? And in neutral, yet. Tally wanted to sock Collins. Hard. Sheriff Birdsong must have sensed that. He not only entered the room first, he kept his big body between them.

Collins was wearing a hospital gown and sitting in bed watching TV when the sheriff and Tally walked in. There was the bulge of a bandage on his side. Unlike Jonah Monday, Harold did not have an IV drip. He was propped on his pillows outside the covers, his legs side by side. He had on the Game Show Network and was watching a rerun of *The Match Game*. He used the remote to mute the sound.

"Not brain," Collins said. "Eyeballs."

"Pardon?" the sheriff said.

"A man blew his nose so hard his 'blank' popped out,'" Collins said. "The contestant said 'brain.' I say the celebrities wrote 'eyeballs.'"

"I would have said 'tongue,'" Tally told him. "Speaking of which, I'm glad to see yours is working."

Collins didn't answer. He continued to stare at the TV.

"How do you feel?" the sheriff asked.

"Like a new man."

"Harold, are you on anything?" Tally asked.

"Not that I'm aware of," he replied.

"You seem like you are."

Collins finally looked away from the TV and at the sheriff. "How is everyone else from the cave?"

"All right," he said. "Jonah Monday is asleep."

"You'd think that after all this time he'd want to be awake," Collins said.

"Then you know what the lab reports found?" Birdsong asked.

"No. But I know he'd been there a long time. What did they find?"

"All of us have traces of pollutants in our saliva and perspiration, in our lungs, in our blood. There is residue in the skin and hair, everything from fluoride to aspirin to food preservatives. This man had none of that. The only foreign substances anywhere in his body were soot from wood-burning fires and both rock and silver dust in his nasal passages."

"And those cuts," Collins said.

"Yes. As though pieces of skin had been sliced out and never grew back, but didn't bleed until we found him."

"The reason being it was not flesh until she restored him," Collins said.

"Your creature."

"Not mine," Collins insisted. "Ours. All of ours. Our legacy."

That was spaced-out. If Harold wasn't medicated, Tally felt, then he had followed Medusa to some kind of zen hideaway.

"Did you learn anything else about the creature when you were in the cave?" the sheriff pressed.

"Yes," Collins said. "I learned that as long as we stay out of the cave she won't be coming back."

"How do you know this?"

"She told me," Collins replied. "Shut the entrance and make sure no one goes there. That was done once, probably by whoever found Mr. Monday. It needs to be done again."

"Why?" Birdsong said.

"I can't tell you," Collins said.

"Can't?"

"If I say 'won't,' you'll try and find some way to force me. So it's best to say 'can't,' " Collins said. "What I can tell you, Sheriff, is that if anyone tries to go in there they will be stopped like Mr. Monday was. And this time there will be no recovery, I suspect. Best just to shut the door and forget there's a cave."

Birdsong did not look happy. "What was the creature that attacked me? Do you know?"

"She is not someone you want to know better, or at all," Collins said.

Tally had never heard Collins like this. She came from behind the sheriff. She wanted to look hard but couldn't.

Collins looked at her. "Tally—I'm so sorry for not calling," he said.

"Yeah, well . . . I was kinda surprised. And worried."

"And angry," he smiled faintly.

"That too."

"I knew you would be."

Harold looked at her. There was something in his eyes she had never seen. Doubt? Fear?

"Sheriff, can Harold and I have a couple of minutes alone?" Tally asked.

"Sure," he said. "Mr. Collins, we'll talk later. I'm going to close the cave. But whether you think I want to hear it or not, I'll need a better reason to give the county than 'I said so.'"

Collins did not reply.

Birdsong nodded at Tally. "I'll be checking on the other patients. Please come and see me when you're done."

"I will," she said.

The sheriff smiled and left, closing the door behind him.

Tally crossed her arms and stood at the foot of the bed. She looked at Collins. He shut the TV, put the remote on the nightstand, then began to sob.

"Harold?" Tally said, utterly surprised. "Harold, what's wrong?"

"I can't—" he said, as the sob became a wail.

The young woman rushed to Harold's bedside. She held him and he pushed his face into her shoulder and clutched her tightly.

"Harold, it's okay. You're back, you're with friends."

"I can't . . . handle . . . it," he said between gasps.

"Handle what?" she asked. "Harold, talk to me. What happened in there?"

"Another wormhole—"

"You expected that."

"Not this."

"Not *what?*"

It took several long seconds before Harold could compose himself enough to speak again. When the sobbing subsided Tally released him and he sat back, looking at her through swollen lids.

"It was Medusa," he said. "Or at least, the creature we have always called Medusa. She took me to the back of the cave where there was a wormhole. It was clogged with grease."

"The same grease that collected beside the petrified people?"

Collins nodded. "It's a form of clay."

"How do you know?"

"I *know,*" he said emphatically. "It is made of the same stuff as we are. The same stuff as all living things. That's why the oil from my fingers gave the spider a few moments of life. It was like running something off a battery."

"Then what about the gun, the other non-living things?" Tally asked. "Why were they affected?"

"We are all over them," he said. "Our oils, our fingerprints, our skin cells, our hair, what we exhale, our perspiration. They are our issue in all ways."

Tally understood everything but the last statement. She let it sit. "Did you learn anything about Medusa?" Tally asked. "Is she alone?"

Collins laughed humorously. "Medusa is very much alone. And the power she has—I don't think it originates with her. I believe it comes through the wormhole, to her, to her eyes."

"What makes you think that?"

Collins choked back another round of tears. "I went through the grease with Medusa. It was night. She wanted me to stay in the cave so we both took a nap."

"Medusa coiled up and went to bed?"

"Yes," he said. "That's exactly what she did. But in the morning she was gone. I believe she wanted me to wait for daylight, so I would see."

Collins stopped. He stared off—into the past, Tally guessed.

"What happened then?" Tally gently urged.

"I watched the sun rise across a valley. I don't know if it was the most beautiful place I've ever seen, but it was definitely the most tranquil."

"What would have made it more beautiful?" Tally asked.

"A challenge," he said. "There was nothing rugged or dangerous about it, no edges like the mountains in Hawaii, no thunderclouds like you see over the ocean. Do you know what I mean?"

"You find beauty in asymmetry," she said.

"Exactly," he said. "This place had none of that."

"Were there other Gorgons?"

"Not that I saw," Collins told her.

"What did you see?"

"Deer, birds, squirrels. All normal, except for her." His expression cracked again and his breathing quickened.

"Something about her bothered you?"

He nodded.

"What, Harold?" Tally asked. She held him again. "Why does she upset you so much?"

"It . . . it isn't her," he stuttered. "Not entirely."

"What else?"

"The loss. The overwhelming loss. I didn't see her, at first," Collins went on through tears he could not stop. "I left the cave and looked for her. I was supposed to, I guess. I saw a tree and walked toward it. She was there, wrapped among the dead, white branches. She looked at me but she did not seem sad or repentant. I don't know. Maybe that is part of the punishment."

"Punishment for what?"

"For what she did, for what we did," Collins said. "Have you ever been to an orchard, Tally?"

"Sure. My parents used to take me apple picking in the fall."

Collins laughed. "Fitting."

"Excuse me?"

"I used to go apple picking too," Collins continued. "It was always a big family outing in Connecticut. So I know what an apple tree looks like, even when it's charred all to hell."

"Medusa was coiled in a dead—" Tally said, then stopped. She let it sink in for a moment. "You can't be serious."

"I am, Tally," he said.

"You can't be—*it* can't be," Tally said. She felt her blood cool several degrees. Her forehead and cheeks grew cold.

"Why not?" Collins asked. "We were expelled once from Paradise and will not be allowed back in. Through Medusa, God sees to that."

"Harold, there has to be another explanation."

"Why?"

"You're saying you went to Eden, you saw a snake, you saw an apple tree, you saw a beautiful garden and—I can't believe that. I just can't."

"Tally, Medusa brought me there so I would come back and make sure people stayed away from the wormhole, from the entrance," Collins said. "She must have felt she could communicate with me, just as I felt that with her. That was why she did it this way. To stop the attacks on people who came too close."

Tally shook her head but words were not forming inside. Thoughts were not coming loose from a suddenly flooded brainpan.

"The grease," Collins went on. "It's the 'dust' from which we were made. Life stuff. Ashes to ashes stuff."

"You're saying the statues *are* what Adam *was*," Tally said. "The clay formed in God's image."

"That's what I'm saying."

"And the power, the eye blasts? They come from—?"

Collins didn't have to answer.

"I've been trying to think of other explanations since I got back, something that would fit the world as I know it," Collins said. "That's why I didn't call. I didn't know what to say. How do you process this? How do we pursue our investigations? What do we tell the public, that we found the train stop just short of heaven? That the light of God shines through the eyes of a serpent? That the Bible is right and so is Darwin? That's actually the most confusing part."

"What do you mean?"

"Tally, we have found two wormholes, each of which take us to what appear to be alternate origins of men. One brought me to prehistory, where it appears that evolution got us to where we are today. The other took me to a place where we were formed from grease, a snake creature tempted us, and we were driven through a cave and ended up here, and in Greece, and in who knows what other locations around the world? Which one spawned us? Or did we come from both? Did Neanderthals come from one, Cro-Magnons from another?"

"Harold—before I even start to think about all that, I've got to ask. Are you sure this happened? Are you sure you saw what you're describing?"

"You mean, is this another potential knocked-on-the-head delusion?" Collins asked. "Tally, I experienced the fall of man. I felt it in the walls of that cave, this sense of sadness. I saw it in the dead tree, saw all death of everyone everywhere. I can't prove that but I felt it."

"Assuming you did," she said. "What now?"

"I don't know."

"You were obviously very affected by this. I am too, albeit once-removed which gives me a slightly different perspective."

"What are you saying?"

"We started this project to understand wormholes," Tally reminded him. "I don't see how that has changed."

He looked at her. "You don't? Tally, I stood at the foot of God."

"So did Moses and he became a leader—reluctantly, I might add."

"The bush he saw was burning," Collins said. "There was hope. Mine was burned-out, dead."

"So what are you going to do? Put a rotten apple

around your neck and stop people in Times Square, tell them to sin no more?"

"Tally, this isn't a joke."

"Harold, I know that," she said. "I also know that this has obviously been a stressful few days and you're on information overload. But withdrawing from me is counterproductive. You're an explorer, Harold. A scientist. You've given your life to the pursuit of knowledge."

"I don't think you understand. There is a superior being who works through Medusa to turn us to the dust from which we apparently arose. Whether it's God or a King Medusa or an alien being, it is *out* there."

"So?"

"So, it makes me feel like a pathetic little monkey. If we could go back through the wormhole and talk to him or her or them, it would be different. There would be something to learn. As it stands, anyone who tries to go back will get cremated. Even if you walk backward through the grease, mirror in hand, what do you do when you get to the other side? Pitch a tent and wait for an audience? Conduct tests on the dead apple tree? Gas Medusa and take her to a laboratory? Grovel and apologize for what Adam did, beg forgiveness?"

"Some of that actually sounds pretty reasonable, just what a scientist should do," Tally said.

"Assuming he wasn't scared down to his heels," Collins said. "Tally, I always looked at this stuff as a fairy tale. Now I don't know what to do. This isn't just a scientific mystery anymore. It's *the* mystery. We're messing with the big one."

"No. You're sitting in bed whining about being afraid of messing with the big one," Tally said.

"Guilty. And not ashamed of my fear."

"And yet look at the things you *did* learn. God, or whoever is out there, doesn't want to kill us. Medusa restored the individuals she'd attacked—even one who had apparently been frozen for a century. She let you see what was on the other side so that more people, and dogs, and spiders, more of God's children, would not be hurt. That doesn't sound like an agenda built on wrath and retribution."

"Maybe not, but it *is* about having a big impediment dropped in the way of your research. If Eden is true, and the rest of the Bible is true, then all the answers are there. Anything I might do just doesn't seem to matter."

"Why not? So these events happened," Tally said. "We already knew that Noah's flood was an historic event. The scars are there, in the geologic record. We knew that the Hebrews were slaves of Egypt, that Old Testament tyrants lived and died. We know there was a Mary and a Jesus and a Peter. Now, it appears, we know there was an Eden. But it's all subject to interpretation and context. It doesn't mean the Red Sea actually parted. It means everything needs to be examined freshly. If you want to study Scripture, that's fine. But whatever you find out there will still be interpretive. You became a scientist to collect facts. Don't be afraid, Harold. Be challenged. I can think of one thing, off the cuff, that should give you hope."

"And that is?"

"There's no mention of dinosaurs in the Bible, yet you saw one on the first journey," Tally said. "Was that a dream?"

"No."

"That means the Bible may not be a complete record

of life in all dimensions. There is reconciling that needs to be done, and it needs to be done by a scientist," Tally said.

"I don't know," Collins said. "Do you realize that if the Garden of Eden is real there's a high probability that heaven and hell are also out there and that one day I may stumble into them? I've been thinking maybe that's how Lucifer fell from heaven—through a wormhole."

"That sure fits the wormhole profile."

"Yes, and it's *so* way more than I bargained for."

"Air pollution was more than Henry Ford bargained for, and aerial combat was more than the Wright Brothers bargained for, and the atom bomb was more than Einstein bargained for. Unfortunately, here they are. The alternative is the Dark Ages."

An eerie calm had come over Collins during the last few minutes. He sat there shaking his head. "I just don't know about this. I'm going to need a whole lot of juice and reflection to rev myself up."

The two were silent.

"Can I get you anything?" Tally asked after a moment. She resisted adding, "Apple juice?" She was one for gallows humor; Harold was not.

"I'm okay, thanks."

"Is that why you were watching *The Match Game*?" she asked. "Looking for order in randomness?"

"It was on when I turned the TV on."

"Oh. Well, that just goes to show how wrong a person can be interpreting data," Tally said.

They were silent again.

"I really appreciate your coming," Collins said. "I hope you don't get into trouble."

"I won't. I took a personal day," Tally said. "My boss was happy to give it."

More silence, though less than before.

"I wonder," Collins said.

"About?"

"Medusa fired a parting blast at my back, one that restored everyone in the cave. I wonder if it restored everyone around the world?"

"You mean, are statues in museums suddenly coming to life and wondering where they are?"

Collins nodded.

"That will startle a few silver-haired patrons," Tally said.

"I'm also thinking, if ancient legends talk about multiple Gorgons, then there must be multiple wormholes into Eden," Collins went on.

"I guess, though many ancient myths predate the Bible. You have to wonder whether the Old Testament scribes were telling original tales or reinterpreting them. Now that I think of it, Greek mythology had the golden apples of the Hesperides. And there was a dragon watching over the garden where they grew, as I recall. That could have been a Gorgon."

"Common origins for divergent stories," Collins said.

"Which is not so uncommon," Tally said. "And if there are wormholes all over, snakes and apples may show up in other cultures as well." She moved closer again and took Collins's hands in hers. "Maybe you can't go back to that one place, at least not right away and probably not through that wormhole. Maybe you'll find a trace of grease and discover that it contains the building blocks of life. That isn't the end of the mystery, Harold. It's just the start. Answer a question?"

"I'll try."

"How much worse would you feel if you hadn't gotten

through the door? If the whole statue thing remained a secret?"

"I don't know."

"I do," Tally said. "You would have been frantic and unbearable and wanting to come back with more money and equipment. None of which would have gotten you more than a mirror and a flashlight. You did a good job, Harold. It was not the last step, it was one more step."

" 'One small step for man . . . ' "

"Exactly like that."

Collins leaned his head back and looked at the ceiling. "I'm scared. It was one thing to have this potential roller coaster through time, to be able to explain phenomena like the Loch Ness Monster and Medusa."

"You thought that would be fun."

"Yeah. And I thought we'd be adding chapters to scientific knowledge, not rewriting the religious beliefs of civilization." He smiled flatly. "I sure don't have the budget for it."

Tally had spent all her pep talk getting this far. She didn't know what else to say, other than, "The long term will take care of itself. What about the next few hours? Any chance you'll be heading back today?"

"I'll have to talk to the sheriff—tell him some of this."

"I agree," Tally said.

He thought for a moment. "Let's do that and then go back."

"Good. My ticket is for—"

"I don't mean home," Collins said.

"What, then?"

"You're right," the young man told Tally. "If I let this situation beat me I'm useless."

"You lost me—"

"Let's go back to the cave. Together."

Tally lost what little blood was left in her face. "Now I think you're going schizo on me."

"Am I?"

"Man of Bible, man of science."

"Both men in search of answers," he said. "Come on."

"I don't think so—"

"Why?" Collins asked.

"For one thing, I'm scared. For another, those are your contacts over the rainbow and I don't want to cut in on your—"

"Bull. This is a big story. You're a journalist. It's a match." Collins got out of bed and went to the door. He yanked his clothes from the hook. "Tally, we need to go there."

"And do what?" Tally asked.

Before ducking into the bathroom with an armful of clothes he replied, "See what Medusa does."

CHAPTER 45

*H*AROLD COLLINS, BOY *coward*.

That's what had whipped through Collins's head repeatedly, like a fast-orbiting satellite, as the conversation with Tally progressed. It was a modest improvement over the I'm-not-worthy thoughts that had been piling on since Collins had reentered the wormhole for the trip home. At least it forced him to get out of bed. Tally was right. Whoever said science was safe, or easy? The Curies had radiated themselves to death. Magellan had died trying to circumnavigate the globe. Benjamin Franklin had risked electrocution to help tame electricity. And it wasn't as if Collins didn't know how to protect himself. What the *hell* was he lying here fretting about?

The fear that I've overimagined what science can do

and that my immortal soul is in danger. That thought was more frightening and sobering than the idea of dying in the line of duty in the jaws of a dinosaur.

But men did brave and silly things, often—was this true with him?—so as not to be embarrassed in front of women, even women with whom they didn't have a traditional romantic relationship. What did army surgeons say in the old, pre-ether days? That it took six strong men to hold down a soldier whose arm or leg had to come off, but only one woman.

Also—and it was a strange feeling for Harold—he had reached a point where he was disgusted by his own weakness. He had never *been* weak; but then, intellect had been enough to get him through most things. Even arguing with Samuel Bordereau, Collins had always had reason and right on his side. And sometimes he'd gotten mad, which had helped. Here he had let shock, fear, exhaustion, and various combinations of them cripple him.

Till now. Till he had started thinking about Medusa. Till he had started to wonder about something he may have overlooked.

He dressed, then joined Tally, who had gone to say good-bye to Sheriff Birdsong. The sheriff had finished checking on the others, all of whom appeared to be in good shape. None of them remembered anything between "passing out" and "waking up." Birdsong took Collins aside by the nurse's station.

"So, Dr. Director," Birdsong said. "What can you tell me about the cave?"

Collins sighed. "It leads to what I believe is another dimension, where a monster of Greek mythology stands guard so that people don't come through."

Birdsong nodded. "That's it."

"That's all I know for certain."

"You were a little less objective a few minutes ago."

"I was overwrought," Collins replied. "Sheriff, the cave is a dangerous place. It was closed for a good reason once before. It should be closed again."

Birdsong nodded again. "I've got friends with the EPA," the sheriff said. "I'm going to work the 'mysterious gas' angle, call in favors if necessary to get the cave and the case closed." He looked Collins over. "Obviously, you feel fit to travel."

"I'm all right," Collins said.

"I'll square your checkout with the doctor."

"Thanks."

"Meanwhile, is there anything off the record you can tell me about?" the sheriff asked.

Collins hesitated. "You won't go up there yourself?"

"Only to make sure the wall is built bigger and stronger."

Collins exhaled. "There are spirits beyond the cave, sheriff. Spirits that were known to your ancestors and to mine. They have asked us politely, through me, to let them be."

"I believe you and I'll respect that," Birdsong said. "I assume you'll be going back to the cave."

Collins was surprised. "What makes you say that?"

"Your car is there."

"Ah. Yes," Collins said as Tally walked over.

"It's funny," the sheriff said. "You're the scientist and you encounter something deeply spiritual. I'm the one with an animal spirit that walks beside me, yet I was deaf to the voices."

"What animal spirit walks with you?" Tally asked.

The sheriff smiled and pointed to his name tag.

"Of course," Tally said, wincing.

Birdsong extended a powerful hand. "Mr. Collins,

Ms. Randall—it has been an honor meeting you, and I wish you success. If there's anything you need I'm here to help, officially or unofficially."

"Of course," Collins said. After releasing the sheriff's hand he gave him a business card. "Likewise with Mr. Monday. I have a feeling he is going to need all the help you can provide."

Birdsong said good-bye to Tally and the two New Yorkers left the Sedona Medical Center.

"Nice guy," Tally said as they walked to her car. "A real gentleman."

"And he didn't roll his eyes at a damn thing."

"It's the Native American upbringing," Tally said. "I bet your mom's family would be the same way, with their Hawaiian heritage."

"Oh yeah. Sacrifices to the mountain gods were a Sunday night tradition in the Waipahu household," Collins said.

"Animal or human?"

"Human, of course."

"Animals are so 'compromise,'" Tally said.

It was a relaxed but oddly forced conversation, the social equivalent of whistling past a graveyard. The two slid into the car and were silent as they headed to the Boots and Spurs to check Collins out. The Wyndhams were fine, but confused. Collins told them that the sheriff was looking into a gas leak of some kind that originated in the mountains and caused them to pass out.

"Must've been something like nitrous oxide," Joe Wyndham said as he walked them to their car.

"That's not been ruled out," Collins said. Which was true. Because it wasn't being considered at all.

"Meg swears she saw snakes flying through the air, but I think it was too much wine at dinner," Wyndham said. "Mr. Collins, you didn't go running around here with snakes, did you? Looking for toast to put one on or something?"

"No," Collins said. "Just the tarantula."

"That was strange, this whole thing was, but we sure hope you come back. Both of you. You look like you could use some color, miss. A few days by the pool would fix that."

"I'd love it."

"We'll give you a special rate," Wyndham winked. "The pretty lady's package. Discount and a piece of Meg's jewelry. Think about it."

"I will," she promised.

Collins and Tally hurried to the car. Collins actually envied Joe Wyndham his safe overview. Gas. Visions. Unusual but not unprecedented. Unnerving but not soul-shaking.

The two drove to the highway, to the mountain, to a spot that had put awe in Collins's soul and terror in his spine. His brain kept his body moving forward but as they neared the site that motion was fueled by bravado, not conviction. When they finally saw it, an elbow-shaped silhouette against the pale-blue sky, even the bravado lost traction. They parked the car and got out. The air was dry and dusty. It smelled like dirt. It wasn't room-freshener sweet, like the air in Medusa's valley.

You can't even call it Eden, can you?

Collins razzed himself.

Collins was literally shaking as they went to his car. He retrieved the flashlight and both mirrors, and then went to the trunk. He took something out and tucked it in his belt. Then he went back to the front where Tally was waiting. She took his hand and squeezed it.

"You doing okay?" she asked.

"Surviving."

"You know, I brought a camera," she said. "Should I bring it?"

He shook his head. "If I'm right, you won't be needing it."

"Would you mind if I brought it anyway?"

"No," he said.

Tally got her small digital camera from her backpack. She hooked it around her wrist and they started up the path.

The trek to the cave passed quickly, probably because for the first time he wasn't alone. They stopped just north of the entrance.

"Where is the wormhole?" Tally asked.

"It's back behind a bend, to the west," Collins said.

Tally looked out across the plain. "That would make the exit on the east," she observed.

"Correct. Is that significant?"

"Yeah. That's the way the exile went."

East of Eden. *Holy mother,* Collins thought, she was right.

"So how do you want to do this?" Tally asked.

"The physical drill is this," Collins said, then proceeded to illustrate. He put the flashlight on his shoulder pointing back. Then he turned, raised the mirror, and looked in it.

"We walk backward, just using the mirror," Tally said.

"Yes."

"Got it. But Medusa has claws," Tally said. "The sheriff told me they're pretty powerful."

"I know. That's why I brought this." He pointed to the tire iron. "But I have a feeling I won't need it."

"A feeling?" she said.

Collins nodded. "I think Medusa was telling me more than I got right away. We'll see."

Tally nodded bravely. Then, slowly and cautiously, they began backing into the dark opening.

The cave looked, and felt, different without the statues. It seemed larger, emptier, and carried a little of the melancholy Collins had felt in the other world. He kept his eyes on the bend. As they neared, he moved Tally toward the south wall. She stayed on the exit side of the cave; he was on the interior side. She had the mirror in one hand, her camera hanging around her wrist.

"Are you watching for something in particular?" she whispered.

He looked into her mirror and nodded.

"What?"

He didn't answer until they were just a few feet from the bend. "That," he said, as a delicate glow appeared on the other side of the wall.

Tally stopped. Collins slowed but continued to move forward.

"Is that her?" the young woman asked.

"Yes."

"What are you doing?" she wheezed.

"I want to see something," Collins said.

"What? A quicker way to be fossilized?"

The young physicist did not answer. Instead, he inched toward the bend. The light grew and came closer. Collins slowed but did not stop. He waited until he was just shy of the bend before stopping. The light also stopped.

"She's doing it again," Collins said.

"Doing what?"

"Not coming around," Collins told her. "Not attacking.

The first time this happened to us Medusa came to the inn to get me. She realized I knew something the others did not."

"Snake-woman's intuition?"

"Who better to sense a person's inclination than the serpent of Eden?" Collins asked.

"Good point. What is she sensing now?"

"Something I didn't have before," Collins answered. "I completely missed the other reason Medusa didn't attack me earlier." Collins lowered the mirror and came around so he was facing Tally. He looked at her face and at the light beyond. "If the biblical accounts are correct, then the serpent 'fell' with man. Only she wasn't banished from Eden."

"My gosh. She was imprisoned."

Collins nodded.

"So you're saying what?" Tally asked. "That she wants your help? The serpent, the ultimate tempter, wants you to save her!"

"That's what I'm thinking. She's spent eternity scrunched in the Tree of Life. She can only leave to enforce God's will. Or at least, that's the story we've assigned to this being, to this place."

"You're saying there could be more."

"Not *could be,* Tally," Collins said. "There is a lot more, as you said back at the hospital. For one thing, the cave was reopened from the inside. An accident? Maybe. But it could also have been caused by Medusa. Maybe she wants out." Collins walked to the bend.

"What are you doing?" Tally asked.

Collins didn't answer. He put his back to the wall and stretched his right arm along the rock, the mirror in hand. The light dimmed as he moved the glass around the bend. The glow faded considerably and he fixed the mirror on the face of the Gorgon. Only the eyes of the snakes were glowing, and those faintly. Medusa's eyes were in their natural state. He studied her expression. He saw for the first time her shame. Something that was highlighted by every moment of every spotless Eden day. Men did not realize their flaws because the world around them was imperfect. But this creature—

Collins lowered the mirror and stepped around the corner. He held her eyes directly for a moment, giving her his trust and a moment that told her he understood. Then he took Tally by the elbow and turned her slowly toward the entrance of the cave. She walked quickly, her expression taut, her eyes on the daylight, her camera dangling from her forearm, forgotten.

The cave would be sealed. Medusa would go back to waiting, though perhaps now she would nurse something other than regret. For the first time since the beginning, perhaps she would have something else.

Hope.

CHAPTER 46

TALLY RANDALL AND Harold Collins sat across from one another at the outdoor table of the Parkhut. It was eight-thirty in the morning. It was a cool morning and they were the only ones out here, Tally huddled over coffee and Collins working on his second decaf double espresso. Dr. Jackson would not be joining them. Tally had not bothered to call him. She didn't know what she would say.

The day before, they had driven to the airport in their separate cars and had come back to New York on different planes. Which was just as well: Tally hadn't felt like talking *or* listening. To anyone. About anything. Tally wasn't a religious woman and she didn't fear that they were messing with the Old Testament God. She was also an editor who loved the Bible as literature but knew how allegories worked, how stories could be spun to persuade, control, or civilize the masses, how translations of dead languages gave us imprecise pictures of the past. That's how Michelangelo's *Moses* ended up with horns instead of rays of light rising from his head and why scholars still debated whether the commandment was, "Thou shalt not kill" or "Thou shalt not murder."

But if the wrath of Yahweh didn't scare her, the snake lady had. This was Tally's first contact with one of Harold's creatures. When he'd gone to the bend in the cave she'd seen the reflection of Harold's mirror in her mirror. Something scaly was out there. Something that didn't resemble any creatures extinct or non- that she had seen in the museum. A Gorgon. It was disturbing that she should doubt the validity of a book that so many people believed, yet find a Greek myth entirely credible.

"That would be like a Federalist suddenly showing up on the next presidential ballot," she said.

"Pardon me?" Collins said.

It was the first thing Tally had said since they'd ordered and done the "how-was-your-flight-did-you-sleep-okay" drill.

"I was just thinking about an upside-down world in which myths are real," Tally said.

"Well, that may be overstating things somewhat," Collins said. "It's like you said about Noah's flood. One aspect of mythology being true doesn't make the entire canon fact. The existence of Medusa doesn't mean we'll find a flying horse or a cyclops somewhere else."

Tally frowned. He was right. She just hated knowing that a monster was real and not having a biological place to put it. Ontology had never been her favorite branch of metaphysics.

Their food arrived. Collins dug into his corned-beef

hash with sunny-side-up eggs. Tally jabbed off small pieces of her Spanish omelette. Being in the Southwest had put a taste in her mouth for hot peppers.

"So what do we do?" Tally asked.

"You have a magazine to put out," Collins reminded her. "This is my full-time job and my full-time headache."

"Yeah, but you can't expect me to go back to business-as-usual."

"You have to, Tally. You can't let this preoccupy you."

"Don't be insane," she said.

"I'm being serious. This is like when presidents are about to launch secret attacks or rescues. They still have to go through their planned day, posing with Girl Scouts and having egg rolls—on the lawn, I mean, not Chinese—and all the usual stuff. Because if they let on that something big is about to happen it'll mess things up for the mission and the country."

"I'm not the president," she reminded him.

"If you were, this would be easier," Collins said. "We'd have all kinds of staff to help us. I've got to re-search Greek mythology as well as snake and paradise stories from other cultures. And that's just for starters. I want to read newspaper stories, or accounts on ancient tablets, of anomalies in those areas that might have given rise to those tales, areas that might harbor wormhole en-trances. I want to check on different kinds of phenom-ena that might mesh with what I've already seen."

"So we may not know anything else for weeks, maybe months," Tally said.

"Right. And if you carry this around to the exclusion of everything else you'll go nuts. And you won't be any closer to understanding it. Only methodical research can do that."

Tally frowned again. Collins was right again.

"To change the subject, I wanted to say that I really appreciate what you did, coming out to help me," Collins said.

"I'm glad I could do it," Tally said.

"It meant a lot to be able to bawl all over you."

"I appreciated the trust," Tally told him.

"I also want you to know how much it helped UNIT Omega," Collins added. "You had a fresh perspective, gave me the push I needed to go back up there. If you hadn't done that I'd still be lying in that medical center bed or roaming around Sedona with a puss."

"Nah. You'd have bootstrapped yourself out of there."

"Eventually," Collins said. "Probably after my mother called. You know, she never let me stay in bed when I was sick? She thought that activity was a good way to fight a fever."

Tally grinned. A quick hit of the mundane brought her brain back to the real world. She took a few bites of omelette.

"How is it?" Collins asked, nodding at the plate with his chin.

"Good. So what do you think?" she asked.

"About?"

"The wormholes. The destinations. You must have thought about it on the plane ride."

"Yeah. It wasn't as if watching the movie was an option."

"So if you had to guess, what is this all about? Did you move through space or time or both."

"Tal, I just don't know."

"You said the flora and fauna on the other side of the Sedona wormhole were similar to those in our own world—isn't that a clue? You obviously weren't in another dimension."

"That isn't necessarily true," Collins replied. "The air was breathable, the geology seemed the same, so wherever I was life would have evolved along similar lines. Physics are the same throughout the universe. I mean, if I had seen a hummingbird the size of a 737, that would tell us that I had shrunk."

"Or that it had grown."

"No," Collins said. "The wing-to-body ratio still has to provide lift. A giant hummingbird would need exponentially larger wings which would mean increased musculature to support those wings which would mean even more musculature to support the increased musculature."

"Got it," Tally said. Collins was right a third time in a row. The world had indeed gone mad.

"As for strict time travel, that's also possible. The sun rose and set there as it does here, the moon looked the same, and the animals I saw in the valley of 'Eden' were familiar. Ten thousand years ago, the world and the skies *would* have looked pretty much the same as they do now."

"Except for the presence of Medusa," Tally pointed out. "But she may have lived, at some point. There are plenty of extinct life forms. Some we only know from one or two fossil fragments."

"Right," Collins said. "Maybe we haven't found her remains because she was cooked in her own light. For all we know she became part of a mountain, or curled up into a boulder somewhere. Maybe her features were eroded by time."

Tally drank coffee as she considered how little they knew. It was the classic example of "The more you learn, the more you realize you don't know."

"Medusa aside, we really need to find more wormholes," Collins said. "Two points only define a line but three points give you a plane, and a plane is something you can stand on. With three or more locations we can compute angles, area, and volume, use them to figure out where other event horizons might be located."

"And I thought geometry would never come in useful," Tally mused. She studied him for a long moment. "You're psyched about this, aren't you?"

"Let's call it 'guardedly hopeful,'" he said. "Who knows? The next wormhole could be worse than the first two."

"Or better."

"Or better," he agreed. "You're absolutely right."

Finally, Tally thought.

They finished their breakfast with a helping of mundane things about their lives and families that they had never discussed before. It went down easy. When he wasn't obsessed with wormholes and monsters, Harold Collins was a good listener with a dry sense of humor.

That was good to know. She had a feeling they would be working together for quite some time. As they left the restaurant—Collins's treat—Tally was guardedly optimistic, a little excited, and a whole lot scared. And wondering one thing above all:

What was next?

EPILOGUE

HIS BROWN EYES were ancient, wise, and very, very tired. They were thickly lidded with leathery, gray skin. His limbs were long and powerful and covered with fine, white hair. His arms and legs, too, were weary. But he could not stop now. There was much to do before he went home.

The ferocious winds raised fine, sharp-edged particles of ice and spun them into wild, dusty eddies. They bit at his exposed feet and fingers, at his large lips and the tops of his ears, at the wide bridge of his nose. They caused those bloodshot eyes to tear so he shut them. He didn't really need them. It was nearly dark and, besides, he could feel and smell his way through the tall, cold crags.

His massive shoulders hunkered into the wind as he

moved up the slippery cliff-side pass. Over one of those shoulders was the sack containing the thing he had come for. The thing one of them always came for.

Surefooted, he reached the cave, which was little more than a ragged gash in the face of the cliff. Breathing deeply to compensate for the thin air high in the mountains, he pushed the bag in first then followed it in, moving sideways to fit his great body through the opening. He wiped his eyes with the sides of his hands then turned them out toward the dying light. Toward the mountains.

This had once been their home. Not just these peaks, but the land below. He remembered how it was for those who had come before, and for a moment his peaceful eyes flashed anger.

Then the Yeti turned and disappeared into the darkness.

One man has just discovered an
international threat that no one could
have prepared for—or imagined...

Unit Omega
by
Jim Grand

In charge of investigating unusual
scientific phenomena for the UN,
Jim Thompson is the world's authority
on the unexplained.

But when a world-renowned scientist
reports a sighting of the legendary
Loch Ness Monster, the disturbance
turns out to be much bigger—and more
dangerous—than the folklore
ever suggested.

0-425-19321-7

**Available wherever books are sold
or to order call: 1-800-788-6262**